ALL THE
SECRETS
WE KEEP

OTHER TITLES BY MEGAN HART

Captivated (with Tiffany Reisz)
Taking Care of Business (with Lauren Dane)
No Reservations (with Lauren Dane)

Order of Solace series

MEGAN
HART

ALL THE
SECRETS
WE KEEP

A NOVEL

Montlake
Romance

Published by Montlake Romance, Seattle

www.apub.com

Amazon, the Amazon logo, and Montlake Romance are trademarks of Amazon.com, Inc., or its affiliates.

ISBN-13: 9781503942783
ISBN-10: 1503942783

Cover design by Shasti O'Leary Soudant

Printed in the United States of America

This book is for the hungry ones. Feed yourselves.

CHAPTER ONE

Theresa Malone had made a lot of mistakes in her life, but that didn't mean she wasn't capable of making a few more. One of them was sitting across from her right now with a glass of whiskey on the table in front of him and a smirk that looked like every kind of bad idea. She'd invited Ilya Stern to Dooley's tonight, so she had nobody but herself to blame. She ought to have known he'd be no different with her than he was with anyone else. Charming and difficult.

"You are bound and determined to make my life miserable, aren't you?" She frowned. "C'mon, Ilya. Why? What good is any of this going to do? You're delaying the inevitable."

"It's not at all inevitable, Theresa. And it'll make me feel better." He sipped from the glass with a grimace and set it down before leaning back in the chair to link his fingers behind his head. His grin was hard and didn't soften his expression at all.

Theresa drew in a slow, calming breath. "They're not going to offer you more money or any kind of guarantees beyond what they already have. You're coming across as greedy."

"Oh," Ilya said with a purposeful leer, "I'm very greedy."

Theresa pressed her lips together to keep from smiling. This wasn't funny, and though it was easy to see exactly how her former stepbrother had earned his reputation for being an alluring rogue, she wasn't going to succumb. He could treat her the same way he treated every other woman in his life, but that didn't mean she was like any of them.

She leaned forward. "You're going to screw yourself over. That's all that's going to happen. They're going to build that hotel and those condos up all around you and not put one cent toward developing the dive shop or diving area, and, in fact, they will do their very best to make sure that you can't do anything, either. Your business," she said, "is going to wither and die and leave you with nothing."

Ilya's brows rose, and that tilting smile vanished. "Damn, that's harsh. Why you gotta be so cold, Theresa? What do you have wrapped up in all of this, anyway?"

That was a good question. She had put her reputation on the line to get this deal together, gambling on all the pieces falling into place just right so that maybe she could come up for air instead of drowning in years of debt. She'd first convinced her former boyfriend Wayne Diamond to sign off on the offer to buy the dive shop and quarry Ilya and his ex-wife, Alicia, had owned together by telling Wayne the owners were eager to sell. Then, offer in hand, she'd encouraged Alicia to sell her 60 percent. Ilya was the only one she hadn't been able to convince, and she was running out of both ideas and time.

"I mean, why do you care," Ilya asked when she didn't answer, "if my business crashes and burns or I end up in the hole, or what? What's it to you, really?"

"Why wouldn't I care? It's not like we're total strangers. You act like I should just sit back and watch you screw yourself out of what could be something really good for you." The words slipped out of her, almost so low she couldn't be sure he'd be able to hear her over the ambient noise in the bar, even with her leaning closer.

Ilya frowned and leaned across the table. "You don't owe me anything, you know. If anything, my family's the one that owes you. My mother's the one who kicked out you and your dad without more than a few hours' notice, then erased you from our lives like you'd never been a part of them."

She couldn't say anything about that; it was true, even if Ilya didn't quite understand the entirety of what had happened back then. The truth was Theresa didn't, either. She'd given up trying a long time ago, even if some small part of her had always remained tied to the Sterns and that time when she'd been part of their family. In fact, that winding thread of incestuous entanglement was exactly why she wasn't just laying out to him why, exactly, she was so desperate to make this deal happen. Whether she liked it or not—and she definitely didn't—her connection with Ilya's family had in many ways directly led to the mess she was in right now.

"Of course," he said, with one of those grins that had laid waste to women for years, "considering what a pain in the ass my mother is, maybe you guys got out lucky."

Lucky was far from what Theresa would've considered herself, but she shrugged, dipping her chin in response. They shared a look, longer than necessary. His gaze held hers, dropping for a second or so to her mouth before his lips thinned and he looked away. Ilya sat back, raising his glass and draining it before slamming it on the table.

"You're buying, aren't you?" He waved over the waitress for another. "One for me. Not for her. She doesn't drink. Right?"

Theresa rolled her eyes. "Yes."

Ilya shrugged. "Suit yourself."

Theresa gathered the papers she'd spread out in front of them both shortly after arriving, before Ilya had waved them away and told her flat out he wanted more money and written promises regarding the plans for Go Deep and the quarry property. She put them neatly into the folder she'd brought along, then closed it and slid it across the table toward him. He gave her a look.

"I'll take the requests to them," she said. "But you should realize this isn't a negotiation. They've settled with Alicia for her majority share, and they're going to move ahead with the project, no matter what."

"Screw them," Ilya said evenly. "And you know what? You, too."

That was it; she was done.

Theresa got out a pair of twenties—all the cash she had in her wallet. All the cash she'd have for the next couple of weeks until her commission check from the first part of the sale cleared. She tossed the money on the table and stood. She didn't bother saying good-bye. Her heart was pounding, her throat closing, her eyes burning. The last thing in the world she wanted to do was give him the benefit of seeing her upset—and how familiar did that feel? Years had passed, and the difference now was that instead of Ilya teasing her about the posters on her wall or stealing the last slice of pizza, holding it above her head so she couldn't reach it, he was actively pushing the point of something sharp into her soft places in order to get a reaction out of her.

Outside in the parking lot she gave herself a few seconds to breathe in the night air, fresh with the promise of spring. At her car, she opened the trunk to sort through a few of her bags, looking for her pajama pants. At the sound of a male voice behind her, she jumped, hitting her head on the edge of the trunk and letting out a cry.

Blinking against the pain stars blooming in her vision, she whirled. Pepper spray, dammit, where was . . . oh. "You scared the hell out of me!"

Ilya had backed off a step, hands held up. "Sorry. Shit, Theresa, ease up."

She took in a breath and put a hand on her head, rubbing away the sting. "What do you want?"

"I was hoping you'd give me a ride home."

"After what you said to me?" She laughed harshly. "You *must* be drunk."

"If I wasn't, I wouldn't need a ride. And I'm sorry," Ilya said in the tone of a man for whom apologies had always worked in the past. "I shouldn't have said it. I didn't mean it, really. I know you're just doing your job."

She hesitated, wishing she could tell him to screw off. There weren't any ready cabs in this rural town. None of those phone-app car services. There was no way he'd be able to walk home, and that meant risking he'd decide to drive himself if she refused. She didn't want that on her conscience.

"I know it's out of your way," Ilya said while she was weighing her answer. He shuffled his feet in the gravel and had the grace to look at least a little bit embarrassed, that earlier put-on charm dissipating. "I'd owe you. Not enough to agree to that deal. But I'd owe you."

Theresa sighed. "Fine. Get in."

She realized too late that the passenger-side seat sported her cosmetics case, pillow, blanket, and—oh . . . there were her pajama pants. She bent across the center console to start moving things into the backseat so he could get in. Ilya helped, then slid onto the seat.

"What's up with all this stuff? Your landlord still fixing the ducts or whatever he was doing before?"

She'd forgotten she'd told him that lie a few weeks ago when she'd been staying at his house after Babulya's funeral. She shrugged, not looking at him. "I've been on the road for a while. For work."

When he snapped on the radio, she didn't say anything. It was better than trying to make conversation. She sensed him looking at her but kept her eyes on the road.

"Was your hair always that curly?" Ilya asked.

Theresa's brows knit. "Huh?"

"Your hair." Incredibly, he reached to touch it. "It's so curly. And soft."

She burst into laughter, shivering at the touch of his fingers and pulling away as best she could while keeping the car on the road. "You're drunk."

"It looks good," Ilya said. "I like it."

She frowned at that. "Okay, well, thanks. I'm glad to know that my personal appearance is up to your presumably high standards."

Ilya laughed, low. "Salty."

She didn't answer that. She'd decided sometime ago that she was finished owing men her smile or her good humor or anything else. His stare still burned into her, but she ignored him. They drove in silence for the next few minutes until she made the last turn onto Quarry Street.

"Still wigs me out sometimes," Ilya said as they pulled into the driveway. "All the houses."

Theresa peered through the windshield, turning on the wipers to swipe at the faint drizzle that had misted the glass. Before Babulya's death, Theresa hadn't been back to Quarry Street for decades, and the changes had been extreme. It made it easier for her, a little. Reminded her she wasn't coming back to the past; she was only visiting. "Things changed, for sure. That's what they do."

"Yeah," he said quietly. "That's what they do."

CHAPTER TWO

By the time they pulled up in front of his house, the whiskey had settled in his gut with a low, roiling reminder that he meant to quit drinking any day now. Ilya didn't *feel* drunk, but that was part of the problem. He hardly ever did, not until he got out of the car and the ground tilted under his feet so that he had to grab the door to keep from tripping.

Ilya turned his face to the sky for a moment, letting the late-night rain tickle his closed eyelids. He opened his mouth, tasting it. So maybe he'd die from the poisons in the water, whatever. Something else could kill him first, and worse than that.

"Life," he said aloud like an answer to a question Theresa hadn't asked. "Life's what kills us."

"Oh my God." She sighed, and he looked at her. She'd gotten out of the car and was leaning on the roof. Her hair—that cloud of soft, dark, curly hair—was getting wet. She pointed at him. "You need some help getting inside?"

"No, nope. I'm good." He closed the car door. From across the street, a faint movement in the window of the Guttridge house tempted him to drop trou and send a full moon Dina's way. If she was watching, she deserved it.

Theresa came around the car and took him by the elbow. "C'mon."

"Sure, sure, let's go prove to my mother what a disappointment I am, okay?" He didn't try to fight off her grip, even when she steered him around the small lip on the front walk that would surely have reached out to trip him if he'd been trying to walk on his own. "Again."

"Again," Theresa agreed.

Ilya stopped and turned to look at her. "I was being sarcastic. Self . . . self-defecating."

"Oh, that's exactly what you are." Theresa's brows rose, and she shook her head as she tugged his arm. "All over the place. C'mon. Inside. It's wet and chilly out here."

In front of them, the house with its dark windows was an unneeded and despised reminder that nobody was waiting up for him.

"She didn't even leave the lights on for me!"

Theresa huffed something under her breath and led him to the front door, where she waited for him to fumble in his pocket for the keys that insisted on hiding from him. Rain slipped down the back of his neck beneath his collar, trickling down the line of his spine and making him shiver. She must've been impatient, because with another of those sighs, she pushed his hand aside and dug deep into his jeans to pull out the keys.

"Is that a key in my pocket, or am I just happy to see you?" It was a stupid joke, but he laughed at it.

Theresa looked at him for a second or so with her hand against him. The only barrier between her fingers and a few of his intimate parts was the pocket's thin inner fabric. Then her fingers curled around the metal and dragged out his keys fast and hard enough to scrape him through the material. Ilya winced and yelped, but Theresa ignored him.

She opened the door and guided him inside, then hung the keys on the hook by the front door. "There. Now you won't lose them."

"I never put them there," Ilya said with a gesture at the hook.

"If you put them on the hook," she said calmly, "you won't have to hunt for them in the morning."

Then there was silence, unbroken except for the rhythmic plink, plink of water dripping off them both and onto the floor. A little unsteadily, Ilya reached for the newel post and found her shoulder instead. His fingers squeezed. He pushed the wet hair off her face with his other hand.

"I'm sorry I said you should screw off," he said.

She snorted softly. "Whatever. It's not the first time you were ever awful to me."

"Was I awful to you?" he asked her, weaving a little, his fingers slipping down her shoulder to squeeze her upper arm like that would keep him on his feet. "Back then, I mean? Was I a terrible stepbrother?"

For a moment she didn't answer. "We barely had time to be siblings, really. You weren't great, but you could've been worse."

"You grew up," he said.

Theresa smiled, finally, and he hadn't realized until that moment how hard he'd been trying to get one of those out of her. "You're drunk. Let's get you some water and then to bed."

"It's been a little while since a lady said that to me." Ilya wove a little bit, squinting to focus on her face.

Theresa rolled her eyes. "That's not what I've heard."

In the kitchen, she drew him a glass of water from the tap and ordered him to drink it. Clear, cool, fresh. The liquid hit the back of his throat and slid down like heaven. He gulped, waiting for his stomach to protest, but everything stayed settled, and he held out the glass for another fill. He drank that one, too, watching her over the rim as she leaned against the counter.

"Who's been talking about me?" he asked her.

Theresa eyed him, then went to the fridge to pull out a can of cola. She cracked the top and sipped, letting out a long, slow, appreciative sigh. "People talk. That's all."

"You moved all the way to the next town over, and you're saying people talk about me?"

"Miranda Dillon," she said.

The name sounded familiar, but that didn't mean anything. She could've been someone who came to Go Deep to dive. She could've been a local news reporter. She could've been his kindergarten teacher. Something in the way Theresa looked at him suggested something else, probably a one-night stand. Lots of those were blurry in his memory, like most everything else at the moment.

When he didn't answer her, Theresa finished off the cola and tossed the can into the recycling bin. "You don't even remember her?"

"I . . . is she blonde?"

"Good guess. Yes. That's your thing, huh?"

"What's *your* thing?" Ilya tried to sound serious, but the words came out mixed and mumbled.

Theresa laughed. "I'm not going to talk to you about my thing, Ilya. It's late."

It was, but he knew better than to try to go to bed just yet. That would lead to a sick head and stomach in the morning. Besides, he wanted to know what kind of guy she was into. Why it had suddenly become so important to him, Ilya had no idea. Only that it was.

"You like a strong dude, I bet. Like a muscle guy? No, no." He shook his head. "Like a professor. That sort. A smart dude."

"Oh, brother. Let's get you upstairs. I'll help you get to bed."

"So long as you promise . . . promise not to take advantage of me." He blinked and straightened, attempting to put on a haughty attitude, but dammit, that was hard when the world was tilting. "Shit. I *am* drunk."

Theresa sighed. "No kidding. C'mon."

"I can make it by myself." He shrugged off her grasp, determined not to be pushed into doing something he didn't want to do. Too many women in his life had tried to make him do stuff "for his own good." He was tired of it.

She laughed at that, a trill of giggles. "Sure you can. Like the time you huffed too many whippets and tripped on the last step and got a concussion?"

"You remember that?" Ilya touched his forehead reflexively, remembering the pain. His nose had bled. Niko had laughed himself into hiccups, but Theresa had brought him ice wrapped in a dishcloth. Funny, the things he could remember when there were so many others he'd forgotten. He looked at her. "Yeah, you were there."

"I was there," she agreed, and hooked her arm beneath his to lead him toward the hall and toward the front stairs, not the steeply pitched and creaking back set.

He flicked the wall switch at the bottom of the steps, turning on the light in the upper hallway. He put his foot on the bottom stair, his hand on the railing.

"You're going to wake everyone," Theresa said.

"Ask me if I care. Couldn't even leave a light on for me. They deserve to be woken up." The words came out muttered and slurred. He was so tired, and she'd been right about bed being the best idea, but he wasn't going to admit it. All the way up the stairs, one foot at a time, down the hall. He stopped in the bathroom and fumbled with his zipper so he could take a long, hard piss, which rattled in the bowl. He didn't bother to flush.

In his bedroom, he fell face forward onto the unmade bed. He felt her hands slipping off his shoes, one at a time. Heard the thunk of them on the floor. He wanted to thank her, but with his face pressed into the pillow and his mouth open, already drooling, the most Ilya could manage was a grunt.

The bed dipped as she sat next to him. "Do you need anything?"

He shifted, meaning to answer her, and somehow found her hand with his. Their fingers linked. He kissed the back of her hand, since his words weren't working any longer.

She laughed again, softer this time. "Ilya."

"Your hands are soft. Your hair is soft. Everything about you is so soft, Theresa."

"You . . ." She sighed and withdrew her fingers, then hesitated, leaning forward to stroke his hair. "Go to sleep."

He found a few new words at the last minute, when she was already almost out the door. "Are you, too?"

"Am I what?"

"Disappointed in me." He was drifting . . . drifting.

"Why would I be?"

"All . . . the women in my life . . . mother, Alicia . . . they're all disappointed in me. Are you?" The question came out of him like a belch in church, unexpected and unwanted and embarrassing. He wished at once he could take it back.

Theresa's low chuckle eased him. Kept him from continuing to fight the waves of sleep overcoming him. Her voice soothed him.

"No," she said.

"Why are you taking care of me? I'm a mess."

The last thing he thought he heard before sleep claimed him was her lilting, laughing answer.

"Maybe that's my thing."

CHAPTER THREE

Then

They'd made out for hours, but that girl was never going to let Ilya in her pants. He was going to spend the rest of his life with his balls aching. He should have given up long ago. Gone out with someone else who'd at least agree to jerk him off. When it came right down to it, though, Ilya knew he could date a dozen—no—a hundred other girls, and not one of them was ever going to be Jennilynn Harrison. He'd never met anyone else like her, and even at seventeen, he somehow knew he never would.

What if he asked her to be his girlfriend, like be legit? If they held hands in the school hallway, went to dances? She'd wear his class ring, he thought as Jenni easily slipped his hand away from between her legs with the same skill she always did. Kiss him at the lockers before the homeroom-bell rang.

When he asked her that question, she laughed aloud. "Us? Dating? Like a real thing?"

"You don't have to make it sound like such a bad thing," Ilya answered, irritated. "Yeah, us. A real thing. Dating."

"Out in public?" She'd snuck in through the back door when everyone else was asleep. This had always been a secret.

Ilya sat back against the couch. "Yeah."

"Don't you like us being like this?" she purred, reaching for him, her mouth open.

He held himself away. "Look, if we're going to keep doing this in secret, but you won't even let me touch you, and you won't touch me, what's the point, Jenni?

She got quiet. Her face was hard to see in the shadows, but the soft snuffle of her breathing told him she might be crying. He didn't want to make her cry, but on the other hand, she pissed him off. She was always doing that. Teasing him, then getting angry when he called her on it. She tried to manipulate him with some kind of emotional response, and Ilya wasn't into that, not at all.

"See, I knew that was all you wanted," she said.

"Of course it's what I want," Ilya snapped with a tug at the crotch of his jeans, trying to make some room. "What guy doesn't want to get laid?"

"But you want me to be your girlfriend?" she shot back. "Go on dates? Be a couple?"

Ilya frowned. "What's so wrong with that?"

"If all you want is to get laid," Jenni muttered, "why bother with the rest of the bullshit? All that hearts-and-flowers crap. So, what, you can get your dick sucked on the regular? And after that, what? When you figure out that you're done with me, you can dump me and go get laid by someone else?"

"What's your problem?" Ilya put an arm's length of distance between them in case she decided to smack him or something. "What, are you on your period?"

Her reply came on a hiss, the sneer he couldn't see on her face clear in every word. "Oh, right, because a girl gets mad, that means she's on her period. Did it ever occur to you that maybe I'm just tired of all this shit from guys like you?"

"Guys like . . ." He knew she'd been out with a few other guys, but hearing her actually admit it put his stomach in knots. "Guys like who?"

"Just . . . all guys." Jenni flapped her hands at him, shadows upon shadows. "You all want sex, and that's it."

Ilya leaned forward to rest his elbows on his knees so he could scrub at his face. "I just told you I wanted to make you my girlfriend, Jenni. Take you out. Make it a real thing, not some kind of secret sex thing. Why do you have to twist it around like that? You're the one making this into that sort of thing. Not me."

"And what happens when you want to break up with me?"

He looked at her, trying to turn the shadows and darkness into a face, her face. "What makes you think I'd want to?"

"It's what happens," she said in a small and broken voice. "And then what?"

"Jenni . . ." He reached for her, but she kept herself out of reach, so he stopped reaching.

"It's what happens," she said again. "So we'd have this thing for a little while, and then you break up with me—"

"You could break up with me," Ilya retorted.

None of this was going how he thought it would. He had to swallow hard against the rush of nausea and the chills. He clenched his fists, digging the knuckles into his knees. He wanted to kiss her, that was all, but the way she looked at him made him think she might bite him if he tried.

Jenni swiped at her tears. "Whatever. Then we hate each other."

"How could you think I would ever hate you?" Ilya shook his head.

"Well, it's not like you *love* me," she spat.

The words had been there, on the tip of his tongue. If only they'd been able to move past his teeth. But . . . love? That was a huge thing to say out loud. And what happened then, Ilya thought, once he said it? He wouldn't be able to take it back.

Love was forever.

"I have to go." Jenni got up. "This is all bullshit, Ilyushka."

He frowned. "Don't call me that."

15

"Maybe I just won't call you *anything*," Jenni whispered, not moving away. She stood in front of him.

He could have reached for her again. She might have let him touch her this time. He thought that if he did, they could fix this thing between them that felt so determined to be broken, but he couldn't quite make himself do it. It was too much like giving in to her, when he didn't feel like he was the one who needed to surrender.

Without another word, Jenni left him there. He heard the whishing noise of the back sliding glass door open, then close. After that, silence. He waited a few minutes more to get his body under control before he decided to go upstairs to bed, where he suspected he wouldn't find it easy to sleep.

In the kitchen, a dark silhouette startled Ilya enough to shout. "What the—"

"Shhh, you'll wake your mother, and I'll have to explain to her what you were doing down here in the middle of the night with a houseguest." Barry sat at the kitchen table in nothing but a pair of sagging boxers. He had a bottle in front of him. Clear liquid inside. An empty shot glass that he filled while Ilya watched. He pushed the glass across the table toward his stepson. "Here. Sounded like you could use that."

"You were listening?" Worse, maybe he'd been watching? A rush of disgust had Ilya crossing his arms.

"I came down because I heard a noise."

"Did . . . did Jenni see you?"

Barry shrugged and tipped back the vodka from the shot glass with a smack of his lips. "She went out the back door, but yeah. Probably."

"Dude . . ." Ilya was at a loss for what to say. His mother had married this guy, who seemed decent enough, but he was hardly a father figure. If Barry thought Ilya needed some kind of advice, he was going to be disappointed.

"She called you Ilyushka," Barry said. "Isn't that what your grandmother calls you?"

Ilya gave him a wary look. "Sometimes. Yes."

"In Russian, it's how to talk to someone with fondness, right? Like a nickname."

Ilya shrugged. "Yeah."

"Ilyushka is what you'd call someone you love," Barry said, and poured himself another shot. He didn't offer it to Ilya this time, merely tipped it up in a salute before downing it. "Just saying."

"I'm going to bed." For a moment, Ilya thought Barry would call him back, but he climbed the stairs in darkness and silence and made his way to his bedroom, where he tangled himself in the sheets and was asleep, despite his fears of insomnia, within minutes.

CHAPTER FOUR

"Are you disappointed in me, too?"

Ilya's words had echoed in Theresa's dreams all night long, and she couldn't figure out why.

She woke without being rested. She'd intended to stay in the guest bedroom that she'd used the last time she slept here, but it had been full of construction supplies for the repairs she knew Ilya's younger brother, Niko, was doing. The bed had been covered in boxes, while tools and paint cans had been scattered on the floor. The couch in the Sterns' den wasn't the most comfortable in the world, but it was better than the backseat of her car, which was where she'd been sleeping for the past two weeks.

Theresa had spent the past nine months or so crashing on couches and guest rooms with a series of excuses to her friends, all so she didn't have to tell them the truth. She didn't have an apartment to go to, and she couldn't afford a hotel room. She could barely afford to cover her cell-phone bill or buy gas. There were only so many stories she could tell her friends, and only so many friends to tell the stories to.

She'd planned to wake up before anyone else did and slip out so she could avoid any questions. She must've been more exhausted than she thought, because what woke her was not the soft bleat of the alarm on her phone but the sizzle and smell of bacon frying and the sputter of coffee brewing. Theresa stretched and sat, noticing the light slatting through the blinds. It was late.

"Hey." Niko stood in the doorway, his hair sleep rumpled and a mug of coffee in his hand. "Good morning."

"Morning."

He didn't look surprised to see her crashing there, which either said a lot or not much at all. The idea that she somehow belonged there enough not to cause speculation felt strange and yet oddly comforting. Theresa yawned behind her hand and took the elastic from her hair to redo the messy bun. Her mouth tasted like an ashtray, which was stupid since she hadn't smoked a cigarette in years.

"What time is it?" she asked.

"Almost eleven. Ilya's still passed out."

She'd expected as much. They hadn't gotten home until after two, and he'd been pretty hammered. "I gave him a ride home last night . . . it was late. I crashed on the couch. I hope that's cool."

Niko lifted the mug. "It's not my house, but I don't imagine it's going to be an issue. Coffee's in the kitchen."

She swung her legs over the edge of the couch, very aware that she wore a sloppy T-shirt and a pair of pj bottoms with pineapples on them. The pajamas alone spoke to at least some level of intent or advance preparation for a sleepover, but if Niko noticed, he wasn't pointing it out, and she wasn't going to bring it up.

"Thanks." She shuffled past him into the kitchen and helped herself to a mug, adding sugar and cream and sipping with a grateful sigh. Sometimes the worst part of everything was how hard it was to get coffee in the morning. She let the heat bathe her face, aware the Niko had come into the kitchen behind her. "Where's Galina?"

"No idea. She wasn't home last night."

Surprised, Theresa turned. "No?"

"She has a new *friend*. Or more than one. Who knows? She does her own thing." Niko smiled and shrugged. He offered her the plate of bacon, setting it back on the counter after she'd taken a piece.

Theresa crunched the bacon, tilting her head at the flavor, and sipped the coffee, contemplating this. "Huh. Turkey bacon?"

"Yeah . . . my mother's finding her religious roots. No pig allowed." Niko laughed.

"Wow." Theresa knew that Galina had taken on some of the Jewish traditions after her mother's death, but this seemed a little more extreme. "She's keeping kosher?"

"In her own way. An observant person wouldn't think so."

"What do you think about it?" Theresa nibbled again on the strip of turkey bacon. It wasn't bad, but it wasn't like eating *real* bacon. On the other hand, she wasn't too proud to turn down a free breakfast.

Niko turned off the burner and slid the pan off the heat, then took a drink from his coffee. "I lived on a kibbutz for years. It's not like I don't know how to keep kosher."

That wasn't exactly what she'd meant. Theresa studied him. "Are you religious now?"

Niko laughed, shaking his head. "Oh, far from it. No, I've never been. I chose to live at Beit Devorah, so it was respectful to follow the rules, but it was never anything I felt mattered to me, personally. I traveled too much to keep kosher and observe Shabbat, at least if I wanted to eat and get anywhere on time."

"I don't know much about it," she admitted.

Niko shrugged. "It's complicated. But if my mother wants to decide she's going to be religiously observant, I'm not going to argue with her about it."

"No. I wouldn't, either. From what I remember about her, it's not likely you'd win." Theresa had finished half her mug without thinking much about it, and she went to refill it. She breathed in the steam, grateful for this simple thing, this comfort she didn't need to struggle for.

Niko took a carton of eggs from the fridge, along with a stick of butter. He pulled a pan from the cupboard. "Scrambled?"

"Yeah. Sure." She put a hand on her stomach, feeling the hollowness there. Her last full meal had been a grilled chicken salad at lunch yesterday. "You have any bread? I can make toast. Oh, how about potatoes? Hash browns? I can cut up some onions."

"Check out the freezer. I think there are some frozen breakfast potatoes in there."

Niko moved aside a bit so she could also put out a frying pan and add a thin layer of oil. She spread out the frozen potatoes while Niko took care of the eggs. He whisked them with a little milk, some garlic, and some chopped scallion.

"Fancy," Theresa said, watching.

Niko laughed. "Where I lived, everyone had assigned turns to work in the kitchen, no matter what other job you had. The idea was that you'd appreciate it so much more if you understood the amount of work it takes to feed people."

"It's a good skill to have." She took his place at the stove to turn over the potatoes, then gave him space to finish the eggs. "So how long are you planning to hang around? Are you going back overseas?"

He glanced at her as he set three plates on the table. "No. I'm staying here. The house needs a bunch of repairs, stuff I can handle so Ilya doesn't have to. Or my mother, I guess, since she's set on staying here, too. I have a little bit of time before I have to get a job. I'm going to guess that finding a permanent job as a beekeeper around here isn't going to happen, so I'll have to look for something else. That's one thing I'll say about the kibbutz. You were guaranteed a job, a place to live, food, clothing. Made things easier."

"Is that what you did? Keep bees?" For some reason this delighted her.

"Yeah, that's where I settled. How long have you been doing this real estate development stuff?"

Less than a year, she thought. A job born of desperation and necessity, cobbled together out of her own grasping, clutching, and climbing. There were days when she tried to be proud of what she'd begun and how well she'd succeeded at it so far, relatively speaking. Maybe she'd be able to feel that way once she no longer had to sleep in her on-the-verge-of-breaking-down car because she couldn't get the credit approval to rent an apartment.

"I worked a bunch of different jobs while I was in college, to help pay my way, and by the time I graduated, I figured out I was really good at organization, completing tasks, keeping people on track, putting things together that might not have been the obvious way. I was not very good at accounting, which is what I got my degree in, so I moved around for a while, trying to find a place that fit. I tried retail, real estate, insurance sales, even some multilevel marketing." She shuddered at that, remembering, and Niko laughed. "Then about three years ago, I started working for Diamond Development in their human resources department, then in their research and development department."

She didn't mention that she'd also dated and then subsequently broken the heart of the company's owner, and that had begun the downward spiral that had led her to where she was right now.

"I realized," she said after a second, "that I was really good at making connections between people who had things other people wanted to buy or build or make. So here I am."

"Cool."

They both sat at the table. She ran her fingers over the scarred top, remembering the pattern of scratches and gouges. Galina had been putting Niko to work repairing and refurbishing a lot of things in this old house, but she hadn't replaced any of the furniture. Theresa circled the dark ring in the center.

"This is from the time Ilya wanted to make popcorn, and he caught the pan on fire. He set it down here."

Niko looked at it, then at her. "Yeah. I'd forgotten that. How did you remember it?"

"I only actually lived here for about six months, so I guess you have a lot more memories of this house to sort through than I do. The things that happened here stuck kind of hard. When I come back here . . ." She looked around the kitchen. "I feel kind of like I'm a teenager again."

"Yowch," Niko said. "That can't be great."

She laughed softly. "It wasn't all bad. There was Babulya. Living as part of your family was certainly a strong influence on me, no doubt about that. Everything we go through makes us who we become. Right?"

His brow furrowed. "Yeah. You got that right."

They dug in to the food, eating in silence for a few moments. Theresa chewed slowly, savoring it, enjoying the flavors and also filling her stomach gradually. This meal could last her until dinner, if she ate enough. She could save her stock of granola bars and the giant jar of peanut butter for another time.

Niko pushed back from the table with a satisfied groan and rubbed his belly. "That was good. I'm stuffed. So, hey, what happened last night?"

"Hmm?" She paused to show him that her mouth was full, hoping to avoid this conversation, but Niko seemed happy enough to wait until she'd finished chewing and swallowing to get an answer. "Oh, I was meeting with your brother to see if I could convince him to just sign the damned deal already. Get him out of the dive shop before they really start getting to work. I tried to tell him that it's not going to go well for him. They're totally capable of making his business completely fail."

She used to think Wayne's ability to destroy other people's lives in the pursuit of his own goals was his worst character trait, until she'd learned how easy it could be, when it came down to self-preservation.

"Shit." Niko looked stricken. "You think so?"

"They're planning to break ground on the hotel in a couple weeks, and the condos before that. Ilya is asking for more money and guarantees about the shop, which there's no way they're going to honor. I tried to tell him. He wouldn't listen." She took her last swig of coffee and sat back from the table to admit defeat in the face of all that food.

"More money," Niko said. "Figures."

"All I can say is that he's got three weeks to take their offer or they're no longer going to honor it, and I fought to extend it that long. If he doesn't take the deal, they move on with construction, and it's not going to work out very well for him."

"He's going to hold on to his forty percent," Niko said. "He's stubborn."

"That forty percent gives him the shop, the parking lot, and access to the docks and underwater fixtures but doesn't prevent them from making it impossible for anyone to get to the shop, or if they start tearing things down or removing them and not replacing them . . ." Theresa shrugged. "There won't be any customers to take lessons."

The ceiling creaked overhead. Both of them looked up. Niko smiled, and after a few seconds, she did, too, even though she didn't much feel like it.

"In three weeks," Theresa said, "none of this will be my problem anymore. But I sure wish he'd change his mind before then."

CHAPTER FIVE

Then

In the Stern house, Theresa had a room all to herself. There was a bed with a fluffy comforter and soft sheets. A dresser for her clothes, only hers—no sharing with her dad, three drawers for her and three for him. The bathroom situation wasn't the greatest—one for the entire household, including two teenage boys who made a big mess and never cleaned up after themselves. Aside from that, she loved living there. She was grateful for it; that was the truth. Every day.

She'd come home from school to find Babulya in the kitchen slicing red beets and boiling chicken bones to make stock. The fact that there was someone at home to make any kind of meal on a regular basis was also one of those things Theresa appreciated. Homemade soup, even the weird kind that Babulya made, was a luxury compared to the days of canned soup and stale saltines. Off-brand cereals. Soured milk.

It was one of the things, back in the first days when her dad had started seeing Galina, that Theresa had clung to. Whatever might have been happening at home, and it was usually on the verge of awful, she could look forward to the weekend and spending time at the Sterns'. Even if she had to sleep on the couch and deal with teenage boys who either teased or ignored her.

"Like this?" she asked now, slicing the beets and onions carefully, the way Babulya had demonstrated.

"Doesn't have to be so fancy." Babulya smiled. Her reading glasses were pushed on top of her head, the chain connected to the stems dangling around her neck. "But is good to know how to make good cutting. How to . . . be clean with it."

The old lady's thick Russian accent sometimes made it hard to understand her, but Theresa nodded like she understood. She went back to slicing, trying her best to keep the beet slices all the same thickness. Pretty. Why? Why not, she thought as her fingertips stained red from the juice. If you could make something nicer than it had to be, what was wrong with that?

"Borscht? Ugh." Ilya came into the kitchen to snag a cookie from the jar, ducking away from Babulya's flapping hands. "Can't you make, like, chicken noodle or something?"

Theresa finished the last of her slicing. "Maybe you should learn how to cook it yourself, if you're going to complain."

"*Pfft.*" Typically, Ilya could barely be bothered to pay her any attention.

It could have been worse. When Theresa's father married Ilya's mother over the summer, Niko'd been kicked out of his bedroom so Theresa could have it. He'd moved into the attic. The brothers had fought about that—each had wanted the space with its slanting ceiling and cobwebs. They both could've been nasty to her about it instead of each other, but they hadn't. Sure, they teased her sometimes, but they were brutal to each other.

Babulya chased him out of the kitchen, scolding, but fondly. She caught sight of what must've been a weird look on Theresa's face, because she wiped her hands on her apron and pulled a cookie from the jar to hand over. Theresa took it with her pink-stained fingers. It was chocolate chip, and it was delicious.

"I teach you to make these," Babulya said. Later, as they measured and sifted and laughed while they made the dough, she said, "Boys are good, but a girl . . . a girl in the kitchen makes my heart happy."

Together, they made dinner. Borscht. Bread. Cookies. The cooking gave Theresa a sense of satisfaction and of settling in that nothing else had since she and her dad had moved in. Sitting at the dinner table with everyone around, a family, she began to think it was all going to be okay.

Until one day, it wasn't.

CHAPTER SIX

The sound of voices woke him, but the smell of food was what brought him downstairs. The sight of Theresa sitting across the table from his brother took Ilya by surprise. For a moment, he wondered if he was still dreaming or had somehow slipped backward in time to just after Babulya died, when Theresa had ended up staying with them.

"Hey," she said when she saw him. "Umm . . . it was late last night. I crashed here. Better than falling asleep at the wheel and crashing my car."

"Don't look at me. It's not my house, as my mother's been so kind to point out over and over the past couple months." Ilya scratched at his bare chest idly, narrowing his eyes at her. "Coffee?"

Niko pointed wordlessly to the counter. Ilya helped himself, then fixed a plate from the veritable feast someone had made. He took a seat at the table, looking up only when he felt the weight of two sets of eyes on him.

"What?"

"You look like shit," Niko said.

Theresa pressed her lips together against a smile. "You look better than I thought you would, to be honest. You were sort of wrecked last night."

Frowning, Ilya raised his mug in one hand and his middle finger on the other. When Theresa and Niko burst into laughter, he managed a grin. The coffee was hot, fragrant, delicious. Not that it mattered. He'd have guzzled gas-station swill, if that was all there was.

"Could get used to this," he said around a mouthful of eggs and bacon. He gave Theresa an eye. "You do it?"

"Some. Mostly it was Niko." She sat back in her chair, her plate almost empty, and rubbed her belly. "I won't be hungry for hours."

Niko also pushed his plate away with a sigh. "I need a nap."

"It's not even noon," Theresa said.

Niko grinned. "Yeah, so what? That's why it's a *nap*."

"Have you heard from Alicia?" Theresa got up to take her plate to the dishwasher. She filled her mug with more coffee and leaned against the counter, one leg crossed over the other.

"Nice pajamas," Ilya said. "And no. She's off on her world adventures—good for her."

Theresa sipped. "I was asking Niko."

Ilya paused with a forkful of food halfway to his mouth. He looked at his brother, who took that moment to get up and take care of his own plate. Ilya put the fork down and twisted in his chair to look at the two of them.

"Yeah, bro, *have* you heard from Alicia?" he asked. "I mean, might as well get it all out in the open. It's not like it's a secret anymore."

"It's not?" Theresa caught herself, adding, "I mean, what?"

Ilya gave her a level look. "Huh. So you knew?"

"I . . ." Theresa cleared her throat. "No, not really. I mean, I thought. Maybe."

Niko frowned. "You did?"

"I accidentally saw you guys . . . umm . . . it doesn't matter." Theresa made a show of sipping her coffee to keep from having to speak.

Ilya tossed up his hands. "Well, shit. Did everyone but me know?"

"Know what?" This came from Galina, shrugging off her jacket in the doorway.

The kitchen was becoming a freaking clown car. Ilya dug back in to his pile of food, speaking with his mouth full. "About Niko and Alicia."

"Oh, for a long time," his mother said. "Before they knew it, probably."

"Mom." Niko shook his head, then hung it, looking defeated.

Galina laughed. "Hello, Theresa. Nice pajamas."

"She gave me a ride home last night and then crashed on the couch. Where were you?" Ilya asked, regretting the question immediately. She'd probably tell them all exactly where she'd been and what she'd been doing, and that was a level of detail he absolutely didn't need.

"I had a similar situation," Galina said breezily with a wave of her hand. "Although regrettably, I hadn't thought ahead to bring pajamas."

Theresa shrugged. "I had some things in my car."

"You have everything in your car, by the looks of it when I peeked in the windows." Galina gestured. "Pour me a mug of coffee."

"I'm in the middle of a . . . move," Theresa answered.

She sounded embarrassed and annoyed. Ilya didn't blame her. His mother had that effect on him, too.

Galina took the mug Niko handed her. "How's that going, dolly?"

Theresa frowned, and her shoulders squared. "Fine."

Ilya watched the exchange, chewing slowly. He took the time to swallow so he could interrupt before his mother could keep up her interrogation. "Got yourself some new, fancy place? Did you buy one of those mini mansions over in Bent Hills? Oh, no, I bet you got yourself one of the time-share condos they're going to be putting up in my campgrounds. Can't wait to spend that commission, huh?"

Everyone turned to look at him with varying degrees of distaste on their faces. Theresa's was the only gaze he met. He didn't give much of a damn if they all thought he was being a dick about it. He *was*.

"It takes a while for stuff like that to clear," was all she said. She turned to Galina. "Would you mind if I took a shower before I left?"

"For the price of babysitting my son, a little hot water seems fair. Especially now that Nikolai has made it so much nicer." Galina waved a hand. "Help yourself. Of course it's all right."

"I'll just get some stuff from my car." Without so much as another glance in Ilya's direction, Theresa left the kitchen.

Ilya looked at his mother and brother, both of them giving subtle variations of the same expression. Yep, they both thought he was being an asshole, all right. He shoveled another fork of eggs into his mouth and said with his mouth full, "Can you give me a ride back to Dooley's so I can pick up my car?"

"Sure," his brother said.

CHAPTER SEVEN

A month had never seemed like such a long time to Niko. Even during the worst times in his stint in Antarctica, knowing that even if he wanted to get out and leave there was no way he could, he'd never felt quite this restless. Eager. In four days, Alicia would be coming home.

What that meant for the two of them, he wasn't sure. He'd encouraged her to go on her trip without him, but there'd been a lot of lonely nights over the past three and a half weeks when he'd stayed awake, staring at the ceiling of his attic bedroom and thinking about how much he missed her. He'd been following her social-media accounts. Pictures of her grinning in front of landmarks. Snapshots of her artistically lit food. He'd been unable to stop himself from scanning each to see if there was a man in them, someone who showed up more than once, even in the background. Someone who'd been taking the place Niko had wasted so much time before claiming.

His phone chimed just as his eyes were finally closing. He almost ignored it. Anyone who texted him this late deserved to wait until morning, and it was probably someone from home—from Beit Devorah—he reminded himself. No longer home. They sometimes forgot the time difference. It chimed again, though, and he knew if he didn't at least check it, he wouldn't be able to get to sleep.

I'm home, the message said. Come over.

He didn't bother texting a reply. Or getting dressed. He shoved his feet into a pair of battered flip-flops and threw on a hoodie over his pajama bottoms. He did stop to brush his teeth and run a hand over the bristles on his chin and cheeks, but he didn't shave. That would've taken too much time.

He was out the front door and across the street, eyeing the Guttridge house next to Alicia's. The light in the living room was on, and he suspected nosy neighbor Dina was twitching aside the curtains to look out, but he didn't care. He rapped lightly on Alicia's front door before turning the knob and letting himself in.

"Alicia—"

She was in his arms before he could finish calling out his greeting. Her mouth on his. His hands fell naturally to the swell of her hips, his fingertips skating bare flesh along the top edge of a pair of soft leggings. She tasted like mangoes. Sunshine. Sweetness and light.

"I missed you," she said into his kiss.

Niko didn't say anything, concentrating solely on her flavor and the feeling of her against him. His hand slid beneath her hair to cup the back of her neck. His other gripped her ass, round and firm and so perfect his body responded at once.

"Nikolai," Alicia said.

He rubbed himself against her. "I missed you, too. Can't you tell?"

"Doesn't mean I don't like to hear it." She broke the kiss long enough to take a breath, even as she molded her body to his. "Mmm. I can definitely tell you missed me."

She took him upstairs, both of them shedding their clothes along the way. They barely made it to the bed before they were naked, touching, kissing, stroking. Loving.

He hadn't forgotten the way her body curved, but a month of travel had reshaped her. Niko ran his hands up her thighs and over her belly, which had been softer before she left. He cupped her breasts, letting his thumbs tweak her nipples into tight peaks, and reveling in the sounds she made at his touch. He was hard enough to ache already, but he wasn't about to rush this. Not after so long.

His first taste of her lips had been sweet, and that flavor was echoed when he moved lower to sample between her thighs. She cried out, already lifting her hips to meet his mouth. Her fingers tightened in his hair. He wanted the anticipation to linger, but she was tipping over the edge in only a few minutes. She urged him upward, capturing his mouth in a greedy kiss and reaching between them to fit him inside her.

That first moment of joining urged low groans from both of them, and Niko pressed himself up on his hands to get a little control. Alicia wasn't having any of that. She hooked her heels around the backs of his thighs and pulled him deeper into her so that he was helpless not to thrust.

"I missed you," she said into his ear as her nails scored lightly down his back. She gripped his ass, pulling him harder against her.

"Missed you, too," he managed to say, even though forming words had stopped being easy.

It didn't last long enough. He held off until she cried out his name, and he felt her body tighten around him, then spilled into his own pleasure that blocked out everything else for an endless thirty seconds. When he opened his eyes to look into her face, Alicia was smiling.

"I missed you." Niko kissed her. "Like crazy."

CHAPTER EIGHT

Then

"When I was girl in Russia, I never asked Mother why on Fridays we had white bread, and on all other days only brown. She never spoke of being Jewish. It wasn't allowed, you know." Babulya handed Theresa another egg to crack into the bowl. "But she made the Jewish bread every week. Many times I'm sure she went without or had to scrimp, save, barter for the eggs and white flour and the butter. But she always did it."

"Now you do it." Theresa threw the eggshells into the trash and turned back to watch as Babulya added some softened butter and salt to the center of the flour.

Babulya nodded. "Yes. Now I do. And you do, too."

"I'm not Jewish, though. Is that okay?" Frowning, Theresa dug her hands into the mess in the bowl when Babulya waved at her to start mixing all the ingredients.

"None of us here in this house are very Jewish," Babulya said. "But we eat the Jewish bread. Is fine."

When the dough had become smooth and thick, only a tiny bit sticky, Theresa put it all back into the bowl and covered it with a clean dish towel. At the sink, she washed her hands carefully, then cleaned up the measuring cups and spoons they used while Babulya sat at the table with a glass of hot tea and milk. It would take a few hours for the dough to rise, and then they would braid it and cover it in an egg wash and poppy seeds before baking it.

"It's one of the best parts of the week," Theresa said when she took a seat across from Babulya at the table. The old woman was already dealing out the cards for a game of War. "Friday-night dinner. And especially the challah."

Babulya smiled, showing the gaps between her teeth. "Someday you will make for your own family."

"Oh . . . I don't think I'll ever have a family." This was something Theresa had thought about a lot over the past few years. "I don't want kids. They're a huge pain and hard to take care of."

Babulya looked surprised. "What is this? No children? You're young. You should wait. But to say you want none, ever?"

"I don't really want to have to take care of anyone else." Theresa snapped down a king, confident she was going to take this round, but Babulya had a matching king. They had to go again at war.

The old woman held her cards close to her chest, not putting down the next. "Children are a blessing, Theresa. You'll change your mind when you have good husband who takes care of you."

"Oh," Theresa said as she carefully laid her next card. A jack this time. Good, but beatable. "I don't want one of those, either."

Babulya snorted laughter. "You will change your mind."

"You don't have a husband," Theresa said.

"I had one," Babulya said. "One was enough."

"I don't really even want one." She watched as the grandmother placed a three, and then she scooped up the pile of cards, adding them to her deck underneath. She looked up to see Babulya frowning. "Well, I don't."

"Without husband, how will you have children?"

"I guess I could have kids without a husband, you know." It was a little edgy, talking to Babulya like this, like admitting it was okay to have sex without being married. Theresa wasn't sure she'd ever have sex, either. It seemed like a lot of work and effort for very little payout and a whole lot of problems.

"But . . . without children or husband, Titi, who will you make the challah for?"

It was the first time Babulya had ever called Theresa by a Russian nickname the way she sometimes did with Ilya and Nikolai. Unexpectedly, Theresa's throat closed and her eyes stung. This was the first time she felt as though the old woman might truly consider her to be a granddaughter and not some interloper hanging on the outside.

"I could make challah for you," Theresa said.

Babulya smiled. "What a good girl you are. I will not be here forever. And then what will you do?"

"I'll make it for myself," Theresa said with a shrug. "That'll be okay."

CHAPTER NINE

His whole life was crumbling all around him, and what was Ilya wasting his time doing? Sitting in Alicia's old desk chair, looking up tanks on the Internet. It was easy enough, relatively speaking, to get one. If you had the money to pay for it.

He'd have to settle for a school bus, he thought as he scrolled through several pages on a website. Take off the front and back doors to make it safe. Remove the seats so that divers could swim all the way through it. He'd sink it far enough away from the helicopter to keep it interesting, although the bus itself wasn't going to attract anyone. Most every dive site around had one.

A tank would bring people in.

He wasn't idiotic enough to put any money down on one, though. Not because of the expense—in the past he'd taken out loans and lived on hard-boiled eggs and tuna for nearly a year to make upgrades to the Go Deep dive site. But why would he waste his time and money acquiring, hauling, and sinking a tank when it didn't look likely he was going to have any kind of summer business this year at all?

The number of divers who used Go Deep, even during its best years, had never been impressive. There were several abandoned quarries with dive sites in the tristate area. He and Alicia had put a lot of effort into providing clean, economical facilities for divers here in central Pennsylvania, but Go Deep had always survived more on providing lessons and trips to exotic dive locations than on-site competition with the fancier, better-equipped dive sites.

The ones with water parks, for example, Ilya thought somewhat bitterly as he closed out of the website and brought up his e-mail instead. The ones with higher-end camping facilities and RV hookups instead of splintery picnic pavilions and outdated jungle-gym equipment. Easier access to highways instead of a tangled set of country roads winding through a small, rural town. None of those other places had a tank, he thought. He could be the first.

It wouldn't matter, would it? He opened a string of e-mails from the new majority owners of Go Deep and immediately closed them. They'd only included him as a courtesy. Owning 40 percent of the property entitled him to that, he guessed. But not much else.

The clock was ticking down on his chances to take the deal they'd offered. Two more weeks. After that, Diamond Development was going to come in with their 'dozers and raze the campgrounds to build time-share condos. Hell, after that, they were going to do it whether he signed or not.

He'd seen the plans. They intended to build economy units just down from the luxury resort hotel that was going in higher on the hill. The whole shebang was going to have fully equipped recreational facilities and tended grounds and activities planned year-round. Boating, water skiing, with sleigh rides and ice skating in the winter. Stuff like that. It was going to do really well in this area, which did not boast any other family-oriented, classy resorts of the sort. There were even optional plans for a water park.

Go Deep was going to be one minuscule part of all that, and if he could get even the tiniest portion of that business, it would be worth putting up with this other bullshit. Yet Ilya knew he wasn't going to gain anything but headaches. Sure, he still owned the shop, the parking lot, and everything he'd sunk into the water, along with his docks and water access, but the construction plans called for an almost complete blocking of his access road. Not to mention that once they put up all the new construction, his already shabby shop was going to look so much worse in comparison.

He wanted to blame Alicia for all this. When it came right down to it, if she hadn't caved, he wouldn't be where he was now, ready to lose what he'd spent his entire adult life building. Of course, without Alicia and her money, he would never have had anything to lose in the first place.

"Hey, man." Niko rapped his knuckles on the edge of the door frame. "Quitting time."

"Easy for you to say."

His brother rolled his eyes. "Like you're really working, anyway? C'mon. I thought we could grab some dinner."

"You buying?" Ilya grinned, incapable of really hating his brother any more than he could harbor an unending fury against Alicia.

Well, at least not until he remembered the two of them were together. Romantically. The idea of it unsettled him and pissed him off, maybe because it didn't make him jealous, and he felt like it should.

He pinched the bridge of his nose, leaning back in the desk chair that Alicia had picked out, the way she'd chosen everything in this office because it had been her space. She'd been the one to decide what items to carry in the shop, to make the class schedules, to order the coffee filters. She'd even designed the logo with the giant goldfish on it, a tribute to the fish her sister had won at the carnival so long ago, the one that supposedly had survived and grown to monstrous size. Alicia had been the one to keep Go Deep running, much the way she'd been the one to keep their marriage from dissolving . . . at least for a while. And what had he done? He'd been flash and fantasy, the idea guy with the big dreams she'd ended up doing the work for to make a reality. She'd given up on him, and now she'd given up on the business.

He couldn't blame her.

He was a mess and probably always had been. Why anyone had ever given him the time of day, Ilya would never understand, but it seemed that women were drawn to the damage in him like bees to nectar. First Jennilynn . . . and with that thought, he stopped thinking. Put the idea of her out of his head. That, and that of her sister, the woman he'd married for better or worse. It had all been worse, in the end.

"I wouldn't have to, if you'd take the deal," Niko said. "You'd be flush, then."

Ilya gave his brother a faint grin. "Theresa sent you, huh?"

"No, Alicia did," Niko said. "She said I needed to talk to you."

The very last thing in the world Ilya wanted was the kind of talk he suspected his little brother was angling for, but at the same time, he wasn't going to say no. Maybe they needed to get this shit out on the table, once and for all. "Fine. You're still buying."

"First round. Sure," Niko said easily enough with a grin. "I'll even drive."

Dooley's Pub had a decent-enough bar menu, along with a number of "traditional" Irish dishes. Ilya ordered shepherd's pie. Niko got some French onion soup. Both ordered Guinness.

"*Vashee zda-ró-vye,*" Niko said when they clinked their glasses together.

"Whatever that means," Ilya answered, though he knew it meant "cheers" or "to health" or something like that. It had been Babulya's phrase, though Galina had sometimes said it, too.

"It means drink up and don't be an asshole," Niko told him.

They both sipped the drinks and settled into their chairs. The waitress who'd been on duty the previous week when Ilya had been here with Theresa came over to the table. "You're back."

Usually, Ilya would've taken that flirtatious smile for exactly the invitation he was sure she meant it to be, but tonight something kept him back from it. "Yep. I'm back."

41

"Did Kelly take care of you already?" The waitress gestured at the glasses. "She took your order and everything?"

"Yeah," Ilya said easily, not making eye contact. She got the hint and excused herself. He lifted his glass and caught a look from his brother. "What?"

"You're a force of nature, man."

Ilya laughed, surprising himself with the humor. "Nah."

"I always envied that about you," Niko said.

"Well," Ilya replied after a second or so, "it's not like it worked out all that great for me in the long run. Seems to me that you got the best of the deal."

Niko nodded and drank. "Yeah. I guess I did."

Kelly brought their food to the table with little fanfare, but Ilya welcomed the break in the conversation. He dug in to the sizzling platter of mashed potatoes and spiced ground beef while Niko merely let his soup rest.

Ilya looked up. "You're not hungry?" he asked.

Niko shook his head, smiling. He waited a moment, then said, "Listen. About . . . things."

"You're both grown-ups." Ilya finished his drink and signaled to a waitress who may or may not have been theirs, but it didn't matter so long as she, or someone, brought him a whiskey. Neat. He was going to need it.

"Yeah, well. We all are, theoretically. Which is why I wanted to talk to you about things that are going on. Because we *are* adults," Niko said. "And because you're my brother."

This would've been a hell of a lot easier with some whiskey in him, but as it was, Ilya managed a small smile. "You feel you gotta tell me something, but do you, Niko. Really? Do I really need to know?"

"I love her," Niko said.

Ilya closed his eyes for a second or so. In that time span, like magic, by the time he opened them, the waitress had returned with his glass of whiskey. He took the chance to down it, grimacing at the smooth sting, before he said, "Of course you do. I wouldn't expect it to be anything less than that."

Niko frowned. "Ilya . . ."

"Look." Ilya wished for water, but there was none, and the waitress had gone. He slicked the whiskey from his teeth with his tongue and fixed his brother with a look he hoped wasn't threatening. "Me and Alicia . . . it was . . . we shouldn't have gotten married. You were right. You told me I was crazy to think I could get over Jenni by marrying her sister, and you were absolutely right. You were a dick about it, but you weren't wrong."

"I didn't mean to bring that up."

"It's the truth," Ilya said. "Maybe if we'd been different sorts of people, me and Alicia, we'd have worked it out. But we weren't. We shouldn't have gotten married. She'll tell you the same thing."

Niko coughed and shifted. "But you did. It happened. You can't take it back. "

"Lots of things happen. Are you going to let it stop you?" When his brother didn't answer, Ilya shrugged, trying to make like it didn't matter. It did, of course. He couldn't help that.

"I love her," Niko said again in a low voice that was nearly drowned out by the caterwauling of the girl at the karaoke stand in the pub's back room. "I think I have since we were kids."

The beer and the whiskey had settled into a slightly warm buzz in Ilya's brain. Nowhere near drunk, but it was enough. He smiled at his brother, feeling the way his lips stretched across his teeth. More a snarl than a smile.

"The two of you . . . it's messed up, for sure. But no more than anything else, I guess," Ilya said, thinking of Jennilynn. Marrying the younger sister of his dead ex-girlfriend had seemed to make sense at the time, but there was no question it was its own level of mess. Still, he forced himself to give his brother a long, steady look. "But I *did* love her. No matter what happened or whatever she might've told you about us, or what she thinks . . . I really did think we were doing the right thing."

"I know. People make mistakes."

Ilya looked at his brother. "If you hurt her . . ."

"What will you do?" Niko asked evenly, not rising to the bait. "Kick my ass? Fair enough. But I don't intend to hurt her."

"Not like I did, is what you mean, right? You think you're better for her than I was?"

His brother smiled. "Yes."

The thing of it was, even though he might not have wanted to admit it, Ilya knew it was true. "Just about anyone would be, I guess. Even you."

Niko very carefully gave his brother a double bird, the middle fingers on each hand stabbing the air before he lifted his glass again. Ilya laughed at the gesture. Something twisted inside him, then lifted. It might not ever go *away*, he thought. But he could at least try to let it *go*.

The waitress appeared again. Niko ordered a beer. Ilya asked for water and hoped he wouldn't regret not going for something stronger.

"Why'd you come back here, really?" Ilya asked finally.

Niko shrugged. "Babulya was dying. I wanted to pay my respects."

"Why'd you stay?" It seemed a fair enough question, even though by the way his brother's expression twisted, Ilya thought Niko didn't really want to answer.

"At first, for you."

Ilya snorted. "Right."

"It's true." Niko fixed him with a steady look. "You were the one who stayed here, taking care of her. Mom had gone off to South Carolina, doing who knows what. And I was gone most of the time, all those years."

"Alicia was the one who took care of Babulya. Not me." Ilya took a long pull of his water but met his brother's eyes squarely. "She's the one who figured out she needed to go into the home, the one who found it and arranged it. She's the one who visited her. Not me. And it's too late for me to change any of that now."

"I'm not asking you to. Or to beat yourself up over it. You asked me why I came back and why I stayed. I told you the truth." Niko shrugged.

"And now?"

"Now," his brother said, "I stay for her."

Ilya dragged his fork through the remains of his dinner. "How come you didn't go with her when she went away? I thought for sure you would have."

"She needed that time. To get out there. Do some things. I wanted her to have that. I wanted her to be sure that when she came back, she wanted to be here."

Ilya sat back in his chair, mouth slightly agape. The beer, the whiskey—he wasn't drunk, but he felt like he'd been shot up with something that made swirling, patterned lights blink on and off in the backs of his eyes. He stared at Niko, then gave his head a small, bemused shake.

"I think I just figured out what love is supposed to feel like," he said.

His brother laughed. "You never knew?"

"No," Ilya said seriously. "I don't think so."

There was silence between them for a moment. Niko put his spoon into the soup, breaking through the cheese barrier to release some steam from the broth beneath. He looked at Ilya.

"You still have time," he said.

Ilya snorted. "Okay, Mary Sunshine."

"Just saying."

Ilya rolled his eyes and dug his fork into his dinner to take another bite. "Whatever."

"So . . . is this going to be okay?" Niko asked.

"Yeah. I guess so. Sure." Ilya shrugged, cutting his gaze. It might be. It might not. But Niko was his brother, and Alicia would always be family.

They ate and drank and shot the shit about stupid things. The house and its repairs. Their mother. The weather. The conversation wasn't easy or light, but it wasn't awful, either. It was maybe even better than he'd deserved, Ilya thought, when Niko's phone blinked with a message, and he watched his younger brother's smile at the sight of whatever words were on the screen.

"You gotta go?" Ilya asked. "She's waiting for you."

Niko hesitated but nodded. "She's not ordering me to come home, if that's what you think."

"But you want to. So go." Ilya grinned and shot a look toward the flirtatious waitress from before. "I can find something to keep me occupied. Don't worry about it. I'll find a ride home."

Niko was already gesturing for the check, but Ilya shook his head. "I got it."

"You sure?" Niko frowned. "I can grab this one."

"I got it," Ilya repeated.

"You should take the deal," Niko said quietly. "Take the money, man. Get out from under that place and move on."

"It's not as easy as that."

Niko shook his head. "It could be."

Could it, Ilya wondered when he and his brother had hugged it out and Niko went on home to do whatever he planned to do with the woman Ilya had once called his wife. Could it be that easy, really? To let it all go?

"Another of these," he said to Kelly with a tap on his empty whiskey glass and a smile that set her back a step or so before she returned it. "Keep 'em coming."

CHAPTER TEN

Theresa's phone buzzed from its place in the center console of her car. She'd plugged it in to charge but had turned off the car engine so that she wasn't wasting gas. The night air in April could still dip low enough to be considered chilly, but under the weight of a few blankets and wearing fleecy pj bottoms and a heavy sweatshirt, she wasn't worried about being too cold. With the inflatable car mattress in the backseat, she wasn't even particularly uncomfortable.

She fumbled for the phone to glance at the screen, assuming it was her father. He had a way of forgetting what time of day or night it was, his messages rarely urgent and never frequent, but generally inconvenient. At first, the name on the screen confused her, and Theresa had to rub at her eyes to make sure she was seeing it correctly. Then she sat up in the backseat of her car, the blankets tangling around her feet, to hold the phone closer to her face. Another text buzzed through as she looked.

With a sigh, she thumbed her screen to pull up the message and hit the "Call" button. It rang several times before, finally, a familiar voice answered. From the background noise, she could guess where he was.

"Hey," Ilya said, "Niko left without me. Do you think you could come get me?"

Theresa stifled a yawn and looked at the time. It wasn't terribly late, at least not by bar standards. Far from last call, anyway. She'd only fallen asleep maybe half an hour before. And, frankly, she *was* already in the car.

"You're at Dooley's?"

"How'd you know?" He sounded joking, lighthearted. Not slurring his words or anything.

Still, she still had a question for him. "Why me?"

"You did it for me the last time."

"I was *with* you the last time." She was already crawling over the center console and into the front seat.

"Because," Ilya said after a second, "I know you'll do it without expecting something in return."

"I don't know about that part. See you in twenty minutes." She disconnected the call and deflated the mattress, an act she'd managed to get down to a science. She started the car, taking a moment to pull her hair into a high ponytail and check her face in the visor mirror for signs of sleep. She didn't bother to change her clothes. Hey, if people could go discount-store shopping in their pajamas, she could drive to a bar parking lot to pick up her . . . whatever Ilya was to her.

It took her a few minutes longer than she'd expected to get to Dooley's. She spotted him immediately, pacing outside the front doors. A tall man wearing a pair of faded jeans and a black Henley that clung to his lean frame. His dark, shaggy hair, the color of expensive black licorice, glistened a little from the misty rain that had started falling. Theresa flicked on her windshield wipers, watching him as she pulled up.

"Hey," she called, when it looked like he hadn't seen her. "Get in."

Ilya bent to look in the window. "My mom told me never to go with strange ladies."

"I have candy," Theresa replied at once, easily, laughing.

He'd earned all the gossip, she thought as Ilya went around the front of her car to the passenger side. He was charming, but effortlessly, so that you couldn't help but respond even when you knew you shouldn't. He'd always been like that, she remembered, but as a boy he'd sometimes stuttered in the execution of his charisma. As a man, Ilya Stern worked it, and hard.

"Thanks for coming to get me." He slid into the passenger seat and closed the door. He shivered dramatically and shook his head, flinging water everywhere.

"Hey!"

He grinned at her. His hair hung in wet strands over his forehead. Drops of water slid down over his skin, and with a swift motion, he licked a few off his lips. The motion mesmerized her. He smelled like springtime rain and the promise of flowers ready to bloom.

He was definitely no longer the boy she'd known.

Theresa forced herself to look away from him. Her fingers gripped the steering wheel tighter than she needed to; she made herself loosen her grasp. "Let me get you home."

"Not home."

Frowning, she glanced at him. "Huh? Why not? Did you and Niko have a fight or something? Is that why he ditched you?"

"We didn't have a fight. He left me because he wanted to get home to Alicia, and I told him to go."

"Is that why you don't want to go home?" she asked quietly.

"I don't want to go home yet because I'm starving. Let's go to the diner. My treat. Consider it my pickup fee." Ilya gave her one of those deliberately seductive grins that he probably used on everyone, although when she didn't return it immediately, his faded a little. "Unless you have somewhere to be."

She *was* hungry. It seemed like she always was, even when she'd just eaten. Somehow being unsure of where she was getting her next meal had kept her appetite at a constant simmer. "It's very late. Where would I have to be?"

"I don't know. Maybe you were on a date." His glance fell to her pajama bottoms, her hoodie, then up to her messy ponytail. "Or not."

"I was not on a date."

"That's good to know."

She gave him a hard side-eye, not sure what he was trying to get at but not trusting his motives. "I was trying to sleep."

"Sure, that's what all the good boys and girls should be doing this time of night."

"Clearly that leaves you out." Theresa put the car in drive, turning left instead of right out of the parking lot. Heading to the diner. From beside her, she heard Ilya's soft chuckle.

"But you came to get me, anyway? Aw, thanks. I owe you."

She glanced at him again. "Definitely. Put your seat belt on."

He did without protest. They drove for a minute or so in silence, sliced into even pieces by the whoosh-whoosh of the wiper blades and the thrum of the tires on the damp streets. Ilya leaned forward to look out through the windshield, and alternating bands of light and shadow from the street lamps cut across his face before he settled back into his seat.

"If it's going to rain, it should just rain," he muttered. "Thunder, lightning, that whole business. Not this soft little excuse for a storm."

"Is it supposed to storm?" She slowed, for a moment uncertain which road to turn on to get to the diner but following Ilya's lead when he pointed at the cross street in front of them. She felt him look at her but kept her gaze on the street ahead.

"I don't know. I just wish it would."

In another few minutes they were pulling into the diner's parking lot. The restaurant had a name—Zimmerman's—but nobody ever called it that. It had always been, and would always be, simply the diner. Open twenty-four hours. Breakfast all day.

"I haven't been here in years," Theresa said as she found an empty parking spot and turned off the ignition. She twisted a little to look at him. "I think the last time I ate here was with you and Niko, actually. We came here after the musical Alicia was in. Jenni worked here. She brought us extra fries and pudding for dessert."

On the roof above them, a spatter of harder rain made them both look up. From far off came the slow, rolling rumble of thunder, though she hadn't seen any flash of lightning. Ilya grinned. After a second, so did she.

When he opened his car door to get out, though, she hesitated. "Wait."

"Huh? Don't tell me you changed your mind. I need coffee and eggs. Bad."

"I can't go in there like this." She ran her hands over the thighs of her soft pajama pants.

Ilya laughed. "It's not like you'd be the only one."

"I do have some dignity left. I haven't yet totally given up on life." She'd meant her words to be blithe. A joke. They came out a little cracked, a little rough, a bit too raw.

Ilya didn't laugh again. His voice was softer when he answered. "Sure, Theresa. Okay. We don't have to go in. Tell me what you want. I'll get takeout."

"I have, umm . . ." She cleared her throat, not looking at him. If she did that, she was afraid she'd break down altogether, which would be ridiculous and useless. This was Ilya, after all. "I have some clothes in my umm . . . gym bag. In the trunk. You go in and grab a table for us, okay? You know there's almost always a wait. I'll throw something on and come in."

"Theresa." Ilya spoke quietly but with confidence. A man used to women looking at him when he called them by name. She did not so much as glance his way. "Are you okay?"

"I'm fine. Go on."

For a second she thought he was going to refuse, but then he got out of the car. His body broke the beams of her headlights as he crossed in front of them. The rain had started falling even harder. Quickly, she got out and went around to the trunk to find her bag. A pair of jeans, socks. The T-shirt and sweatshirt she'd been wearing would be okay, she thought distractedly as she tried to finish fast enough to avoid leaving the trunk open so long her entire collection of worldly belongings got soaked. She slipped her feet into battered tennis shoes and gathered her small purse and keys.

By the time she made it into the diner lobby, her hair was dripping and the hems of her jeans were damp, but at least the rain hadn't managed to penetrate her sweatshirt. Just as the glass door swung closed behind her, another roll of distant thunder tickled her eardrums. This time, she also saw the flash of lightning reflected in the diner's back wall of mirrors.

Ilya had snagged a small booth for two in a back corner. The diner still featured little jukeboxes at each table, and he was flipping through the selection with a look of concentration. He glanced at her when she slid into the seat across from him.

"Ordered us both coffee. Hey, you got any quarters?"

She ran her hands over her hair to smooth it, tightening the elastic band. With a paper napkin, she wiped off her face. "No."

He looked at her then, with one of those grins that lit his eyes and showed off straight, white teeth. She couldn't remember if he'd worn braces the way she had—two years of metal torture in her mouth, until her father had stopped being able to pay the bills on the work and she'd had them removed. She'd worn them again as an adult, paying for them herself in order to fix what had been left undone the first time around.

"It's really going to storm," Ilya said at another rumble of thunder, closer this time. "Awesome."

With steaming mugs of coffee in front of them, and a typical diner menu that featured hundreds of choices, Theresa let herself relax into the booth. She scanned the menu, wondering if she should order something that would keep overnight in the car so she could eat it for breakfast the next morning. Two meals in one.

She decided on a diner standard: veal parmigiana. It came with crusty garlic bread, salad, and a side of pasta, as well as dessert. Choice of tapioca pudding or ice cream. Ilya ordered breakfast, as he'd planned, and also the diner's special: loaded waffle fries.

"Sorry, hon, we don't do those anymore," the waitress said.

Ilya looked surprised. "What? No more garbage fries? Since when?"

"Since the new owners took over." The waitress shrugged. "Been about six, eight months."

"What happened to Reggie Zimmerman?" Ilya asked.

The waitress gave him an apologetic smile. "I only started working here a couple months ago, so I don't know. Sorry. I can bring you nachos instead, with a side of chili and onions?"

"Nah." Ilya leaned back in the booth to put an arm up along the back. When the waitress left, he said, "I'll save room for dessert. Something from the dessert case, something good."

"What, you don't like tapioca pudding?" Theresa laughed.

"Tapioca pudding is like eating custard with caviar in it."

She grimaced. "Ew. No way. I love tapioca pudding!"

"You're welcome to it," Ilya said, then added, "You know who liked to make homemade tapioca pudding?"

"Babulya," Theresa answered. "I know. She taught me how."

"She never taught *me* how to cook anything." Ilya reached for a straw from the holder on the table and stripped it of the paper to twist the plastic tube tight around his fingers. He held it out to her. "Flick it."

She'd forgotten how they'd all done this. She flicked it hard with her fingers, crowing at the way she made it pop. It ruined the straw, of course, split the plastic so you couldn't drink from it, but it felt somehow . . . triumphant. Her grin softened when she caught Ilya's gaze on her. They stared, not speaking.

"We used to come here all the time," Ilya said finally.

"You and her." Theresa nodded, thinking back to those long-ago years.

Ilya's eyebrows rose, but he didn't ask her to clarify whom she'd meant by "her."

He said, "I meant all of us. But yeah. Me and Jenni. It was the place to be."

"Even the kids from Central came here." Theresa had not. In high school, there'd been no extra money for hamburger platters or milk shakes after school dances, and besides, she'd never gone to those. She might have if they'd stayed in Quarrytown. Or not. There was no way to know and no sense in dwelling on it.

Ilya took up the straw paper and tied it in a knot. Then another. He looked around the diner. "It looks the same here, but . . . not as nice."

"It *is* a little shabby." Theresa looked around.

The retro decor was no longer really vintage, just old. Several of the booths had duct tape covering tears in the vinyl. The mirrors along the back wall had gone dark with age, the silvering worn off in places, leaving disconcerting blank spots in the reflections. The place was crowded with a mix of patrons of all ages, most with coffee mugs in front of them.

The food arrived on worn, thick white plates that bore the scrape marks of thousands of forks. She dug in to her veal, disappointed at how tough it was. Not burnt, just overcooked. The pasta was limp, the sauce more like watery ketchup than real Italian marinara. The salad consisted of iceberg lettuce and a few carrot shreds and a couple of croutons. Literally two.

Ilya paused with his fork halfway to his mouth, noticing her hesitation. "No good?"

"It's fine." She cut into the veal and ate another bite, hoping it was going to taste better than it looked. And it was fine. It just wasn't . . . good.

She ate it, anyway, because she was hungry, and because she wasn't about to waste a meal. She set the salad and pasta aside, along with the garlic bread. She could eat them later. The shoe-leather meat would fill her up but leave room for the pudding.

The conversation was brief as they chewed and swallowed. Not awkward or strained. She noticed that. Sitting across from Ilya, Theresa didn't feel as though she was somehow expected to run a long string of words, small talk, to keep this from being weird. Nor did he ramble on like he expected her to listen.

It wasn't a date, Theresa reminded herself sharply. They weren't strangers, really. He wasn't trying to impress her, and she was not looking to be impressed.

But once, just once, when she let herself linger over the sight of the way the tendons in his forearm twisted as he spread jelly on his toast, Theresa wondered what it must be like for those women who did go on a date with Ilya.

"How's the pudding?" he asked when the waitress had brought a Styrofoam container for Theresa's leftovers, along with a cup of the dessert.

Theresa pulled her spoon through the creamy white custard and tasted it. "Good."

Ilya shuddered theatrically and turned to the waitress. "Can I get a piece of the chocolate cream pie?"

"Sorry." It seemed to be the theme of the night. The waitress shrugged. "We have apple or cherry pie, chocolate cake with peanut-butter frosting. Also vanilla or chocolate ice cream. Chocolate, vanilla, and tapioca—"

"I'll take a look at the case," Ilya began, but stopped at her look. "You're kidding me. No dessert case?"

The waitress's entire expression wrinkled. "Sorry."

"Man." Ilya sat back. "This place used to have the best desserts around. Mrs. Zimmerman made them."

"Well, she died."

Theresa blinked. Her spoon clattered against the side of her pudding cup. Ilya let out a small noise of surprise.

"No dessert, thanks. Just the check." He pulled a few bills out of his wallet and tucked them against the bill. He waited until the waitress had taken the check and money and left their earshot before saying, "I should've had the pudding."

"You can have a bite of mine. I'm stuffed." She offered him her spoon, not thinking that he'd take it.

Ilya's fingers closed around her wrist to keep her hand steady as he leaned toward the spoon, mouth open. He'd captured the mouthful of pudding on the spoon before Theresa could react. He looked up as he finished the bite, gaze holding hers as his tongue swiped across his top lip to catch the little bit of cream that had lingered.

He didn't let go of her wrist. She didn't pull away. They stayed that way until a flash of lightning and thunder made them both jump.

"We should get going," Theresa said.

Five minutes into the drive back to his house, the rain had made it almost impossible for her to see the road. That, along with the increasingly frequent slashes of blue-white lightning and ear-splitting thunder, was enough for Theresa to be white-knuckled on the steering wheel. By the time she pulled into his driveway, she was tense, fingers aching and jaw sore from clenching it.

"You should come in until this passes," Ilya said. In another flash of lightning, his eyes glinted.

For a few seconds too long, Theresa let herself get a little lost in the intensity of his stare before she looked back out the windshield. "I should get home."

She had no home to get to, but he didn't know that. The thought of driving again, even if it was only to the big-box store parking lot where she'd be able to park unmolested overnight, was enough to tighten her grip on the wheel again. Sleeping through this storm was going to be hard, too. Her hair was still wet, and she would have no place to dry it.

"Theresa," Ilya said, the way he had in the diner. This time she looked at him. His expression was curious. More open and honest than she could ever recall seeing it. "I don't want you to crash your car because you were good enough to bring me home. Again."

She chuckled and shook her head. Lightning lit the car's interior, bright as day, and she prayed hard for a moment to whatever greater power the universe provided that he didn't look into the backseat and see her pillow and blankets, the deflated air mattress.

"C'mon in until the storm lets up."

She nodded. Ilya counted to three, and they both got out, slamming the car doors and racing for the front door. They got there seconds ahead of another flash and crash, and Ilya pushed open the door so they could stumble into the entryway.

Theresa wasn't surprised when he kissed her.

Somehow she seemed to have been expecting it. The looks. The touch. His reputation, if nothing else. She'd been waiting for Ilya to pull her into his arms, one of his hands flat between her shoulder blades so he could bend her as he captured her mouth the way he'd taken that spoon of tapioca pudding. Savoring, lingering, tasting.

Breathing hard, they both ended the kiss at the same time and moved a step apart from each other. Outside, the storm seemed to be moving away. The plink of water dripping off them onto the hardwood floor seemed very loud. Theresa put her fingertips to her lips.

"Don't do this because you're trying to get back at him. Or her," she said quietly against her own touch. "This isn't the same thing at all."

"I'm not doing it to get back at either of them," Ilya said. "Maybe just at you."

She was the one who kissed him this time, pushing him back a step so that he bumped the newel post. Her hands anchored on his belt loops, her fingers hooking them for a moment, holding him still so she could explore his mouth with hers.

They didn't break apart so abruptly this time. Softly, easily, ending with a brush of lip on lip, they parted. A moment or two after that, she let go of his belt loops so she could put another half step of distance between them.

"You want to talk to me all the time about how I don't know you? Well, you have no idea who I am," she said. "Not a single damned clue, especially if you think that kissing me will make me feel bad about convincing Alicia to sell. It won't change my mind about *you*, either."

"I'm sorry, Theresa."

It was not what she wanted him to say, but the kicker of it was that he sounded sincere. Theresa nodded and shivered. Her clothes were soaked through. She went to the door and looked out through the door's side windows.

"It's still coming down really hard," she said as though nothing had passed between them but the most casual of conversations.

She couldn't decide if she was angry with him for the kiss or at herself for the one she'd given him. All she could be sure of was the lingering flavor of coffee and sweet jelly, and the memory of his heat against her. Behind her, she heard the shuffle of his feet on the bare wooden floor, and she tensed, waiting to see if he would touch her. Disappointed, a little, when he didn't. Maybe only because it denied her the chance to refuse him.

"It's a forty-minute drive back to Elisabethville," Ilya said, naming the town he didn't know she no longer lived in. "I can't make you go out in that. Stay here tonight. You can have my bed."

She turned to face him.

"I'll be on the couch," he said, seeing her expression. "Not like last time. You should have the bed."

Snuggled beneath blankets that had covered him? Her head on the pillow that had cradled his? The sheets would smell of him. Sleeping in his bed without him in it beside her would be as intimate as those kisses they'd shared, yet would make her feel as distant as a stranger. She didn't want to go out into the storm, not even to get her pajamas, but she most definitely did not want to sleep in Ilya's bed alone.

"The couch is fine. I'll need something dry to wear, though. And a hot shower first." If she took one tonight, washed and combed her hair, she could braid it before she went to sleep. It would still be damp in the morning, but it would be tidy and professionally appropriate for the cold calls she'd planned to make.

"Sure. Of course."

She followed him upstairs, where all the doors in the hallway were closed except for the one to the bathroom. She took the oversize sweatpants and T-shirt he was lending her and let herself linger in the shower, using up their hot water far beyond what seemed polite. With the almost-scalding spray beating down on her shoulders, she could close her eyes and pretend everything was going to be all right.

It wasn't going to be, she thought when the water started to go lukewarm and she got out, drying herself with a towel embroidered with daisies that she swore she remembered from when she'd lived there as a girl. Nothing was going to be okay, not for a long time, anyway, and some of that wasn't her fault, but some of it was.

She came out of the bathroom wearing Ilya's clothes, her hair clean and braided so that it hung down over one shoulder. The rain still pounded the roof, but no light flashed through the windows at either end of the hall, and she heard no more thunder. She knocked softly at Ilya's bedroom door, opening it at the sound of his voice.

"I changed the sheets," he said. "You really should take the bed."

"I can't do that, Ilya."

He shook his head. "No, really. I feel like shit, making you sleep on the couch—"

"It's fine. I really don't mind."

"The bed's big enough for two." The offer might've sounded lecherous. Maybe was meant to be. He only sounded hesitant.

She could tell him that the lumpy couch was better than an air mattress in the backseat of her car. That she'd showered here not because of the chilly rain but because the other option would've been pits-and-privates in the bathroom of the discount store in the morning, early enough so that nobody would walk in on her. That she had enough money in her bank account to make the minimum payment on her outstanding loan and monthly bills, but nothing beyond that, and she chose to keep making those loan payments because every time she did, it chipped away a tiny bit at the seemingly insurmountable problem of getting her credit score above three hundred. She could have told him that almost everything she owned was in her car or a storage unit that was about to go up for auction if she couldn't manage the back payments on it by next month. She could tell him this wouldn't have been the first time she'd let a guy take her to bed simply so she'd have a place to spend the night.

At nearly two in the morning and wearing his clothes, Theresa didn't have it in her to be honest.

"I don't think it's a very good idea," Theresa said. "Do you?"

"I'm not known for my good ideas." An unmistakable heat flared in Ilya's gaze.

No hesitation this time. Definitely an invitation. One he'd no doubt made to countless other women who'd taken him up on it. Theresa was not about to share his bed. Especially not after that burning pair of kisses at the front door. How could she? What would she do? Screw him with his mother down the hall, his brother on the floor above them? In the house where they'd once lived as brother and sister? Theresa had made a lot of dumb choices in her life, but she was *not* going to make this one, no matter how tempted she was to explore the heat that had become so palpable between them.

"I really have to be up early." That was the truth.

"Okay, then. Good night, I guess." He sat on the edge of the bed. He waited until she got to the doorway before he said in a low voice, "Theresa."

She half turned. "Hmm?"

"Why did you come and get me?"

"Because you asked me to," she said. "Why was I the one you called?"

Ilya smiled. "Because I knew you'd come."

CHAPTER ELEVEN

Then

"Wake up, girl. C'mon."

Theresa fended off the tugging hands and grabbed at her comforter. She tried to burrow back into the pillows. It had to be a nightmare, but no, again the blankets were yanked away, and her father's hands were shoving. Pulling.

"Get up—now. Pack your shit. We have to go."

Theresa, bleary-eyed, sat and gathered the blankets to her chest. "What's—"

"She's kicking us out." Her father was hollow-eyed, hair sticking up all over the place. He stank of nervous sweat, and his gaze darted around the room without settling too long on any one place. He paced, grabbing things and throwing them in a giant black plastic garbage bag.

If she didn't get out of bed and stop him, he was going to ruin her stuff. He'd done it before. Lots of times. "Dad, stop, I'll get it."

He tossed the half-full bag onto the floor in front of her. "We have an hour."

"Or what? What happens in an hour?" She was already bending to scoop up the bag and put it on the bed, then pulled her suitcase from beneath it. This was probably the reason why she'd never put it in the basement along with everyone else's. Maybe she'd always known, somehow, that she'd need it like this. Suddenly, in the middle of the night.

"She said she'll call the cops." Her father ran both hands through his hair. "Let's go."

"Why is she going to call the cops?" Theresa put the empty suitcase next to the garbage bag but turned to face him. She wanted to ask him what would make his still-new wife threaten him with the police. What had he stolen from Galina that would make her toss them both out like this? Money? Or something to sell for money? Galina was not the sort of woman to allow it, not even once. "What did you do to her?"

It was the wrong question. He whirled to face her, fists clenching. "Just pack your shit, Theresa. Whatever isn't packed in forty minutes, you leave behind."

There was no way she'd be able to fit everything in this room inside the single suitcase, not even if she used the garbage bag, too. She'd lived here for a little more than six months, and in that time, Galina had been generous to her. She claimed it was because she'd always wanted a daughter to spoil. A pretty bedspread and curtains, a shaggy throw rug, posters for Theresa's bedroom wall like the ones Alicia and Jenni had across the street. Thinking of Jenni now made Theresa frown, the older girl's death still raw, and a nightmare all its own.

Were these things important enough to her to take along? Was she even allowed? Theresa thought, her brain no longer fuzzy with sleep. Or would Galina accuse her of stealing them? Theresa focused. Pinpointing what, exactly, she needed to take and what she would have to leave behind. Her father had left the room, thank God, because his pacing and hovering were distracting.

She folded clothes quickly, pulling out what she'd need most from the drawers of the dresser that had been in this room when she moved in. Underwear. Socks. If she had to wear the same jeans for weeks at a time before they could get to the Laundromat, clean panties and socks made it easier. She pulled out a dark-green, short-skirted dress. Galina had taken her shopping to buy Theresa "pretty things." The things her father had never known she'd want or need.

She would not cry.

The dress went in the suitcase, even though it took up too much room. T-shirts, jeans. The sweaters and pajamas she shoved into the garbage bag, careful not to stuff it so full that it would tear.

It took her thirty minutes to pack up everything she could possibly fit. The suitcase. A backpack. Her gym bag. The plastic trash bag. Her entire life in these four bags.

The sun was still an hour or so from rising when she hauled her suitcase out to her dad's car. When she went back into the house to get the rest, Babulya was sitting in the kitchen. Theresa had been heading for the back stairs but stopped at the sight of the old woman in her head scarf, her gnarled hands resting on the table in front of her. Babulya had packed up a paper plate of cookies wrapped in plastic.

She would *not* cry, Theresa thought.

"These are for you. And take the sandwiches from the refrigerator. You'll be hungry. Maybe not now," Babulya said in her thick Russian accent. "But later."

Faintly from the living room came the sound of muffled shouting. A skid of furniture legs on the wooden floor. Babulya didn't look in the direction. Her gaze was steady on Theresa's face.

"I don't know what happened," Theresa whispered.

Babulya shook her head. "Is Galina. Is your father. Not you."

"But I still have to go with him. She's kicking us both out, not just him."

"Theresa!" Her father shouted and was hushed at once by Galina's lower, but no less angry, voice.

Babulya opened her arms, and Theresa went to her. In the old woman's embrace, she closed her eyes and thought of how it felt to be, even for just a little while, safe. Part of a family.

"Is not you," Babulya repeated, and kissed Theresa's cheek. "Never worry that it was you."

In the end, it made no difference. Whatever her father had done, Theresa also had to pay the price for it. They were out of the Stern's house before sunrise, their belongings tossed into the back of her father's beat-up Volvo, and in a rattrap motel in the next town by breakfast time. Whatever had gone down between him and Galina, he wouldn't talk about it to Theresa.

He talked about it on the phone to his soon-to-be ex-wife, though. Muttered conversations while Theresa lingered in the bathroom so she didn't have to come out and pretend she wasn't overhearing. Her father had done some shady things in the past, but whatever he'd gotten into this time must have been worse than anything. This was something he wasn't going to get out from under; that was evident as three weeks passed before they moved from the motel into an equally crappy apartment close to the hospital where he had not yet, miraculously, lost his job.

Theresa never asked him again what he did to Galina to make her throw them out.

CHAPTER TWELVE

Alicia had only been home for a couple of days, but it seemed like a million years had passed since the last time she'd stood in the farmer's market in Thailand, eating mangoes and sticky rice. A bagel with cream cheese and a large French vanilla latte weren't quite the same, but that didn't make it bad.

The travel had been fantastic, beyond her wildest dreams, but the money from the sale of the dive shop wasn't going to last forever. If she was going to travel again, she'd need to go sooner rather than later, because soon enough she was going to have to start thinking about getting a job.

She sipped the hot drink and set it on the table, shrugging out of her jacket as she juggled her purse and laptop. She'd come to the coffee shop because sitting at home was becoming tedious and suffocating. She figured she'd start researching job possibilities, and maybe another trip, too.

She and Nikolai hadn't talked about what would happen if she wanted to leave again. Mostly, they hadn't talked about what they were doing with each other. She'd come home early to get back to him. He'd told her he missed her. They'd spent every night together since then. She'd caught him looking at her. A lot. Well, she guessed she was looking at him, too. Both of them had carefully sidestepped any discussion of their relationship beyond the here and now.

"Hey, Alicia. You're home! How was the trip?"

She looked up to give Theresa a warm smile. She moved her bag off the opposite chair so Theresa could take it. "Amazing. Life changing. Have a seat. What're you up to?"

"Getting ready to use the Wi-Fi, get some work done." Theresa held up her computer bag. "I don't want to bother you."

"No bother." Alicia looked around the coffee shop, which was now full enough that there weren't any open chairs other than the one she'd offered. "We can agree not to talk to each other, how's that?"

Theresa laughed and slung her bag over the back of the chair. "No way. I want to hear all about your adventures. I saw the pictures on Connex. It looked fantastic."

"It was." Alicia moved her computer so Theresa had room to put hers on the table. Her plate and mug, too. The table was barely big enough for everything. "I'll eat fast, then you can have room for a plate."

"Not grabbing anything, don't worry." Theresa sat. "So, tell me about everything."

They talked for half an hour as Alicia ate her bagel and finished up her coffee. She hit the trip's highlights. The food. The views. The bugs.

Theresa shuddered. "No, thanks."

"Yeah, you think the wolf spiders around here are bad . . ." Alicia grimaced. "Let's just say there are some things I can never unsee."

"Sounds like an amazing trip." Theresa smiled.

"I'm going up to grab a coffee refill. You want something?"

"Oh . . . yeah, I guess I should have something if I'm going to be here for a while. Pay my rent, so to speak." Theresa dug in her pocket for a crumpled dollar bill and a handful of nickels and dimes. "Can you grab me a plain bottomless cup?"

"I got it." Alicia waved away Theresa's protest. "C'mon, it's a buck fifty, I think I can spare it."

Theresa nodded, her eyes widening for a few seconds as her lips pressed together.

Alicia thought something seemed off about her, though she couldn't quite put her finger on what it might be.

By the time Alicia brought back the drinks, Theresa had cleared away the empty bagel plate and set out her laptop. She'd brought an extension cord, of all things, to plug into the outlet closest to them, and she'd plugged both her phone and her computer into it.

"You're prepared," Alicia remarked.

Theresa gave her another odd, offbeat smile and took the empty coffee mug. "I started learning to be prepared when I went freelance. Because I don't work out of the office every day, I needed to find places where I could access the Internet, get charged up, stuff like that."

Alicia waited for Theresa to come back from filling her cup. "Must be nice. Having that freedom."

"It has its pros and cons." Theresa sipped the coffee and set it carefully on the table. "Puts a lot of mileage on my car. Sometimes makes it hard to get stuff done if I'm out and about and haven't found a good spot to roost. It's a little bit like being a traveling salesperson, always on the road."

"Have you thought about getting something more permanent?"

That seemed to be the wrong question, or at least a semi-impertinent one. At any rate, Theresa frowned and cut her gaze from Alicia. She tapped her fingers on her computer lid.

"Sure," she said finally. "Of course. Something with a steady paycheck would be great. Working on commission can be inconvenient. Never really sure if the money's coming in, or when."

"It was like that, owning the shop. We had our regulars, and of course the trips we scheduled always brought in regular money, but so much of it was seasonal." Alicia paused, thinking of how many times she'd budgeted their accounts to the literal penny, holding her breath until some money trickled in. "I'm not sure how I'll feel if I go back to work for someone else, but I won't miss that part. A steady paycheck would be a nice change."

Theresa gave her a wan smile. "Selling your share seems like it was a good choice for you."

"It was the right decision. I'm sorry Ilya didn't go for it." Alicia paused, watching the other woman. "He hasn't changed his mind?"

"He has a couple weeks left, but after that, it'll be too late." Theresa shrugged.

Alicia shook her head. "He's stubborn."

"Yeah." Theresa sipped more coffee. "So you're looking for a job? I thought you'd do more traveling."

"I want to. But I can't live forever on the money from the sale. I'm lucky I don't have a mortgage, at least. Being a lady of leisure doesn't seem to be in my blood." Alicia laughed. "So, yeah, I plan to do something. I'm not sure what yet. It's been so long since I had to think about it. I'm not even sure what I'm qualified to do."

"You'll find something." Theresa glanced at her computer. "Speaking of looking for jobs, I'd better get to work. I have some leads I need to research and stuff."

Alicia waved a hand. "Of course. I'm taking up your time."

Without much fanfare, both of them bent to their laptops. Theresa typed more regularly than Alicia, who'd intended to look up job listings but had instead spent most of her time scrolling through travel blogs. So many places to see in the world. How could she ever see everything? How would she decide where to go next?

"Zimmerman's Diner is going into foreclosure," Theresa said, out of the blue.

Alicia looked up. "Hmm? The diner?"

"Yes. We were there a couple nights ago." Theresa coughed lightly. "Ilya and I."

"I haven't been to the diner in ages. We used to hang out there all the time in high school. Sometimes we'd go right after school and stay there until Galina got off work. She'd pick us up on the way home. Or after the school dances. Wow, what a blast from the past." Alicia thought back to that. "Jenni worked there after she got her driver's license. We all kind of stopped hanging out there, after . . . well. So it's going into foreclosure?"

"Yes. It's got some back taxes owed on it. Nothing outrageous, but sometimes people just don't want to be bothered paying them. They want to dump it." Theresa looked thoughtful.

"That's too bad."

Theresa looked up with a smile. "Not for me. It's exactly the kind of property I should be able to get some interest in."

"You like what you do." It wasn't a question, but it seemed to take Theresa aback.

She nodded thoughtfully. "Yeah, I do. It's not exactly what I thought I'd be doing, but it's going all right. I think it might work out for me."

"That's a good thing."

"Yeah. Yes," Theresa said more firmly. "It really is."

"I hope he changes his mind," Alicia said suddenly. "I've tried to tell myself I don't care, that it's his business and he's no longer my problem."

"You were married for what, ten years? And part of each other's lives for longer than that. It would be strange if you just stopped caring."

Alicia frowned. "I know, but still."

"Do you . . . are you still . . . you're not in love with him anymore. Obviously." Theresa paused. "I mean, you and Niko are together. Right?"

Hearing someone else say it made it feel more real and also more like a dream. Alicia grinned. "Yeah. We are."

"That has to be a little complicated."

"No kidding. Plus, if it all works out, I'll have the joy of getting Galina back as my mother-in-law." Alicia snorted softly. "Lucky me."

"No kidding." Theresa's phone rang, and she pulled it out of her bag to silence it quickly. Whatever she saw on the screen must've disconcerted her, because her expression twisted. "Shit."

"You okay?"

"I have to take this outside. Can you watch my stuff?" Theresa was already getting up, closing her laptop lid, and grabbing her bag.

Alicia waved. "Yes, sure. Go. I'll be hanging out here for a bit."

Twenty minutes later, she looked up from her online scrolling to realize Theresa had not yet returned. Alicia got up to peek out the coffee shop's front window, searching. She thought she caught a glimpse of curly black hair standing by a car parked toward the front of the lot. When another ten minutes passed without Theresa's return, Alicia sent the other woman a text. Theresa didn't answer it. She waited another few minutes but, concerned, figured she ought to make sure everything was okay.

She packed everything up, tucking her own computer into her bag and Theresa's laptop into the protective sleeve she'd left on the table. Making sure she hadn't left anything behind, Alicia grabbed both bags and went out. She found Theresa standing by her car, a battered gray Volvo that had seen better days.

Theresa was crying.

This was awkward. Alicia cleared her throat to catch the other woman's attention, and when that didn't work, she reached out to touch her arm lightly.

Theresa turned, swiping at her eyes. "Hey. Sorry, that took longer than I thought."

"What's going on?"

"It's nothing. I mean, it's not nothing, but it's fine." Theresa rubbed again at her eyes, using the tips of her fingers to blot away her smearing mascara.

Alicia frowned. "It doesn't look fine."

"It'll be okay. Really." Theresa put on a watery smile that did nothing to convince Alicia.

"I brought your stuff." She held it out.

"Thanks." Theresa took the bag and set it on the trunk of the car. She sagged suddenly, shoulders hunching. "Thanks."

"Look, I'm sure it's none of my business, but you definitely don't look fine. You look terrible," Alicia said.

Theresa looked at her. No smile this time. She wasn't crying anymore, although she looked like she could start again at any minute. "I'm going to lose the stuff in my storage unit, which is everything I own that doesn't fit in my car, minus the stuff my ex was keeping for me in his garage and which he put out with the trash when he figured out I wasn't going to get back together with him."

"Oh . . ." Alicia wasn't sure what that meant.

Saying that seemed to break a dam, because now the words came fast and hard. "I'm six months behind on the payment. I don't have the money to pay the fees. I was counting on my commission check to be deposited this week, which would cover some of what I owe, but there's been a delay. I don't want to say it's my ex's fault, but I wouldn't put it past him to have screwed up the numbers on purpose somehow, just to cause me trouble. They reissued it, but it won't hit my account until the next pay cycle, which is in two weeks. I don't know how they think I can live for another two weeks on the change I might be able to scrounge up from underneath my car seats. I'm so screwed, Alicia. I thought it was all going to be okay, but it's not. I am totally screwed."

"I'm sorry. Can I help you?" At the sight of Theresa's bleak expression, Alicia felt her own stomach twist. Something was very wrong, but she had no idea what it could be. She'd known the other woman for a number of years, she realized, but knew very little about her. Still, she was family. There had to be something Alicia could do. "Can I lend you the money for the storage units?"

Theresa barked out a humorless laugh. "It won't matter. Thanks, but I'm so far beyond all that."

"Are you sure? How much do you owe?"

"Alicia," Theresa said wearily, "I'm literally fifty thousand dollars in debt. I am never going to get out from underneath this. Never."

CHAPTER THIRTEEN

Then

"Do you know how proud I am of you?" Theresa's father was in a good mood. He'd shaved, put on clean clothes. So far as she could tell, he wasn't using, at least not at the moment.

When he hugged her, Theresa closed her eyes and let him. They'd just returned from her high school graduation. She wasn't at the top of her class, but she did well enough to get a small scholarship to Millersville University. She was going to study accounting. This didn't thrill her, but it felt like a good, steady choice. She'd be able to get a job. She wouldn't have to live in a crappy apartment with roaches in the walls and rats by the dumpster. Not ever again.

"Very proud," her father added when she didn't answer.

"Thanks, Dad." She squeezed him in return, then let go.

It had been a tough year and a half since Galina Stern had tossed them out. Her dad had quit his job at the hospital two months ago, or so he said. Theresa suspected he was fired. Again. You couldn't miss so many days of work and not expect repercussions. He would find something else, he told her. It was what he always said. But he hadn't yet.

He was cooking dinner. Most everyone else she knew was having a graduation party, or at least going out to a restaurant in celebration, but Theresa didn't bother asking if they could do that. He might have said yes, but she'd just feel bad about spending the money. She took off her graduation gown and folded it neatly, along with the cap. She couldn't imagine ever needing either of them again, but since she was the one who'd come up with the money to pay for them, she wasn't willing to simply toss them. Beneath it, she wore the required white dress she also couldn't imagine ever wearing again. She'd bought it at the thrift shop for $3.99, along with the shoes for another three bucks. She hated the entire outfit, but it had done the job.

When she was out on her own, she would never have to suffer with thrift-store clothes or not eating in restaurants. She would make a good life for herself. She wasn't going to mess it up, either. Not with drugs or booze or falling for the wrong person. She'd make the right choices.

Her father's good mood continued over the spaghetti dinner he cooked. He poured them both glasses of cheap red wine even though Theresa wouldn't touch hers. She should have. He'd finish it for her. But what difference did it make, really? He'd drink the whole bottle. They both knew it. And later, there would be a pill or three from the tin he kept in his pocket. She ought to have known better, thinking he'd stay sober at least this one night.

"I'll take care of the dishes," he said when they finished eating. "Don't you have a party or something to go to? You must have a party."

She *had* received a few invitations. Theresa liked the kids at Central High about as much as they liked her, which was to say she had a few dozen casual friends and one or two good ones. Heather's family was in town, but Lia's party was tonight. Theresa could go to that.

"Nah, we can hang out, Dad." Everything was changing. No matter how eager she was to get out of there, she couldn't make herself forget that in a few short months, she wouldn't be around anymore. And then what would happen without her there to take care of things?

Theresa was giddy with the relief of not caring.

Her father shook his head. "You should go out, Theresa. You don't need to stay home with me. It's a Friday night. You should have a date."

"Yeah, sure." She laughed, shaking her head. "No, thanks."

"I don't understand you." He sighed. "When I was your age—"

"I don't see the point in it, Dad. That's all."

Tying herself down to someone now would be stupid, when she planned to leave as soon as she could. Millersville was only an hour or so away, but the rest of her life could take her anywhere. Besides, she thought as she cleared the table and washed the dishes while Dad packed up the leftovers, having a boyfriend would mean taking care of *him*, and she was just about over all that. She didn't ever want to take care of anyone except herself ever again.

"I'll run out and pick up a DVD. What are you in the mood for?" He jingled the change in his pocket—a restless, familiar sign. "Something funny? Scary?"

She didn't want him to go out at all. The DVD was an excuse. He'd probably already put in a call to someone while she was in the bathroom. He would come home flying.

"We can just watch what's on TV, Dad."

It was useless to protest. If she told him not to go, he would argue with her, and it would ruin the night. If she offered to drive him, he would end up lying to her face about what he was doing, and she would have to pretend she didn't know what was going on when he ran in "real quick" to "catch up" with his buddy.

For a moment, though, he stopped fidgeting to look at her. There was love and pride in his eyes. It was like he was really seeing her for the first time in a long time.

"Sure," he said. "Sure, okay."

He made it through forty minutes or so of inane TV before he started to jostle his knee up and down. Tapped his fingers on the arm of the sofa. He polished off the wine and moved on to even cheaper beer, but it wouldn't be long before he was digging in his pocket for the little tin that used to hold mints. If it was empty, he would go out to see if he could fill it.

He did go out a short time later. Theresa no longer wanted to watch TV. In the tiny galley kitchen that always stank of grease and garbage, she cleaned off the counter. Her father had separated out a stack of mail for her, most of it junk. The information from Millersville, about selecting a roommate, and when the first payments were due, she set aside. There were three credit-card offers addressed to her that she tossed in the trash. She'd seen her dad chasing the payments on credit cards, using one to pay off another. She wasn't going to get suckered into that, not if she wanted to start off ahead in life and not always running behind.

There was one other letter, already removed from the envelope. Theresa read it, then read it again to make sure she understood the contents, before looking at the discarded envelope stuck to the back of one of her letters. It wasn't addressed to her, and she was sure her dad hadn't meant for her to read it.

Written in a loosely looping and clearly feminine hand, it looked like it should have been a love letter; it was not. Theresa had no idea why Galina was writing to her father and, frankly, wished she didn't even know there was a letter at all. Whatever happened between them that kept them tied together was none of Theresa's business or her concern, and she didn't want to know any more about it. If her father wanted to spend his life going back and forth with a woman who thought it was okay to put them out on the street with only the clothes on their backs, he was more than welcome.

There was one part of the letter Theresa couldn't stop thinking about. Galina had called her dad out as an addict, something Theresa had never said aloud to her father or to anyone else. Galina's words also laid blame at his feet for something that had happened, something he'd done, unnamed but clearly horrible. Something to do with "all that money" he owed her.

Heart pounding, stomach sick, Theresa went to bed but couldn't sleep. She heard her father come home sometime later. The clatter of dishes in the kitchen. Running water. She tensed at the pause of his footsteps outside her bedroom door, but he didn't knock or try to come inside.

In the morning, sitting across from him at the table, she thought she would ask him why he was still tied to Galina, but in the end, she discovered she didn't really want to know.

◆ ◆ ◆

Once she'd begun unburdening herself, Theresa found herself almost incapable of holding back—except for the part about finding that letter from Galina. That was an entire tale, one she thought she'd never know the full depth of, and she didn't want to get into it. What she'd already spilled was bad enough.

"He opened almost a dozen credit cards in my name while I was in college. He ran up debt I had no idea existed until last year," Theresa said. Alicia had insisted on taking her somewhere to talk. Ironically, they'd ended up at the diner. She hadn't been there in years, and now twice in one week. "He'd been making the minimum payments on the cards for years, but always in rotation. He'd pay a few one month, then a few others the next. Always enough so he didn't totally default. Just enough to completely screw my credit score. I'd never had reason to look at it. I had one credit card that I got right after I graduated from college, which I never carried a balance on because I'd grown up watching him overspend, and I was determined I wouldn't live like that. I bought my cars used, with cash. Lived in the same apartment for years so I didn't need to go through the application process for a new one."

"Damn, Theresa, that's rough. I'm so sorry."

Theresa warmed her hands on the mug of coffee. It tasted burnt, but her stomach was churning too much to drink it, anyway. She shook her head.

"I'd been dating a guy for a couple years. When he asked me to move in with him, I thought it was a good idea, you know? I thought it was what I wanted." She didn't mention that the guy was Wayne, the owner of the company that had bought the quarry.

Alicia snorted soft laughter. "Let me guess. Not all it was cracked up to be."

"Not even close. It was fine at first, but after a while it turned out he was really serious about us. He asked me to marry him." Theresa's fingers tightened on the mug.

"Wow."

She nodded. "Yeah, exactly. When I said no, he didn't take it very well. I'd spent so many years making sure I would never be put in that position again. At least, unlike Galina, he gave me a few days instead of a few hours to get out. That's when I found out that I couldn't get an apartment because my credit score was so bad nobody would rent to me. And wouldn't you know it? I lost my job in a downsizing thing. That was about nine months ago."

Alicia shook her head and gave a low whistle. "I don't understand . . . why are you responsible for this debt? You didn't open the accounts. That's fraud, isn't it?"

"Yes." Theresa swallowed around the lump in her throat. "I'd have to file a police report and declare identity theft. I would have to prove I wasn't the one who'd made the charges. Instead, I consolidated everything into a single payment and closed the other accounts. I've been doing what I can, but it takes time to erase bad credit."

"Like gaining weight. Easy to put on, hard to take off." Alicia frowned. "Sorry. I shouldn't make light. He should be paying, Theresa. Not you."

"He sends me money every month toward it, but my father is not . . . reliable," Theresa said stiffly. "And before you ask me why I didn't just turn him in . . . he's my dad, Alicia. I don't know if I can forgive him for any of this, but he's still my father. I couldn't send him to prison."

"So you've been living in your car?" Alicia waved at the waitress to refresh their mugs, waiting until she'd gone before continuing. "All this time?"

"Only the past month or so. I stayed with some friends, on and off, although I didn't want to tell them this wasn't a temporary thing, so I could only stay for a few days at a time. I stayed with the Sterns for a bit around the time of the funeral."

"I wondered why on earth you'd agreed to do that," Alicia said.

Theresa laughed. It felt genuine. It felt good. She felt lighter, at least a little unburdened by her confession. "It was a place to stay. Food. I wasn't too proud to take it. Now you know."

"But what about the quarry deal? That didn't help?"

"It wasn't as much as I was counting on," Theresa said. "It was enough to take care of the debt I'd racked up over the past few months. Money I didn't want to spend but had to. My cell bill. Car insurance. That about wiped me out, but I need the phone and the car in order to make the cold calls I need to put these deals together. And I'm good at this, Alicia, surprisingly good, but everything is on commission, and so far nothing's really come in the way I need it to. Until then, I have to keep hustling."

Hustle was the right way to describe it, not that she'd admit that to Alicia. The quarry deal had been the best and biggest she'd managed to put together—but only by the skin of her teeth, and her ex-boyfriend's lovesick hope that helping her out would get her back into his life. She'd been lucky the entire deal hadn't fallen through when Ilya refused to sell, but as it turned out, she had a talent for this sort of thing. Wayne might have wanted to pull out to spite her once he knew she'd used his emotions to get him to agree, but his partners were completely on board with the hotel and condo plans. Working with them on this had led to other opportunities she hoped would soon pay off.

Alicia shook her head, frowning. "All of this sucks. No wonder you didn't look happy to see your dad when he came to the house after Babulya's funeral."

"I hadn't seen him since I confronted him about what I'd learned. Yeah, that was . . . awkward." Theresa stretched, rolling her neck on her shoulders. "You're the first person I've told any of this to. Thanks for listening. I guess I needed someone to vent to."

"Are you kidding me? I can't imagine having to deal with all of that. You've held it together remarkably well, better than I ever could have." Alicia leaned across the table. "Look. You come stay with me."

Stunned at this sudden and undeserved generosity, Theresa shook her head. "No, I couldn't . . ."

Alicia held up a hand. "Don't even. I'm in that house all by myself—"

"For now," Theresa said with a grin.

Alicia grinned, too. "For now. And for a while, anyway. Niko and I haven't even talked about making anything permanent, and I have no idea what's going to happen. But I definitely have an extra bedroom, and you're going to move into it until you get back on your feet."

"I can contribute," Theresa said at once, already deciding she was going to take the offer. She had to. This was no time for too much pride. "Not a whole lot. But you won't have to carry me, Alicia. I mean . . . you don't have a job, either. And trust me, you don't want to get behind on things."

Alicia shrugged. "Honestly, my parents left me pretty well set with the house. I have money left from the sale. It will last me for a little longer. If you chip in for utilities and food, I'm good with that."

This gesture was beyond generosity. This felt like true friendship. It struck her, then, why she hadn't asked her other friends to help her out. It had been more than embarrassment. Shame. It had been a deep-seated knowledge that even if she did ask, none of them would have offered her anything close to what Alicia just had. There were friends, and there were people who would always be more than that.

When she said as much, Alicia's brows rose. She shrugged. "Well . . . we've known each other for a long time, Theresa. I mean, just because we haven't been superclose doesn't mean that it doesn't count."

"It would only be for a little while," Theresa insisted, but her heart lifted. She didn't want to cry, but she wasn't sure she was going to be able to hold back.

"It would be for as long as it takes," Alicia said. "Okay?"

Theresa wiped her eyes. "I don't want anyone to know about my dad. The rest of it is bad enough, but please, don't tell anyone what my dad did."

"I won't say anything."

"Not even to Niko. Please, Alicia. It's so embarrassing. And definitely not to Ilya." Theresa paused, considering for a moment the folly of blurting out that she and Ilya had made out by his front door, and that had somehow made things different enough between them that she cared about saving face. Wisely, she kept that bit of information to herself.

Alicia looked wary at the request, but then nodded. "I'll do what I can. And I'll lend you the money for the storage units so you don't lose your stuff."

At that, Theresa could no longer hold back the tears. She tried to say thanks, but nothing came out. Alicia's eyes were bright, too. They both sniffled and grabbed napkins to dab at their eyes.

"Thank you, Alicia. Thank you so much." Theresa shook her head. "I can't even begin to describe what this means to me."

"Don't worry about it," Alicia said. "And, hey, look at it this way. If you're right across the street from him every day, maybe you'll be able to convince my stubborn ex-husband to take that deal."

"Right," Theresa answered. Across the street from Ilya. Every day. Every night, too. Her heart thumped harder at the thought. "That would help."

CHAPTER FOURTEEN

Then

If there'd been men in his mother's life, Ilya hadn't known about it. Hadn't wanted to know about it. The fact that she'd been bringing this joker around for the past couple of months should've set off warning bells.

"She says they're going to get married!"

Ilya paced in Jennilynn's den. Her parents were still at work, and her sister was upstairs in her room with the radio playing loud. Summer vacation just started, but already they were a little bored, wanting to get into trouble. He and Jennilynn had planned to smoke a little weed and watch some shitty scary movies, the kind with a lot of bare, bouncing boobs and blood. He didn't feel like doing any of that now.

Jenni tossed her long blonde hair over her shoulder. "She's going to marry *that* guy? The one from the hospital?"

"Barry Malone. Yeah. That's what she says. Next month. Talk about short notice." Ilya threw himself onto the couch beside her.

"Maybe she's knocked up," Jennilynn said, and ducked away from the cushion he used to hit her. "Stop it, jerk!"

He knew she was teasing him, but he couldn't find a way to laugh. "You wouldn't be laughing if it was *your* mother."

"Aw. Poor puppy." Her frown was also teasing, but something in her voice was soft and tender.

It called to him. Everything about Jenni had been calling to him over the past couple of months. It wasn't like he hadn't noticed her banging-hot body, that long blonde hair, and those blue eyes that could give a guy a boner from all the way across the room before now. But they'd been friends for so long that something seemed wrong about him wanting her that way.

Still, when she gestured for him to come closer, he gave in to her embrace. She petted his hair. The kiss happened almost by accident, though later he would think they both knew all along that it was going to happen. He wasn't sure who pulled away first, but when the kiss ended, her eyes were bright, her cheeks flushed, her lips wet.

He was suddenly, achingly hard. Somehow she was on his lap, his face in her hands and her mouth on his. They kissed and kissed and kissed, and she ground herself against him until he couldn't stand it anymore. He had to push up against her, turn them both until they were on the couch with him between her legs. They were moving and rocking together, and he'd give just about anything if she'd let him touch her bare skin with his.

It was enough to make him forget about Galina and Barry and his daughter, who would be moving in to Ilya's house as soon as they got married. For now, all Ilya could concentrate on was the girl beneath him. The sound and smell and taste of her.

She went still at the sound he made when the heat burst and let go inside him, staining his jeans. She looked into his eyes. Her mouth twisted in a secret kind of smile.

"Hey, let's go to the firemen's carnival," she said. "My mom left me some money to order a pizza for dinner, but if we let Alicia come with us, we can use it there. Call Niko. Babulya will drive us, won't she?"

At the carnival, the four of them gorged on junk food and rode a few of the rickety rides. Alicia and Niko broke off to go find funnel cakes, but Jennilynn stopped in front of the game booth decorated with gigantic grinning goldfish.

"You want one?" Ilya had a couple of bucks in his pocket, and after what happened on the couch, he was willing to get her whatever she wanted.

It took him several tries, but at last he sunk a Ping-Pong ball into one of the small fishbowls. Jennilynn held up the plastic bag, the water swirling with crap, and squealed at the sight of the gold-and-black fish inside.

"I'm going to name him Chester," she said, and gave Ilya a kiss on the cheek.

He'd loved Jennilynn Harrison forever, he thought. He would always love her.

It seemed impossible that he could do anything else.

CHAPTER FIFTEEN

The dive shop didn't have much of a sound system, just a small radio set on one of the shelves behind the front counter, and an MP3 player dock in the office. Ilya supposed Alicia must've listened to music through her computer, but that was nowhere near loud enough for what he wanted right now.

The heavy equipment had come in this morning while he was working on setting up another trip. The constant crashing and noise were making him crazy. That, and watching them destroy everything.

He wanted to listen to some music to drown out all the noise, but the best he could do was tune in to a scratchy soft-rock station that wasn't loud enough to cover up the sound of a squirrel farting, much less three dump trucks and a bulldozer. Muttering curses, Ilya went to the front door to watch. It didn't take long for them to clear away the pavilions and the bathhouse, neither of which had been in the greatest shape to begin with. Still, it stung to see them go down in a clatter of splintered wood that barely filled the back of one truck. The spaces left behind seemed so bare, especially with all the ground torn up. So far they hadn't started taking down any trees, but that would be next, he thought, with another string of under-his-breath curses.

Back inside, Ilya pulled up his computer browser again to check confirmation e-mails. He had sent out the usual e-mail blast and put something up on the shop's Connex page, but of the two dozen or so divers who usually made the trips with him, only four had responded with interest in the one he was planning now. One of the more popular dives was in Belize, a more expensive trip, to be sure, but always well attended. At least it always had been in the past.

Idly, he opened his phone to look at his messages. Specifically, the last from Theresa, which was a simple K. He swiped to delete it before he could stop himself, although he didn't go so far as to also delete her from his contacts. He might want to talk to her again, he thought. He might need a ride home.

He might need . . . something.

He scrolled through other messages, deleting most of them. Some had no contact information, others a simple word-or-two description. Very few had both a first and last name, and the sight of so many hopeful or desperate or angry or dismissive messages connected to nothing, barely even memories, disgusted him. When had he gotten so casual about all this? he wondered. Swipe, delete, swipe, and delete. Why did it seem to matter so much that he wasn't that guy anymore?

It had nothing to do with long, dark, curly hair, golden-amber eyes, and a sharp wit, he told himself. Nothing to do with those kisses at the foot of the stairs. And absolutely not related at all to the fact that Theresa had been there for him when he needed her, something he didn't want to trust but could not make himself forget.

He was so caught up in his phone that Ilya didn't hear the bell over the shop's front door jingle, but at the sound of a hollered greeting, he went out front to greet a familiar face. "Hey, Deke. Good to see you."

Deke had been coming to Go Deep since they'd opened it. Today he wore a pair of battered board shorts, flip-flops, and a tank top, even though the temperature outside couldn't have been higher than the low sixties. He gave Ilya a grin and two thumbs-up.

"Hey, man. Patty's supposed to be meeting me here. We figured we'd get in a dive today, but what the hell's going on over there?"

Ilya went around the back of the counter to pull out the standard release forms divers had to fill out every time they went under. "Someone's going to build some condos over there."

"No shit, man, really? I mean, I thought I heard something like that, but wow, it's really happening? The hotel, too?" Deke scrawled his signature on the form and ran a hand through his shaggy hair. "Get out."

"Alicia sold her part of the business. Yeah. So it's just me hanging on." Ilya punched a few numbers into the register. "You want a daily pass or another season pass?"

Deke shrugged. "I dunno, man. You tell me."

"Shit," Ilya said wearily, thinking ahead to the very real possibility that there wasn't going to be any season. "Tell you what. Dive's on me today. I need to get in the water."

"You sure? Me and Patty, we don't mind paying. I mean, free's good, too," Deke said with a smile, "but I'm not trying to jack you out of the daily rate."

"You guys have been coming to Go Deep since the beginning. And it's just me now, so I get to be generous."

Behind Deke, the door opened again. Patty was already wearing her wet suit, unzipped and folded down to the waist. She carried her tank with her. "Hey, Ilya. I'm gonna need a fill."

"On the house," Ilya said. "Along with the dive."

Patty gave Deke a look. "Huh? You sure?"

"Yeah. Special appreciation gift for longtime customers." Ilya's smile felt like it was going to crack the corners of his mouth. "Consider it a bonus for making it past all the construction."

Patty nodded, expression serious. "Yeah, I heard about the hotel. I wondered if that was going to affect you at all."

"They said it wasn't. But it will," Ilya said.

"Could be good?" Deke asked. "Bring more people in?"

Ilya didn't want to get into all the ways this deal could end up being bad for the business. He didn't want to think about it, to be honest. He wanted to slip into chilly waters and float with nothing but the sound of his heartbeat in his ears.

Less than an hour later, they were all suited up, tanks filled. Go Deep did not permit solo diving. The liability insurance on that had always been far more than they could justify, and even Ilya, who admitted he could be a bit of a bastard when it came to playing by the rules, knew how easily a solo dive could go bad. Still, Deke and Patty had come to do their own thing, so as soon as they were in the water, he held back and waved them toward the sunken helicopter while he went a little lower to let himself drift along his personal favorite attractions.

The 1987 Volkswagen Golf was nothing exciting. It had been Ilya's first car, inherited from Babulya when she decided she no longer felt comfortable driving. He'd driven it for years before no amount of spit or prayers could keep it running. It had become the first attraction he and Alicia sank.

He pushed himself toward it now. The stream of silver bubbles rippled around him as he ran a gloved hand along the pitted metal. At one time, the car had been a deep navy blue, but time had worn it to a dull, deep gray. They'd taken out the seats before sinking it, stripped the insides to bare metal, and taken out the glass to prevent divers from ever accidentally or on purpose putting a fist through it and cutting themselves open to bleed to death in eighty feet of spring-fed water. Now he ran his hands along the side of the car as he swam around it. If he turned slightly, he'd be able to see the looming form of the helicopter where Deke and Patty were exploring. He wasn't expecting to see anything in the opposite direction, and certainly not a flash of orange and black on the car's other side.

He wasn't expecting the push of water being displaced by something swimming close to him. Close and big. Really big.

Ilya had been confronted with sharks, barracuda, and stingrays as big as his entire body. Ugly, aggressive electric eels. But all those creatures were in the ocean, where you'd expect to run into them, where you'd be on guard for them. Nothing like that should be down here. There were quarries that supported fish. Carp, pike, perch, and bass. In the plans he'd looked over from this development corporation, there'd been information in there about seeding the quarry with "fishable wildlife," but he and Alicia had never done that.

Another push of water swirled around him. Something flickered just out of view on the other side of the car. Impossibly, the car itself vibrated, like something was rubbing against it. Something big enough to shift it.

Ilya had been diving for years. He'd taught hundreds of classes, certified hundreds of divers. He knew the dangers of panicking and how to avoid it, but here he was with his breath coming swift and shallow as he flailed in the water, trying to get away from the car. Another thrum came from the Golf. A looming dark form showed itself through the windows, unclear but shimmering.

Nothing that big should be down here. Nothing that could swim or move, nothing that could start toward him. Ilya heard the rush and swoosh of blood in his ears. He knew to stay calm, but right then, all he could think about was getting away.

Despite himself, a shout lurched out of his mouth around his mouthpiece. Bubbles. The feeling he could not breathe. He spun in the water, kicking.

In seconds, firm hands gripped him, and he was pulled gently to the surface, where they broke the water, and he tore away his mouthpiece to gasp in gulps of air. Something brushed his legs, and he screamed hoarsely, jerking them upward while Deke shouted in response. Patty had not surfaced with them but broke a second or so later.

He was going to drown, Ilya thought. He was going to get pulled under and eaten by it. The stories he'd been telling for years were true.

"Chester . . . ," he managed to say.

"C'mon, man." Deke took him under one arm and got him swimming toward the end of the dock. It was only a few feet, a few minutes, and by the time they got there, Ilya was already remembering how to breathe.

Embarrassed, he shook off Deke's help getting up the ladder. He tossed off his mask and sat on the edge of the dock, looking over the edge, convinced he was going to see the gaping maw of an overgrown, mutant goldfish devour Patty. He didn't breathe easy until she was up the ladder, too, kneeling next to him and squeezing his shoulder.

"You okay?"

"I saw it." Ilya looked at her confused expression and started to laugh. "All these years, all the stories—hell, I made most of 'em up. But I saw it."

Patty looked confused. "You saw what?"

"The goldfish. Chester."

Patty snorted laughter. "You're full of it. That was just something you spread around to get people to dive here."

"No. I saw it. It's enormous. It's almost as big as I am. It was behind the Golf." Ilya turned his head and spat. "Shit. I think I almost blacked out."

Patty sat back. "That's crazy."

"I saw it once," Deke said seriously. "Oh, back about seven years ago. I was out with one of the night classes you guys used to run. I was over by the copter. Had my flashlight. I shone it down, you know, just to see if I could get a glimpse of the bottom, but you can't there—it's what, seventy, eighty feet?"

"Something like that," Ilya said.

"What the hell are you both talking about?" Patty asked.

"Back in high school, we all went to the carnival together," Ilya said. "Played that game with the Ping-Pong balls and the goldfish, you know? Jenni Harrison won a fish. A big, fat orange one. She named it Chester.

But she got tired of taking care of it, right, because goldfish are dirty. Their tanks are always gross. So she brought it out to the quarry, and she threw it in. And he's been here ever since. Growing."

Patty pursed her lips. "Hmmm."

"There was a dude in France," Deke said solemnly. "Pulled a thirty-pound goldfish out of a lake."

Patty rolled her eyes. "You're both so full of it."

"I saw it on the Internet, it's true," Deke said again. "And I totally saw the one Ilya's talking about once, right in my flashlight beam. Huge goldfish, swimming away like it didn't give one good goddamn."

"It was a story we told people, but I've never . . . I never saw him. I mean, I didn't really think . . ." Ilya let himself fall back onto the dock, staring up at the sky.

"Now the goldfish on your logo makes a lot more sense," Patty said. "I always figured it was just a fish because, well, *water*."

"No, it's the carnival goldfish named Chester that Jenni threw in the quarry." Ilya shuddered and ran both hands through his hair. "It was huge. It was real. I didn't imagine it."

Jennilynn had gone and died, changing everything, and the fish had lived.

"I believe you," Deke said. "But next time, do me a favor and don't lose your shit over it, man. You scared me. Even if it's really big, it's still only a goldfish. Right?"

It was more than that, not that he'd ever be able to explain it to Deke. Or to anyone. Not even to himself.

"I was stupid," Ilya agreed. "Sorry."

"It can happen to anyone. That's why you don't dive alone." Patty slapped her thighs with both hands and then shaded her eyes to look across the water and the parking lot to the construction. "That's where they're going to build the condos, huh?"

Ilya had taken enough deep breaths by now that he was a little calmer, at least about the goldfish. The idea of the condos had his chest going tight again. "That's the plan, apparently. They don't have to ask my permission."

Patty gave him a sympathetic smile. "It might turn out okay, Ilya. I mean, maybe seeing Chester after all these years when you thought he was just a story . . . maybe that's a sign, right? It's all going to be okay?"

"Sure. Maybe." Ilya had been raised by two women superstitious enough to have put the belief of signs into him. The question was, What did it mean? "You guys going back in?"

"Nah. I gotta get going. But hey, man, about the Belize trip." Deke hesitated. "I know I said I was interested, but I can't make it. It's a lot of money, and I'm trying to save up for a new truck. And umm, well . . ."

"We're getting married," Patty said matter-of-factly. "So I told him that maybe we can go next year, but this year we have a lot of bills. Sorry, Ilya."

There went two of the four who'd expressed an interest. That was it. He was screwed.

"Mazel tov," Ilya said anyway. Just because he *could* be a dick didn't mean he always had to be.

Far out in the water, something splashed. A glint of orange flashed. They all looked, but nothing was there.

CHAPTER SIXTEEN

It would take more than a few days for Theresa to fully settle in so she could feel like she lived here and wasn't merely a houseguest, but it helped that Alicia had been spending a number of nights out with Niko, so Theresa often had the house to herself. Theresa had insisted on talking over everything with her new landlord/roommate—who'd be responsible for what chores, what Theresa was expected to contribute to the household, whether or not it was cool to drink the other's milk without asking. The last thing in the world she wanted to do was find herself homeless again because she'd crossed some line she hadn't known about.

Tonight, Alicia had gone out with Niko to the movies and dinner. She'd told Theresa not to expect her home until around midnight. Theresa had spent the day pursuing leads and checking in with a few new contacts she hoped she could connect with an architect who was interested in turning an old power plant on the outskirts of town into upscale apartments. There was money in that deal—a lot of it—if only she could get all the pieces in the right places. She'd also turned in some paperwork on a small deal that would bring her a few hundred bucks by next week. She'd made it home early, by four, parking in the empty spot in the garage and passing Alicia on her way out.

For the first time in months, Theresa was going to take a night off. No scouring the Internet for properties that looked poised for a cheap sale, no paperwork, no cold-calling, no cajoling or wheedling or flattering her contacts into meetings. She was going to bake some of Babulya's challah bread to use for French toast in the morning and maybe heat up a frozen pizza, take a hot shower, and get in her fuzzy pajamas, then indulge in a book from Alicia's vast paperback library. Many of the titles lining the floor-to-ceiling shelves in the den were from the horror heyday of the eighties—Alicia's father had been a big horror fan. Alicia had added a lot of lit fic and romances to the collection, along with some outstanding science fiction that Theresa was dying to get into. She'd sold off almost all her books at the used bookstore to gain some quick cash, and although she'd often utilized the public library, she hadn't felt much like reading over the past few months.

For the first time in nearly a year, Theresa felt like everything might eventually be all right.

She stripped down in the bedroom that had once been shared by Alicia and her sister. The walls still bore the faint outlines of the posters she'd so envied back then. Boy bands, cartoon cats, a unicorn. The twin beds had been replaced with a comfortable queen-size mattress and headboard, though the scarred dresser looked old enough to be the same. If she stayed here long enough, she'd get her own things out of storage, but for now it was nice to simply have a bed at all. She slipped into a faded terry-cloth robe to walk down the hall to the bathroom.

Unlike the Sterns, Alicia's parents had kept their home in better repair. The bathroom was small and outdated, but everything worked, including the shower. Under the beat of the water, Theresa thought she heard a rapping, but when she stuck her head out of the spray, she heard nothing. Old house, she told herself. At the subtle rumble of far-off thunder, Theresa quickly finished shaving her legs—another practice she'd been skipping too often and was delighted to indulge in now.

Wearing a robe, her hair in a towel, she went on bare feet down the stairs and into the kitchen, intending to check on the challah dough she'd left rising while she combed out her hair and put on pajamas.

At the sight of a blue jeans–clad rear sticking out from the fridge, she jumped, startled. "Hey!"

The guy raiding the fridge jumped, too, hitting his head on the bottom edge of the freezer door. Rubbing it, he glared at her over the fridge door, which he closed at the sight of her. His mouth opened. Then closed.

"Ilya," Theresa said. "What are you doing in here?"

He held up a beer. "I came to . . . this . . . what are you doing here?"

"I'm . . ." She sighed and pulled her robe closer around her throat. "It's a long story. But *I'm* allowed to be in here."

"I'm *allowed* to be in here, too," he said with a grin. "I'm just not *supposed* to be."

"Alicia isn't here." She eyed him, then the beer. It looked like he wasn't planning on leaving right away. She could make him, probably, if she insisted, but the effort seemed like too much work for an evening that had been meant for relaxation. "Grab that pizza out of the freezer, please. While you're standing there."

He did, waving it at her before setting it on the counter. "I was looking for my brother. Figured he was as likely to be over here as not. Guess I was wrong. I sure wasn't expecting to find you."

"They went out." She gestured to distract him from asking more questions. "Grab a baking sheet. They're in that drawer under the oven."

He bent, found one. Pulled it out. Without being asked, he slid open the cardboard box and pulled out the pizza, which was encased in plastic that he tore open so he could put the frozen circle of dough and sauce on the baking sheet. He even turned on the oven and put the pizza inside while she watched.

"Ham and pineapple," he said. "My favorite."

"Don't let your mother hear you say that." Theresa couldn't hold back a smile.

Ilya snorted. "Yeah, because suddenly after her entire life, she's decided to embrace a faith she never paid any attention to before to honor a woman who had abandoned it before my mother was even born."

"People cling to strange things when their lives change," Theresa said.

Ilya leaned against the counter and cracked the top of his beer and waggled his eyebrows at her. "Do you? Cling to strange things, I mean."

"Do you always walk into Alicia's house like you own it?" Theresa asked with narrowed eyes, not rising to the bait. She checked the dough, now soft and fluffy, peeking over the rim of the mixing bowl in which she'd left it. She took it out to place on a second baking sheet she'd already set out.

Ilya didn't answer right away. He took a long, long drink of beer and looked at her. She was very aware of her hair in the towel, the robe clinging to her damp skin. Her freshly shaved legs.

"Old habits are hard to break," he said finally. "You didn't answer my question about what you're doing here. In a robe, no less."

And naked underneath.

"I took a shower." She stood her ground, refusing to let a blush creep up her cheeks. She rolled the dough between her hands, pulling it into three equal pieces.

"You seem to be making a habit of using other people's showers, Theresa."

She cleared her throat, thinking of a response but found none. Uncertain why she simply didn't tell him the truth the way she'd told Alicia. It wasn't anything she had to be ashamed of, she told herself. After all, Ilya Stern had certainly had his share of screwups in his life. Even if he judged her, so what?

It was because of her father. His mother. The thing between them that Theresa knew in her gut had at least partially led to the trouble she was in now. It was a tie between Barry and Galina, and it shouldn't make a difference to anything between Theresa and Ilya . . . yet somehow, whatever it was, she knew it *would* matter. Family might suck. They might let you down, steal your name, put you in debt. But family was family, and each of them, when it came right down to it, would feel their loyalty to their own.

Why it mattered that she and Ilya get along with each other was a whole other story.

He eyed what she was doing with the dough. "What's that?"

"Challah," she answered. "It makes fantastic French toast, and I haven't been able to bake any in forever."

"Babulya's challah?"

"Yes," she said with a lift of her chin. "Her recipe."

He didn't answer at first, then said, "She gave it to you."

"She didn't, actually. She just taught me how to make it, and I remembered." Her voice shook the tiniest bit at the memories of those long-ago days in the kitchen with Ilya's grandmother. The days when Theresa had felt as though she, if only for the shortest time, belonged somewhere, with someone who cared enough about her to make sure she would be all right.

"I haven't had my grandmother's challah since a long time before she died." His voice was quiet, his expression neutral except for the glint of sadness in his eyes.

Theresa remembered how broken up Ilya had been when Babulya died. "Well. It'll be done in about an hour, and you can have some. Okay?"

"Why haven't you been able to bake it in forever?" he asked, circling back around in that way he had of focusing on the one thing she didn't want to talk about.

"I haven't had a place to stay with a reliable oven," she told him, hating that he kept asking questions she didn't want to answer.

"But . . . you're baking it . . . here?" Ilya seemed genuinely confused, and how could she blame him? She was doing her best to keep him in the dark, after all.

"Alicia's got a great oven."

"That doesn't explain why you're using it," Ilya said.

Theresa sighed with a frown, then simply said, "I'm staying here for a while."

"Why, so you can poke me about signing that deal?" Surprisingly, his voice was low, not confrontational. His look curious, but not aggressive. He took another drink and put the bottle on the counter to cross his arms. Waiting for her to answer.

"That's . . . that's not even . . ." She shook her head as she rolled the three pieces of dough into long logs, then pinched them together at the top so she could braid them. "That would be ridiculous, wouldn't it?"

"Why, then?"

She frowned. "Does everything in the world have to revolve around you, Ilya? Did it ever occur to you that not everything I do in my life is about you or that stupid deal? You've made it very clear you're not going to take it, so that's that. Okay? It's over. Done. Now, excuse me. I'm going to put this bread in the oven and then put on my pajamas. You should be gone by the time I get back."

He wasn't. In fact, he'd set the table with plates, glasses, and a bottle of wine from the rack on the counter. The pizza was set on top of the oven, the cheese bubbling.

"The challah wasn't done yet."

"It'll be another twenty minutes or so. And that's not my wine," she told him. "Or yours."

"We'll buy her another bottle. She won't care. I know for a fact Alicia doesn't like white wine," Ilya said. "I'm not even sure what it's doing there."

Theresa moved closer to the table. "That's really not the point, is it? She and I agreed that we wouldn't take what's not ours without asking first."

"Sounds like you really hammered out the details."

He poured himself a glass of wine and filled hers with sparkling water. It meant something, for him to remember. She and Wayne had been together for three years, and he'd asked her if she wanted a glass of wine right up until the night they'd broken it off, no matter how many times she politely or impolitely reminded him she didn't drink. Ilya hadn't impressed Theresa as the kind of guy to pay attention, but he had.

It made her more honest than she'd anticipated being. For a moment she wished she'd had the wine to blame it on. Instead, all she had was a weariness about keeping secrets and the desire to take a chance she might regret.

"I was living with someone. It ended, and he asked me to leave. Kicked me out, actually. I'd already put a lot of my stuff into storage when we were together, but he gave me a day to get my things and leave, which was more than your mother did when she booted us."

Ilya flinched. "Wow."

"He was really mad," Theresa said mildly.

"I didn't know you were . . . it was a serious thing?"

She fixed him with a look. "Yes, Ilya, it was a serious thing. He asked me to marry him, and I said no. It all went downhill after that."

"Shit." Ilya rubbed his mouth with the back of his hand, then laughed ruefully. "Why'd you say no?"

"I didn't want to marry him." Even now, the memory of the conversation with Wayne had the power to make Theresa's stomach squeeze and knot.

"You didn't love him."

Surprised, she shook her head. "Oh, no. I did love him. Just not enough, I guess."

"You dodged a bullet. Marriage is bullshit."

"Careful," Theresa said with a small smile. "You'll make me think you believe that."

"I didn't know you were even *with* someone," Ilya said.

She squeezed the back of the chair. "How could you have known? And you didn't ask. It doesn't really matter, anyway. It's over."

"But I wouldn't have . . ." Ilya lifted his glass of wine, not finishing his sentence, although she could've guessed what he meant.

That kiss.

Theresa went to the vase that held various kitchen implements on the counter next to the oven and grabbed the pizza cutter from it. She cut, then cut again. One more time. She grabbed two gooey slices and brought them quickly to the table, sliding them onto the plates he'd put there before the cheese could drip off.

"So Alicia let you move in here?" Ilya lifted the pizza to his mouth, biting, the cheese running in a long strand from his mouth to the slice.

It was nowhere close to an accurate timeline, but she nodded anyway. "Yes."

"That's generous of her," Ilya said.

She handed him a napkin. "Yes. It is. Very much, and I appreciate it."

She plucked a piece of pineapple from the top of the pizza and put it in her mouth, relishing the sweetness that had mixed with the saltiness of the ham. It was only a frozen pizza, but being able to buy it and put it in the freezer, then cook it for dinner . . . that was a luxury she'd no longer take for granted.

"That story about the landlord," he said after a few seconds. "That wasn't true."

"No."

"Why'd you lie to me?"

She'd been carefully avoiding his gaze, although she could feel it burning into her. She forced herself to look at him, lifting her chin, unwilling to let herself be embarrassed by this anymore. "I didn't want to admit that I'd been sleeping in my car."

Ilya took a long sip of wine and tilted his head to look at her. His eyes narrowed and his mouth pursed for a second as it looked like he tried to parse what, exactly, she was saying. "You've been what?"

"I've been sleeping in my car," she said finally, flatly. She waited for this to feel better, or to feel worse, or to feel anything other than as if she'd just leaped off a cliff without a hint about what lay at the bottom of the drop.

"For how long?" Ilya frowned hard enough to dig a crease between his eyes.

"The past few months, on and off. When I could no longer ask my friends to put me up on their couches, not without feeling like an idiot, or telling everyone the truth that I was completely destitute, I had only my car. Okay, are you happy now?" She drew in a breath, then another. Waiting to feel the impact of her fall.

"No, I'm not happy. Why the hell didn't you tell me this before?" He looked stunned, setting his glass on the table hard enough to slosh white wine all over the sides of his fingers.

"It wasn't any of your business!" She forced herself up from the table, pushing away hard enough to rattle the plates. "I didn't want you to know, okay? I was embarrassed. I was ashamed. I didn't want you to think I was a failure or something."

Ilya was quiet.

"Why did it matter what I thought?" he asked finally.

"I don't know. It shouldn't," she said. "Alicia was nice enough to offer me a place to stay until I could get on my feet. I took her up on it because I had no choice. Just like I accepted your mother's offer to stay there when I had no other choice. Just like I slept on your couch because the alternative was to sleep in my car, and I just . . . couldn't face it for another night, Ilya. This is not supposed to be my life."

She drew in a shaking breath.

"No," he said. "I guess it's not."

Theresa's fingertips skidded along the table's surface, but she didn't sit. Her appetite had fled. This pissed her off more than anything else— that all she'd been looking forward to was a quiet night alone, and here she was, stomach churning, heart pounding.

She went to the oven and pulled out the challah, golden brown and smelling like home. She held up the baking sheet so Ilya could see it before she put it on the stove top. It would need time to cool before she could cut it.

"Here," she said. "We can share it."

Ilya looked away from her for a second, then sat up straight in his chair and fixed her with a steady, unwavering stare. "Fine. I'll sign."

CHAPTER SEVENTEEN

"Stop it." Theresa's dark hair, still wet from her shower, had tumbled all over her shoulders and down her back in thick spiral curls that made Ilya want to tug them just to watch them spring back into shape. "That's low."

"I mean it." Ilya drank half his glass of wine. He looked at the crystal glass. It had been a wedding gift from someone on Alicia's side. He'd never liked the pattern.

Theresa dropped into her chair. Behind her on the stove top, a bit of steam drifted off the golden challah. "Please don't mess with me."

"I'm not. Let's say I had an epiphany. A sign." He thought again of the shadow in the water, the push of it against him. The flash of orange and black. "Do you believe in signs?"

"I don't."

He smiled faintly. "Babulya used to do that thing with her fingers, remember that? She'd poke her fingers at you and spit to the side. *Pfft, pfft, pfft.* It was supposed to ward off bad luck."

"I don't remember that," Theresa said after a reluctant second. "But I believe you."

Ilya sat back in his chair and ran his hands through his hair, scratching at his scalp before clapping both hands onto his thighs. "Do you remember Chester?"

"The goldfish," Theresa said at once. "The one Jenni threw into the quarry."

There'd been women over the years. So many he'd lost count. Not one of them would've known about Chester, other than Alicia. Not one of them would've known about Jennilynn, except perhaps maybe as a long-ago memory of a tragedy that lingered.

"What about him?" Theresa asked, when Ilya had said nothing more.

He studied her face. High, arched brows as dark as her hair. Had he ever known her eyes were such a clear, rich amber? Or had he only paid attention when he got her up close? The memory of kissing her pushed to the surface of his mind; he should be ashamed of that. Regret it. It should certainly feel like it had been a mistake.

It didn't.

"I saw him the other day, when I was on a dive. He's enormous." Ilya held his hands a foot apart, then moved them wider.

Theresa laughed, incredulous. Not that he could blame her. It was a pretty ridiculous story, one he could hardly believe now even though he'd seen the damned thing.

"Uh-huh," she said.

"I mean it," he told her seriously. "For years, we've been telling divers to look for him. Like a gimmick. I think, in a way, it was how Alicia and I could talk about her without talking about her, you know?"

"Yeah. I think I do."

Ilya wiped a hand across his mouth. "But there he was, even bigger than I could have ever imagined. Scared the shit out of me. I've never panicked underwater, Theresa. I've had a few close calls. Some scares. But in all my years of diving, learning, instructing, all the places I've gone, including our quarry . . . I've never been so startled or scared that I lost control. I could've drowned. If I'd gone in solo the way I'd thought about it, if someone hadn't been there to grab me, I might've."

She looked solemn. "Wow. That sounds scary."

"How could that fish," Ilya said, "still be alive after all these years?"

"No predators?" Theresa suggested, but that wasn't what he meant.

He shook his head. "Not that. I mean, you spend twenty bucks trying to win one for your girl, but they're not supposed to live that long. They're not supposed to outlast your relationship with her. They're not supposed to live when . . ."

"When she didn't?"

Ilya said nothing for a few seconds, looking into Theresa's eyes. She didn't speak, either, giving him time.

"We made up those stories like a joke, but they turned out to be real all the time. And this is still the first time I ever saw him, in all these years. Maybe it's just time to give up," he told her quietly. He closed his eyes for a moment or so, thinking of the 'dozers knocking down the pavilion. "I've been trying for years to make Go Deep worth something, and maybe it's time to admit I never will."

"It *is* worth something," she told him. "That's why they're going to give you all that money."

And, blinking, Ilya realized she was right.

The years of dreams hadn't been for nothing. He and Alicia had built something from nothing, and although he would never be able to deny that his ex-wife had been the bones of it all, he was still able to take credit for being at least a little bit of the flesh.

He eyed the bottle but didn't add more to his glass. His head was pleasantly swimming, not drunk, and it was a good place to stop. He hadn't been smart enough to make that choice in a long time, and it made him wonder again about Theresa's reasons for abstaining.

"Why don't you drink?"

"My father is an addict. Pills, though he's been known to overindulge in booze when he can't get access to the drugs." She cleared her throat, her voice scratchy and wavering until she steadied it. "I don't like the way it makes me feel."

"I like it," Ilya said in a low voice, thinking of the times he'd dived headfirst into the drink. He met her gaze. "Do you think that makes me an alcoholic?"

"I don't know. Do you think you are?"

"No. I mean, I don't think so." He turned the glass around in his fingers, then pushed it away, thinking of what she'd said to him after his grandmother's funeral. "I want it, but I don't need it. I guess if I can say no, that means I'm not?"

Theresa tilted her head to study him. "Are you worried about it?"

"Alicia used to say I drank too much," Ilya told her. "She wasn't the only one to say so."

"You do drink a lot. Maybe too much." Her chin lifted slightly, as though she expected him to deny it.

"Does it bother you?" he asked.

Theresa looked as though she meant to answer him but stopped herself. Her brow furrowed, and her eyes narrowed for a few seconds as she looked at him. "It would, yeah. Over time."

She smiled at him then, that crystal-clear gaze digging deep inside him. Somehow, Ilya was leaning over the table and finding her mouth with his, a soft and light kiss that he told himself he meant only as a confirmation. Slightly more friendly than a handshake, that was all. Yet at the whisper of her breath on his mouth, the parting of her lips, he found himself hating the span of the table between them because it meant he couldn't get any closer to her.

She pulled away first, turning her head a little bit. Ilya returned to his seat. Theresa's tongue slid along her lower lip for a moment before she pressed her fingertips to the curve of her smile. Her eyes glinted.

"You're used to getting away with that sort of thing, aren't you?" she asked quietly.

Ilya pressed his lips together, thinking of all those messages he'd deleted recently. "What exactly have you heard about me? Because I think it's disturbing that in all this time you've been hearing all kinds of stories about me, and I've barely heard a word about you."

"Of course you didn't hear about me," Theresa said sharply. "I moved out, and you all kept on going with your lives, and I simply disappeared—out of sight, out of mind. Babulya was the only one out of any of you who bothered with me."

This surprised him. "She did?"

"Yes." Theresa got up and went to the stove to cut the challah into thick slices. She brought over two and handed him one. She bit into the soft bread with a sigh, chewing. "For everyone else it was like I didn't exist. Never had. But she remembered me."

Ilya let the warm bread rest on his palm for a moment before inhaling the familiar scent. Nothing else smelled like challah bread. With his eyes closed, he could pretend the years hadn't passed and his grandmother was standing at the stove, lecturing him. He could pretend a lot of things hadn't happened yet.

But what would be the point? It had all happened, and he had to deal with that. Ilya bit into the bread, tearing off nearly half the slice and chewing. It felt somehow disloyal for him to like it, but damn if Theresa's challah wasn't as good as any Babulya had ever made.

"She never talked about you," he said.

Theresa shrugged and took another bite of challah. "She didn't have to. It wouldn't have made a difference. I was still gone. We weren't a family anymore. It didn't matter."

It should have, Ilya thought. "Still, you did hear stories about me."

"If it makes you feel any better, I didn't start hearing things until after Alicia and I became friends on Connex, and some of her friends started popping up in my timeline and stuff. You sure did manage to get around."

Ilya frowned, imagining threads of comments regarding his manhood . . . or lack thereof. "They talked about me on Connex? Did Alicia?"

"She never did. When I connected with them, some of them remembered who I was, and they would talk to me about you. Ask me questions about you." She gave him a shrug and a bland look and finished off her slice of challah.

"What'd you say back to them?" he asked after some silence had passed between them with nothing but the sound of chewing. He also finished his challah and dug back into the pizza.

Theresa laughed. "I told them the truth—that I hadn't been in touch with you and had no idea what you were doing or who you were doing it with."

This didn't set well with him. He pushed back from the table a bit but didn't get up. He drummed his fingers on the edge of it, instead, then frowned.

"Did they say I was a dick?"

She didn't laugh or smile but instead gave him a slow, assessing look that ended finally with a nod. "Yeah. Sometimes, some of them did. Were you?"

"Yeah," he admitted, not proudly. "Sometimes."

Theresa wiped her mouth with a napkin and then took a long drink of seltzer. "I joined a dating site the day after I broke it off with my boyfriend. For a while I averaged about four dates a week. Some for lunch, some for dinner. Some were overnights, especially in December when it was too freaking cold to sleep in my car."

Ilya blinked. "Wow. Shit. That sucks."

"Does that make me a dick? I didn't force anyone to do anything they weren't willing to do," Theresa said. "I might've made it seem like I was interested in more than I was so that I could get what I wanted at the time, and I'm sure I hurt some feelings. Does that make me a bad person? Or just an inconsiderate one?"

"I don't know," he admitted.

Theresa shrugged. "I never made any promises I knew I didn't intend to keep. That's the best I can say."

"Are you still doing that?"

"Not making promises I think I might break?" Her soft laugh sent a thrill through him, up and down his spine.

"Dating . . . like that."

Her chuckle faded, and she studied him. "Yes. Sometimes. Not as much, since I've started getting more work, but if someone looks interesting, sure."

"Do I look interesting?" It was easy as anything for him to say it, a casually tossed-out comment. Flirting because he found it easiest to talk to women that way, and because they almost always responded.

Theresa sat back in her seat. "What would you do if I said yes?"

"Take you on a date," he offered.

Theresa shook her head but smiled as though he'd charmed her, which *was* his intent. She put her fingertips to her lips, saying nothing. He couldn't stop himself from remembering how it had felt to kiss her. She shook her head again.

"You're not used to being turned down, huh?" she said.

He'd only been half asking as though almost helpless in the presence of an attractive woman to stop himself from taking it a step too far. "I've been turned down plenty of times."

She laughed. "We're not going to date, Ilya."

"Nah." He grinned. "Of course not. That would be stupid."

"It would be imprudent," Theresa corrected.

"It would be a bad idea."

She rolled her eyes and bit into her pizza so that a long, gooey strand of cheese stretched from the slice to her lips. She twirled her finger around it to break it off, then stuck it in her mouth to chew. "Anyway, besides, I already have a place to sleep."

She made him go home shortly after that, and later in his own bed, an arm beneath his head and his other hand resting on his belly while he stared up at the ceiling into darkness, he couldn't stop himself from wondering what he would've done if she'd said yes.

CHAPTER EIGHTEEN

Afternoon delight, nothing better. Niko stretched and yawned, drowsy beneath the blankets. Alicia sighed from beside him and nudged her head against his shoulder. Her hand, flat on his belly, toyed with the curly hairs below his belly button until, chuckling, he had to grab it to make her stop.

"Ooh, you're ticklish," she said. "I'll have to remember that."

He turned his face to kiss the top of her head. "Don't you dare."

"It could be fun," she told him. "Kinky, even."

Niko laughed but kept her hands from teasing him again. Alicia laughed, too, and kissed his bare shoulder before rolling onto her back. She kicked at the covers, pushing them down. When he protested, she knuckled his side gently and rolled over him to get out of bed, then walked naked to the chair in the bedroom corner so she could grab her robe.

"Don't." He pushed up on his elbow. "I like to see you walking around naked."

"I'm sure Theresa wouldn't appreciate it."

Niko fell back onto the pillows. "I thought you said she was working."

"She is, but she doesn't have set hours. She said she'd be back later, but you never know. Anyway, if I walked around naked all the time, you'd get so used to it that it wouldn't be a big deal anymore." She gave him an arch grin and tied the robe at her waist. "I'm going to grab a drink. Do you want something?"

"I'm starving."

She laughed. "If that's a subtle way of asking me to make you a sammich . . ."

"No," Niko said. "But if you want to . . . never mind, I'll get up. But I'm not putting on clothes."

"Fine, let your dingle dangle," Alicia said. "Don't blame me if Theresa comes home and catches you with your willy wagging."

Niko paused with his feet swung over the edge of the bed. "I don't think I realized how much I loved you until you called my dick a willy."

Alicia guffawed, and Niko sat back and enjoyed the beauty of that humor. To him she would always be gorgeous, but laughter transformed her. She didn't protest when he went to her and kissed her, although she gave him a curious look.

"What's that for?"

"Because I wanted to." He kissed her again, letting it linger this time. They'd spent hours making love, and, still, the touch of her tongue on his sent a shiver of delight through him. He nuzzled her neck until she laughed again, softer this time.

"I love you," Niko said.

Alicia pressed her face against his chest. "Love you, too."

Her shoulders rose and fell, and she shook a little. The soft hitch of her breath confused him. Niko pulled away to look at her. "What's wrong?"

"Happy." She wiped at her eyes, then pushed up on her toes to kiss him again. When she pulled away, her gaze was serious. "Niko, there's something I wanted to ask you."

"Shoot."

"I'm thinking of selling this house."

"Are you going to ask me to fix it up first?"

Alicia punched him lightly on the arm. "No! Stop it."

"Well, okay. So you want to sell the house. Then what?"

"Pay my parents back, first of all." She paused with a frown. "I could do that without selling the house, but it wouldn't leave me with much. And they're not *asking* me to pay them back for anything. I just feel like I want to return the money they gave me that had been meant for Jenni's college."

Niko didn't know what to say about this. He brushed the hair off her shoulders. "Okay."

"It was generous of them. It helped me and Ilya get started with Go Deep. And they sold me this house for way less than I would've spent on something else. If I sell it, I can repay them for the money they gave me and get out from under it. I guess that's the thing. I can put things behind me. Move on."

"Moving on sounds good." He settled his hands on her hips, holding her close. "Where do you plan to live?"

She gave him a hesitant, hopeful smile. "I thought you and I could talk about that."

Niko's brows rose. "About living together?"

"Well . . . yeah. Traveling first," she put in quickly. "I want to do some of that. But we'd still need a place to come home to. Maybe more modern. Not out in the middle of nowhere. Maybe not even in Quarrytown."

This gave him pause. "Not even here?"

"We could go anywhere," she said.

Niko kissed her again. "We could go *everywhere*."

CHAPTER NINETEEN

Ilya had brought in the mail, a handful of bills addressed to him, and the rest mostly junk. He'd opened the slim letter and shaken out the check made out to his mother in a nearly illegible hand without paying much attention to it until he realized it had not been meant for him. He looked it over. Fifty bucks, no change. The weird thing was it had come from Barry Malone.

"This is yours," he told her and set the check and envelope in front of her.

It was nearly three in the afternoon, but Galina was eating a buttered English muffin and drinking coffee. She snorted softly as she slid the check toward her. She shrugged, maybe at the amount, and tucked it in her pocket. "Thank you for opening my mail. Apparently I'm so old and decrepit I can't be trusted to do it myself."

"It was by mistake." He wasn't going to let her get to him. "Why's Barry sending you money?"

"We *were* married," Galina said, like that made sense.

Ilya snorted much the way she had moments before. "Sure, a million years ago."

"What can I say? He feels compelled to offer me financial compensation in restitution for being a terrible husband." Her smile broadened, looking wicked. She took a bite of her muffin, crunching. "Where is your brother?"

"I'm sure he's across the street."

"Ah." His mother twisted in her seat to look at him. "Sit. Talk with your mother. I haven't seen much of you for a few days."

He grabbed a can of cola from the fridge but didn't sit at the table. "I've been packing things up at the shop."

"Really?" Galina looked surprised. "Does this mean you sold it?"

If he said yes, she would ask him for money. Perhaps not directly. She was subtler than that. She'd always had a way of getting what she wanted, even without asking outright. Look at the way she was still getting money from her ex-husband of some twenty years ago. Telling her the truth would lead to a fight.

"Yep," Ilya said calmly. "I sold it."

Galina's eyes widened a tiny bit more before she nodded, looking pleased. "Good. I think that's the best thing for you. You've held on to that for too long. What will you do now? Travel, like Alicia?"

"I don't know." The truth was, he didn't love traveling. Sure, the exotic locations and liquors and, yes, the women had always been exciting, but his idea of a good time would always be a hotel with a clean, soft bed and an all-you-can-eat buffet. Trekking through mountains and any kind of wilderness didn't appeal to him at all. It felt like he'd already been most of the places he'd ever want to go.

"You'll figure it out," his mother said serenely and sipped from her mug. "I'll be going out later. Don't wait up for me."

"I don't ever wait up for you," Ilya answered.

She laughed. "I would think you'd be happy to know your mother has friends."

"You've always had friends," he told her. "You're the sort of person who always manages to find some."

Galina's smile became a little pinched. "Why does that sound like you don't intend it as a compliment?"

She was who she was, and always had been. He didn't have to like it, or her. But he couldn't do much to change it.

"Never mind," she said with a wave of her hand before he could answer, not that he had anything to say.

Upstairs, Ilya tossed himself onto his bed and considered pulling up a movie on his laptop, but it had been such a long time since he'd bothered to even log in that the account refused to let him. He'd been using Alicia's for years. He guessed she'd finally changed the password.

Idly, he pulled out his phone and pulled up Theresa's number. "Hey. What's up?"

"I just got home."

"To Alicia's?"

"Well . . . yeah," she said. "That's home, for now. What's up with you?"

"Just following up on things," he said as though that were the truth. "Any idea when it will go through?"

"They got Alicia her money within two weeks. I figure it will be about the same for you," Theresa said.

Ilya nodded. "Okay, I guess that'll have to work. I spent the morning clearing stuff out from the shop."

"How'd that go?"

"Easier than I thought," he said. Murmured voices through the phone caught his attention. "Is that my brother?"

"Yeah, he's over here. They're talking about ordering pizza and playing cards. You should come over."

"Sure. That'll be swell," he told her, his voice thick with sarcasm.

Theresa laughed. "Are you going to avoid them both forever? That could make holidays inconvenient."

"Bah, humbug."

"Come over," Theresa said. "It'll be fun."

CHAPTER TWENTY

Ilya and Niko had gone together to pick up the pizza while Alicia and Theresa dug through the cabinets in the den to pull out a selection of old board games. If Alicia or Niko was upset that Theresa had invited Ilya to join them, neither showed it. Still, she thought she'd better make sure.

Theresa swiped dust off the lid of an ancient version of Clue. "I should've asked first if you'd be cool with me asking Ilya to come."

"No problem." Alicia shrugged and held up Monopoly. "We used to play this for days."

"I'm not sure why I did," Theresa admitted as she set a battered game of Stratego on the table. "He called me to follow up on the offer, you both had just asked me to hang out . . . I don't know. I guess it felt like I should. Kind of like . . ."

"Old times?" Alicia nodded. "Yeah. I get it. Don't worry. Really. Ilya's the one who has to deal with me and Niko being together. It's not like I'm holding on to any lingering romantic feelings for him."

"That's good." She'd said it too quickly, so that Alicia looked up curiously. Theresa didn't want to remember Ilya's kiss or the way his fingers had felt in hers or the fact he'd sort of asked her on a date. Or anything else about him in that way, really. "It's got to be a little weird. But only for a little while, right?"

"I hope so." Alicia sat back to study the array of games they'd pulled out of the cupboard. "I haven't seen any of these in forever. So much stuff in this house . . . it's going to be a huge project to get rid of it all."

Theresa looked up. "Oh?"

"Yeah . . . so, I've been thinking about selling the house. Not right away," Alicia said quickly, although Theresa hadn't made so much as a murmur of protest. "I'd have to clear it out first. Lots of years of stuff here."

"And you want to move on," Theresa said. "I get it."

"I didn't want you to think I was going to kick you out after I just told you it was cool to stay, that's all." Alicia got to her feet with a small groan and a crackle of her spine as she stretched.

Theresa stood, too. "I appreciate it. So much. It wasn't ever supposed to be long term anyway."

Alicia nodded. "It's going to be a lot of work, though."

"I can help. I'm pretty good at figuring out what you need to take and what you can easily leave behind." Theresa tapped the lid of one of the games. "I've had some experience."

"I'd like to live somewhere I can get a pizza delivered instead of having to go out for it," Alicia said. "You know? I'd like to have a movie theater with more than two screens."

Theresa chuckled. "No kidding. Before I moved in with my boyfriend, I lived within walking distance of a couple nice restaurants, and I had three pizza places that delivered, along with a horrible Chinese place. Once I moved in to his house, it was back to flipping a coin to see who'd have to go out to get the food, and he somehow always managed to have an excuse about why it wasn't his turn."

"Maybe that's why you didn't want to marry him," Alicia said matter-of-factly. "If he'd been the one who offered to go, you might have thought differently."

Theresa laughed at first, then paused. Alicia wasn't kidding. She also wasn't wrong. "I couldn't stand the way he chewed. It made me insane with rage."

"Ilya couldn't find anything," Alicia said suddenly, sharply, as though the words hadn't meant to slip out of her. "Flat out refused to look, sometimes. Just said he didn't know where it was, whatever it was. It was infuriating."

"Is that why you broke up?" Theresa coughed lightly into her hand, trying not to sound too nosy.

"It seemed like it at the time. I don't think anyone gets divorced over one small thing. I don't think anyone necessarily gets divorced over one big thing, either. It's all the things together." Alicia frowned. "But what's done is done, I guess. It's not like I can get away from it. The only thing I can do is keep moving forward."

"Yeah. Forward." Theresa thought about that for a second, hating herself for asking the next question. "Do you think he cheated on you?"

Alicia didn't seem insulted or angry. She gave Theresa a thoughtful look. "No. No matter how much of a ladies' man he's been since we split up, I don't believe he cheated on me. Maybe he cheated *with* me, I guess, if you want to count the memory of a ghost."

"Jenni." Theresa frowned, sorry to have brought it up. "You don't think he'll ever get over her?"

"I don't think he wants to," Alicia said. "But he sure needs to."

"Behold, I am the bearer of beverages!" Ilya's voice rang through the den as he appeared in the doorway holding up two six-packs of what looked like craft beer. "My brother brings the pizza. And, ladies, hold yourselves back. We got a Caesar salad and garlic knots! So you may worship us as the gods we are."

"I'm *so* not worshipping you," Alicia told him wryly, but with good humor.

Ilya rolled his eyes and looked around her at Theresa. "I got some fancy iced tea for the teetotaler."

"Thanks." Theresa caught Alicia's surprised look but didn't say more than that.

"Oh, you got anchovies? Thank you, baby." Alicia offered her mouth to Niko for a kiss.

Ilya made a disgusted face and grabbed Theresa as she moved toward the cupboard to pull out plates. Laughing, she tried to pull away, but he was dancing with her, making goo-goo eyes. She gave in after a second, letting him twirl and then dip her.

"Ooh, baby, thank you-u-u," Ilya said in a sickly sweet falsetto.

"Jerk," Niko said without rancor, and planted a long, involved, and exaggeratedly sloppy kiss on Alicia's mouth.

Theresa turned her face at the last minute so that Ilya's attempt at doing the same landed on her cheek. "Don't be a cretin."

He made sure she was steady on her feet before he let her go. "Damn, Theresa. A cretin, really? That hurts me right in the feelings hole."

"I said *don't* be one." She nudged him with an elbow. "C'mon. Food."

Ilya sighed and shook his head, but if he was truly put out by the sight of his brother and ex-wife snuggling, he didn't show it. "Both of you, just so you know, that's how germs spread."

"I'll take my chances." Alicia, eyes bright and cheeks flushed, laughed. "But I'm with Theresa. Let's eat."

Theresa hung back a bit, letting the others go first. When Alicia and Niko had taken their plates into the den, she snagged Ilya's sleeve as he loaded his plate with a couple of slices of pizza. "You okay?"

He glanced over his shoulder. "Huh? Oh. Sure. I mean, it's weird, right? Tell me it's weird."

"It's a little weird. Yes." She took a bottle of the iced tea he'd brought her and cracked off the top to take a drink.

They'd moved toward each other without making too much of it, their voices lowering so Niko and Alicia wouldn't overhear. This close to him, she could see the rim of indigo around his grayish eyes. He smelled like fabric softener, a sensory memory, again of that time so many years before when they'd shared the same house and the same detergent. So he might not ever get over Jennilynn Harrison, Theresa thought. There were plenty of things she wasn't quite able to get over, either.

Ilya smiled. "Whose idea was it to ask me to come over?"

"Mine."

He nodded. "I haven't played board games in a long time."

"Me neither." She grinned. "I bet I kick your butt."

Ilya leaned close and closer, until the soft whiff of his breath gusted along her cheek. "Bring it."

◆ ◆ ◆

Watching Niko and Ilya square off as team members, one trying to get the other to guess a word on a card without using a series of forbidden words, was the funniest thing Theresa had seen in . . . well, a long time. Her stomach hurt from laughing, and she was sure her mascara had become a streaked mess, but none of that mattered. She hadn't been convinced the game-night idea was a good one until now, but man, was she glad they were doing it.

"Time's up!" Alicia slapped the buzzer to turn off the annoying sound. "Losers."

Ilya flipped her both middle fingers as Niko did the same. Then the brothers gave each other high fives. Alicia made a face, and when Niko crossed the room and tried to kiss her, she fended him off. At least for a second or so, before she dissolved into laughter and gave in.

"Gross," Ilya said conversationally as he plopped onto the couch next to Theresa. "You're going to get mono."

"That was the game," Theresa said. "We won."

"Yeah, yeah, whatever," Ilya said. "We gave it up to you."

Alicia shot him the bird. "L-l-looooooser."

It was a lot like it had been back in the day, even if at the same time it was completely not. Theresa recalled a lot more f-bombs being thrown around back then, along with noogies and wrist burns. The good feeling was the same, though. Back then they'd enfolded her into their group effortlessly, if only briefly, and she felt the same way now.

Part of something.

Belonging.

Included.

But only briefly.

She caught Ilya watching her and quickly smoothed whatever expression she'd had that had made him frown. "Rematch?"

"Not for me. I'm beat." Niko shook his head.

Alicia stood. "Me, too."

Theresa and Ilya shared a look. It was obvious that Niko and Alicia had plans that were going to keep them up at least an hour longer, if not more. Not that she blamed them or anything, but the walls were thin upstairs. She wasn't going to go up there for a while. Theresa busied herself cleaning up the game pieces while Ilya, unbidden, took care of the dirty plates and bottles. She followed him into the kitchen when she'd finished.

"So . . . I'm going to watch a movie," she said. "You want to hang out a little longer?"

"You don't have to work in the morning?"

She shrugged. "I make my own hours, and I don't have any appointments until the afternoon. It's only eleven now."

"Yeah, I guess I could hang out. Watch something. Sure." He didn't move, and neither did she.

He hadn't shaved in a few days by the look of the scruff on his chin and cheeks, and suddenly all she wanted to do was rub her palm over the bristles. His hair was silky smooth, his face rough. It had tickled her earlier, and she touched her cheek, remembering. She should've felt caught by his gaze but instead felt only embraced.

He was going to kiss her again, and this time they were alone, so she would let him.

He didn't, and the sweet anticipation tinged with anxiety eased within her. She hadn't misread him. He'd changed his mind. She saw it in his eyes and the tilt of his small smile and the way he let one finger twist into one long curl that hung over her shoulder.

He *wanted* to kiss her again, and maybe that was going to be all they'd ever have. Wanting. Better off for it, she told herself as she let out the breath she'd been holding. They knew there was no good that could come out of acting on this.

In the den, she let him pick the movie while she rearranged the cushions and knitted afghans on the back of the couch to give them both room to sprawl. He chose a recent release full of gunfire and car chases, and despite the action and noise, less than halfway through it, he was yawning broadly. Shortly after that, Ilya had twisted on the couch to lay his head in her lap. Her fingers found the softness of his hair, threading through it. Every so often she let her hand caress downward, giving in to the urge to rub his bristly cheek before moving up again to stroke his hair.

In the TV's flickering blue-white light, she could let her gaze fall to his face every so often. She could trace the line of his brows with her fingertips. She could feel the weight of his head in her lap and see the gleam of his eyes when he looked at her. Neither of them spoke. Words would've ruined this, whatever it was. Speech would've forced them to acknowledge it.

She watched him fall into sleep.

The movie ended, and the room went briefly dark after the credits had finished scrolling. In the darkness, Ilya moved on the couch, shifting to press her back along his front so the two of them were spooning. His breath heated the back of her neck, her hair a barrier to the touch of his lips.

"Thanks for asking me to come over," he murmured.

Theresa didn't answer him. She closed her eyes, listening to the slowing in-out of his breath and relaxing against him. And then, sometime before morning light began its creeping crawl through the windows, she got up and left him there while she went to her own room and her bed, but she wasn't able to get back to sleep.

CHAPTER TWENTY-ONE

Meet me at the diner at one today.

The message had pinged his phone about an hour earlier, but Ilya hadn't heard it. Now he had only twenty minutes or so to take a shower and get over there, and even if he rushed, he was going to be a few minutes late. He shot Theresa a message in return letting her know he was on the way, but he stalled out in his bedroom, not sure what he ought to wear.

It wasn't a date, he reminded himself. They weren't going to do that. Even if he *was* interested in dating anyone on a regular basis, which he wasn't and hadn't been for a long time, it couldn't be Theresa.

"You look nice," Galina said when he stopped in the living room on the way out to tell her he was leaving. "You always did clean up well, Ilyushka."

She sounded drunk, although there was no evidence of her drinking. The pet name was a sign, though, as was the way she lolled on the couch watching daytime television. Ilya ran a hand over his hair, damp from the shower, and looked down at the jeans and T-shirt he'd finally decided were nice enough to make it obvious he'd put in some small effort, but casual enough to show it hadn't been too much.

"I'm going out," he said.

His mother laughed, low and throaty. "I see that. To meet a girl, yes?"

"I'm . . . yeah. Sure." He patted his pockets to check for his phone and wallet and keys. He didn't want to ask, but he did. "You okay? Do you need anything?"

"I'm fine. You can bring back some coffee and cream when you come home. We're out, and your brother used to be sure we had some, but I suppose he has more on his mind these days than whether or not his mother is supplied with coffee and cream."

"Yeah, I can do that." Ilya hesitated, wanting to get out of there, but the old, distasteful compulsion to check up on his mother lingered. "You sure you're all right?"

She looked at him. "Go meet your other woman. I'm fine, I told you."

"She's not—" He bit back the words. Galina was baiting him the way she'd been doing for years, but he didn't have to rise to it. Instead, he nodded and ducked out of the living-room doorway without another word.

He made it to the diner in another fifteen minutes by taking backstreets and avoiding the traffic lights. He pulled in at 1:12 and had no trouble finding a spot in the lot because the only other car there was Theresa's battered gray Volvo. She was leaning against it, tapping a message into her phone, but she looked up with a smile when he got out of his car.

"Hey," she said. "You made it. Good."

Ilya looked toward the building, brow furrowed. "Doesn't look open."

"It's not. They closed last week." Theresa slipped her phone into the bag hanging on her shoulder and clapped her hands together. "Want to go inside and check it out?"

"Like . . . break in? Aren't we a little old to be doing that sort of thing?"

She grinned, and once again Ilya was struck with how broad and beautiful that smile was, and how a man might be tempted to do almost anything to earn another from her. "I have the key."

"How'd you get a key?" He followed her across the lot to the front door.

She glanced at him over her shoulder as she fit the key into the lock in the double glass doors. "I have a good relationship with the Realtor. I took care of a lot of property transactions at my last job. Sometimes she couldn't get to a site at a convenient time for the buyer, so I handled it. She trusted me with the keys. C'mon inside."

Ilya had been inside the diner hundreds of times over the years, but it looked different when it was dark and empty. He waited as Theresa found the bank of light switches on the wall and flipped them on. She gave him one of those grins he couldn't help returning and gestured at him to follow her into the center of the dining room. She spun slowly, looking around and even upward to the ceiling.

"It needs some cosmetic work," she told him. "But I had everything else checked out from some people I really trust, and it's still solid. And the price is totally right. Apparently the Zimmermans want to unload it as fast as they can so they can get out from under the back taxes and just move on."

"Wait, wait." Ilya held up both hands. "What's going on here?"

Theresa's smile faded, though her gaze stayed bright and focused on his. She drew in a small breath, as though gathering courage, but when she spoke, her voice was steady and strong. No hint of hesitation. "I think you should buy it."

"Buy the . . ." Ilya burst into laughter. "Right. I'm going to buy this place? Why would I do that?"

Theresa moved toward the long diner counter lined with swiveling red stools and hopped up to sit on the counter's edge. "Because you need something to do with yourself. You want to own a business instead of working for someone else. And because you'd be good at it."

"Good at running a restaurant? Isn't that like the hardest kind of business to run?" Ilya shook his head. "I have no experience with that sort of thing."

Theresa nodded. "I know. But my job is connecting people with properties I think they'll really be able to turn around and make successful."

"And you think that's me and this place?" Ilya joined her with a hop up onto the counter. They both swung their feet, knocking their heels on the edges of the swivel stools. He nudged her with his shoulder. "Are you for real?"

"Totally for real," Theresa said, and nudged him back without moving away again so that they settled there with their shoulders touching. She looked at him.

He thought in silence for a moment. "It would need to be different than it was. Different menu, still a diner, but lose the stuff nobody eats, and make sure there's always breakfast all day. Keep the retro look. It could be good."

There were bones here. He could cover them with something. He knew it.

"It would be great," Theresa said.

"I don't want to do this alone," Ilya said seriously. "You'd have to come in on this with me."

Theresa looked surprised. "Me?"

"Yeah. You. The one who knows Babulya's secret recipe for borscht. And her challah."

"You think borscht would be a big seller?" she laughed gently.

Ilya smiled. "You know how to make a lot of her favorite recipes, right? What would be better in a diner than some of the meals she used to cook for us? Potato pancakes, borscht, black bread."

"Knishes and piroshki." She sounded thoughtful.

"Lots of Greek diners around," Ilya told her. "Why not a Russian Jewish diner?"

Theresa laughed, tossing her head back for a second before she settled her gaze on him again. "Right. Why not?"

Ilya snapped his fingers, getting excited by the idea. "Challah French toast. Egg-salad sandwiches with macaroni salad. Bagels with lox."

"Matzoh ball soup," Theresa said at the same time he did.

"Yeah," Ilya added quietly. "That."

Theresa nodded again. "I'm not a chef, though. I mean, I know how to make all that stuff, but I'm not sure about doing it for a restaurant. Besides, I already have a job."

"If I can learn to run it, you can learn to cook for it," he said. "And you told me already that you're doing freelance work. So you fit it in around shifts here, or training the cooks. I don't expect you to be the one to actually sling all that hash. Shit, I can't believe I'm actually considering this."

"I told you that's my job. Getting people together with projects they can really run with." She paused. "I ran some numbers for you, and I did have some insider information about that big check you just got. So I already know you can afford this. But I can't."

"Silent partner?" Ilya hopped off the counter to take a walk up and down, looking at the diner with new eyes. From behind him, he heard Theresa also jump down. "We could work something out. You have the recipes. I have the cash. You have the connections. I have the . . . hell, I have the . . ."

"You have the chutzpah," she said.

He laughed and reached out to take her hand, tugging her closer. She came, reluctantly, but didn't resist when he put his hands on her hips. "Hey."

She tipped her face toward his. "What?"

"Who else did you take this to?"

She gave him a curious look. "What do you mean?"

"Am I the only one you brought this to, I mean? The diner. The idea of buying it. Or am I just one in a long list of hopefuls?"

He was asking about the diner, but there was a hint of another question in his voice, one he hadn't meant to ask. At least not aloud. He resisted pulling her closer, the idea of her body pressing against his definitely not even close to being brotherly.

"I brought it to you. Only you." She smiled a little. "Does that make a difference?"

"Just wanted to know if I had any competition, that's all."

Those clear amber eyes narrowed the tiniest bit as her full mouth pursed. "I see."

There was that zing again, the flutter and pull of the need to make her smile. Ilya had been with a lot of women, but very few had made him want to see them laugh. If Theresa had been one of those women, he'd have kissed her in that moment, pushing away the desire to feel something beyond physical pleasure. If she'd been someone else, he would not have hesitated for even a second to seduce her. Looking into her eyes, the curve of her waist beneath his hands, all he could do was force himself to step away from her. He could kiss her, but if he did, eventually everything would be ruined and angry between them, and she would hate him.

He would lose her, he thought with a sudden, stunned revelation, and it mattered more to him that Theresa stay in his life this time around, like a second chance neither of them had bargained for. One he did not want to squander. He took another step back, watching her expression switch from contemplation to confusion.

"You okay?" Theresa furrowed her brow and took a step toward him.

"Yeah. Fine. I'm good. Just thinking about all this." He turned, gesturing at the shadowed dining room. "Do you really think I can do this?"

"I really think you can do this, Ilya. More than that, I think you need it."

That turned him. "You do, huh?"

"You need something," Theresa said seriously. "Why not this?"

He did need something, he thought. He wasn't sure it was a diner; it seemed like maybe it was a woman with dark, curly hair who had no problem keeping him in line. He didn't say that, though. Instead, he nodded. Grinned.

"Why not this?" Ilya said. "Yeah. Hell, yeah. Why not?"

CHAPTER TWENTY-TWO

Then

"There's been an accident." That was what Galina had told them.

Not much more of an explanation than that. Jenni had been missing for a day and a half before they found her body in the water at the quarry. In their swimming spot. Now it had been nearly a week and a half since then, and finally they were allowed to bury her.

Theresa had overheard her stepmother talking to her dad. Jenni hadn't drowned. She'd fallen off the ledge where they'd so often laid out their towels. She'd hit her head on the way down. Broken her neck. She'd been dead before hitting the water.

Drunk. On pills. The murmured conversation between Galina and Theresa's father, huddled together in the living room, shot out small, suggestive nuggets that left Theresa's head buzzing with unanswered questions.

"Listening at doors, you never hear good things." Babulya shook a finger at her, though she didn't look angry. Only sad. "Come away from there."

In the kitchen, Babulya pulled out baking sheets, bowls, and measuring spoons. She instructed Theresa to find the flour, butter, eggs, and sugar. They would make cookies, she said. They would make bread. They would fill their time of grief with busy hands and take the gift of food to the Harrisons, who would surely not be hungry but would still need to eat.

At the funeral, the collar of Theresa's black dress was too tight at her throat. It threatened to choke her, but she couldn't loosen the button because it would cause the dress to gape open. She should've asked her dad if she could get a new one, but she hadn't known it wouldn't fit until she tried it on. Now there was no time. She had to suffer . . . but at least she was alive.

She couldn't believe Jenni was dead. Death was what happened to old grandparents or people on the news. It wasn't meant for your across-the-street neighbor who was only a couple of years older than you. It wasn't meant for someone as pretty and vibrant and enviously alive as Jennilynn Harrison.

Ilya and Niko disappeared from the service. Theresa begrudged the two of them their escape. She was trapped next to her dad, who held her hand so tight he left a bruise.

Later, Babulya invited the mourners to gather at the Stern house, because Jenni's mom, Sally, wasn't able to play hostess. Galina took over that role, shaking hands and accepting murmured condolences. Babulya muttered that it was a kindness as she put out tray after tray of food, but Theresa wasn't sure Galina Stern ever did anything simply to be kind. There was something going on with Galina and Theresa's father, and it had to do with Jenni's death. Theresa just couldn't figure out what it was.

It was far from the first time she'd seen her dad drunk, but it was the first time since he and Galina got together that he was out of control. It wasn't just the beers he'd been guzzling. It was whatever he kept taking from his pocket, the tin that used to hold mints, rattling with pills of various sizes and shapes. Pills that Barry did not have a prescription for, yet somehow managed to acquire.

The house was full of people and the buzz of conversation. Theresa had been helping Babulya serve food while Ilya and Niko, typical boys, snitched booze from the table and didn't help at all.

She found Ilya in the upstairs bathroom, the door unlocked. He'd probably been puking, although he stood in front of the toilet, not hunched over it. He looked at her when she came in.

"Sorry," she said automatically. "I didn't know you were in here."

"I don't want to be in here," Ilya said. "I want to be anywhere but here."

"Maybe you should go to bed." She was used to dealing with her father when he needed to be put to bed, but Ilya proved more difficult to maneuver. He wouldn't go. Stubborn, he dragged his feet and stumbled against her, pushing her into the wall of the hallway hard enough to leave a bruise she found later on the outside edge of her elbow. "Stop it!"

Ilya hung his head, swaying. He muttered something she couldn't make out and again pulled his arm from her grasp when she tried to tug him down the hall to his bedroom. Exasperated, she let go of him as he stumbled toward the attic door and the steps beyond. She should have let him trip on them and hurt himself. She should have left him alone.

She followed, instead, making sure he got up the stairs and into the army cot beneath the eaves without hitting his head on the slanting rafters. His eyes closed at once, but his hand gripped hers and wouldn't let go. He gave a single sobbing breath before his fingers relaxed.

Theresa sat with him for a few more minutes, watching the way his lips parted, his brows furrowed. Ilya's face contorted with grief even in unconsciousness. Her own heart twisted at the sight. Somehow, she felt worse for Ilya than for anyone else.

Downstairs, the murmuring began when Theresa brought a new platter of sliced cheese and deli meat to the dining room. Her dad had burst into braying, gasping sobs. Seated, his face buried in his hands, he raked at his hair and clutched at his own skin while he rocked back and forth. His pain was palpable and embarrassing to everyone in the room, because everyone knew there was no good reason for Barry Malone to be so distraught about a girl he barely knew.

Nobody stepped forward to comfort him, not even his wife, who turned her back with a shake of her head. Galina caught Theresa's gaze from across the room. A dip of chin, accompanied by a small narrowing of her eyes, was a signal for Theresa to come and deal with her father, but what could she do? He was a grown-up. She was a kid. This wasn't her job.

Still, someone needed to get him out of there. He was making everyone uncomfortable. Causing a scene.

"C'mon, Dad." Theresa tugged at his arm.

Her father looked up at her with red-rimmed eyes. "Hey, kiddo. C'mere. Let your old dad give you a hug. I'm so glad you're here. You know that? You know how lucky I am?"

"Dad." She tugged his arm again, her own face heating with the weight of everyone's eyes on her. "Let's go outside, get some fresh air."

In the backyard, her father pulled her into an awkward, suffocating embrace. He muttered incoherently. Grateful she was alive, that nothing bad happened to her—that was all Theresa could gather from his mumbling.

He gripped her by the upper arms, keeping her from moving away. "Promise me, Theresa. Promise your dad that you'll stay out of trouble."

"I'll try, Dad." She tried to tug herself out from his grip, but it was too tight.

"Don't let anyone tempt you into trouble, Theresa. Oh God, oh God. What would I ever do if I lost you?"

"Barry." Galina's tone was sharper than shattered glass. "Get control of yourself. You're making a scene. You're being ridiculous."

"It's not ridiculous. I'm trying to make sure my little girl doesn't end up . . . shit, Galina. I'm just . . ."

"You're drunk," Galina said without inflection. "People are going home. You should come inside and go to bed. Sleep this off."

Without another word, her father pushed past Galina and went inside. Galina let out a long, sputtering sigh. She lit a cigarette and drew the smoke in deep, eyeing Theresa.

"That dress is too small," she said.

Theresa touched the buttons at her throat, which still choked. "Yeah. I know."

"Your dad will be fine."

"I know." Theresa cleared her throat. "Do you know what happened? To Jenni, I mean."

"It was an accident. That's all I know." Galina took in another long drag, the tip of her cigarette glowing fiercely red before she released it from her lips. She turned her head to blow the smoke out of the way, but it still stung Theresa's eyes. "That old quarry's never been safe. I'm surprised nobody's gotten hurt before now."

"She didn't just get hurt. She *died*."

Galina dropped the cigarette to the ground and stubbed it out with the toe of her shoe. "Perhaps she ought to have been more careful."

"Why's my dad so upset?" Theresa asked boldly, pushing, certain her stepmother must know something she wasn't revealing.

"We're all upset, Theresa. Your father drank too much. His emotions got away from him. It happens." Galina shrugged.

The answer didn't satisfy her, but Theresa knew better than to push harder. Galina sometimes lost her temper quickly and violently. In the house, Theresa helped Babulya pack up the platters and containers of food, enough to last for weeks. Much of it went into their fridge and freezer, but Babulya put together two shopping bags of portioned meals in easy-to-heat containers and bid Theresa to take them next door.

It was one of the few times Theresa had ever spoken more than a few words to Sally Harrison, who was always pleasant but often absent. Mrs. Harrison took the food with a blank look on her face, weighing each of the bags in her hands. The containers rattled inside, and Theresa worried for a moment that Babulya had packed the bags too heavily; they would tear and spill everything out into the entryway.

"My God, we'll dine on funeral food for months," Sally said in a bland, blank voice without so much as a hint of inflection to it. "Who could think I would ever be able to eat a bite of any of this?"

"I'll take it, Mom." From behind her, Alicia appeared. She pulled the bags from her mother's clenched fists, gently at first, and then firmly when Sally wouldn't let go. "Why don't you go up to bed?"

Sally turned without a word, leaving Theresa to stare with horrified, embarrassed eyes at Alicia. She wanted to say she was sorry, but that felt so worthless. Alicia was clearly waiting for her to leave so she could put the food away. It was a lost moment, one Theresa remembered for a long time. When she'd had the chance to say something kind, the chance to make a difference and help someone, but had not.

CHAPTER TWENTY-THREE

Theresa had been thinking about Ilya's suggestion that she work at the diner, re-creating and preparing Babulya's signature recipes to give the restaurant its own unique menu. It made no sense. She could cook, but not on that scale, and it was something she did for love. Not as a career. More important, aligning herself with him, tying herself to him, even in the *least* personal of ways—that could not be something she was considering at all.

Could it?

Staring at the ceiling of the room in a bed that did not belong to her, in a house she did not own, and in which she was only a guest by the grace of a woman she'd known long ago, Theresa folded her hands on her chest and took a long, deep breath. Agreeing to this would be insane, but she hadn't stopped turning over the idea in her head since Ilya had offered it.

With the money from her commission, she could pay off a good portion of the credit-card debt, making the rest manageable. She could continue her freelance work and put in hours at the new venture and possibly end up with a decent income. More than that, she could work at something that went beyond the daily grind. Something that left her feeling fulfilled. Excited. It could also leave her financially busted, stressed, and . . . well, she wouldn't go so far as to say brokenhearted, because that meant a level of emotional investment she wasn't willing to admit to. But definitely it could mess with her mojo, and she was only beginning to get back on her feet.

Briefly, she heard the murmur of voices from down the hall, and she turned onto her side, ready to cover her ears with the pillow if she had to. She didn't begrudge Alicia and Niko their rampant lovemaking. How could she, when Alicia had been so generous as to let Theresa move in here? But she'd never been much of a voyeur, and even though she knew they tried to be quiet, the walls were thin.

She'd turned her phone to silent, not worried about missing anything important, but now it lit up and cast a faint blue-white light against the wall. If she'd been sleeping already, she might've missed it. Since she wasn't, she looked to see who had the audacity to text her at this hour. She shouldn't have been surprised. For as long as she'd known him, Ilya hadn't paid much attention to whatever it was he was "supposed" to do.

You know you want to.

She wanted to do a lot of things. Signing on to run a diner with him wasn't necessarily at the top of her list. Then again, it wasn't exactly at the bottom.

I'm sleeping, she typed in return.

His answer came within seconds. You're not. You wouldn't answer if you were.

Theresa pressed her lips together on a laugh, because of course he was right. She thumbed in another message. ZZZZZZZZZ

You're not sleeping. What are you doing?

Thinking about the diner.

A pause. She watched the bouncing dots that indicated Ilya was typing. She should put the phone down and turn over so she didn't see it light up. Instead, of course, she waited with her teeth pressing into her bottom lip to see what he was going to say.

Meet me outside?

Theresa let out the breath she'd been holding. She held the phone in two hands, thumbs poised to reply. No was a simple answer, and she owed him no more than that, really.

It's late, she said.

The next message that came through was a blurry close-up of Ilya's pouting face. She burst into a flurry of giggles at the sight of it and clutched the phone to her chest, a parody of a swooning schoolgirl. Her phone throbbed in her palms with another message. She looked again.

You know you want to.

It was as true now as it had been a few minutes ago. She *did* want to, the same way she wanted to throw all her cautions to the wind and dive into this business project with him. Agreeing to help him with the diner could potentially ruin her financially . . . but somehow agreeing to meet him outside at just past midnight on a warm Wednesday evening at the end of April seemed ever so much more dangerous.

Ten minutes, came the next text, again before she'd replied. Outside.

With a groan, Theresa kicked off the covers. This was stupid, yet there she was, getting out of bed, rustling in her drawer for a sweatshirt to pull on over her tank top. She found a pair of flip-flops and slipped them on. Her hair had been bundled into a loose bun on top of her head for sleep, and she contemplated tugging it free of the elastic band, but it would be kinked and messy, maybe a little damp from the shower she'd taken before bed. Better to leave it up. Besides, it wasn't like she was rushing to meet a lover, she reminded herself. This was Ilya.

Ilya, who'd kissed her in the front hallway of his house. Who'd made her laugh hard enough to forget the last time she'd cried. Ilya, who was asking her to meet him outside in the middle of the night.

She brushed her teeth quickly, trying to make as little noise as she possible. If she could hear Niko and Alicia in Alicia's bedroom with the door closed, it was conceivable they'd hear her messing around in the bathroom and wonder what she was doing up so late. Heart pounding, she slipped down the hall and the stairs and paused at the front door to slowly, carefully, and as silently as possible, click open the lock so she could ease her way outside.

"Hey," Ilya said with a grin, not even trying to whisper.

"Shhh!"

"What? Nobody's even awake."

She frowned and gently closed the door behind her. "And I don't want you to wake anyone up. Okay?"

"It's not like they'd care." In the darkness, lit only by the half-moon overhead, his grin flashed white. "Wait a minute. You care?"

"Yes. I do." She tugged his sleeve to pull him away from the house. "I'm out here, okay? What did you want?"

"Remember how we used to sneak out at night? All of us?"

Theresa could recall a couple of times, no more than that, but something about how Ilya had automatically included her in his memories warmed her. Against her will, but it did. "*You* all did that."

"You were with us. I remember. It was the end of the summer, right after you and Barry moved in." Ilya bounced on the balls of his feet. "We went out to the quarry. It was a full moon. We skinny-dipped."

She burst into laughter she quickly muffled behind her hand. "We did not!"

"I did. I remember." Ilya grinned.

"You probably did. That sounds like something you'd do. But I know I didn't." She tilted her head, studying him. Like on that long-ago night he'd been trying to get her to remember, tonight's moon was full and bright, the sky cloudless. "It can't have been very impressive, I have to say, since I can't remember it at all."

He put a hand on his chest, fingers clutching. "Ouch. Boy, you really know how to dig, huh?"

She smiled but said nothing.

"Well, come on then," he said.

Her eyebrows lifted. "Come on then, what?"

"You and me. The quarry. Skinny-dipping. Right now." He stabbed two fingers downward. His grin got bigger and also more challenging.

Theresa blew out a breath that wafted her bangs off her face. "You're on."

Ilya looked surprised, but only for a second or so before he jumped in place, clapping his hands together. "Aw, yeah. C'mon. We'll freeze our nuts off, but let's do it."

"I don't have nuts, and I'm sure we'll get arrested for trespassing," Theresa said as she followed him across Alicia's front yard and onto the street toward the woods. "You don't own it anymore, remember? And that's if we don't—"

She cut herself off. She'd been about to say "kill ourselves falling off the cliff," but that would've been bad. At the least, insensitive. But more than that, she knew without having to say it how much it would hurt him.

"Come down with the flu," she said instead. If Ilya noticed the momentary awkwardness, he didn't mention it. "But, hey. Let's do it. Why not?"

"Why not!" Ilya cried, too loud, and ducked at her swinging punch that she pulled at the last second. He stifled his laughter and danced away from her. "Sorry, sorry."

"Just go, before you wake the entire neighborhood." She shot a glance over her shoulder at the Guttridge house, anticipating the lights turning on and Dina peeking out through the curtains, but if the nosy neighbor was spying on them, Theresa could see no sign of it.

Together, they jogged to the end of the street. In the past it had ended abruptly, no curb, just cracked asphalt blending into scrubby grass that became the woods surrounding the quarry. At some point, improvements had turned the end into a paved cul-de-sac with a nice curb that nearly tripped her up as she followed Ilya into the trees. Ilya caught her as she stumbled, holding her by the arm. The pair of them dissolved into hysterical, snorting laughter that rang throughout the patch of woods despite her attempts at keeping quiet.

"Watch yourself," he said. "I got you."

She lingered a moment too long in his embrace before pushing herself away. "I'm okay."

"I know you're okay."

In the bright moonlight, his eyes looked darker than usual, or maybe it was simply that his pupils had dilated so much they blocked out the color. He looked at her for less than a minute before taking her hand. Their fingers linked loosely, and she let him hold tight while they wove their way through the scrub pines. Once they were past the first row or so, a curving path of dirt and pine needles opened up, heading toward the drop-off.

"I don't remember a path," she said.

"I made it. C'mon." He tugged her hand.

She followed. "You made it?

"Well . . . yeah. I've lived here my entire life, spent countless hours trekking through the trees to get to the swimming spot. I got too old to keep fighting my way through the brush." He ducked to slap a hanging tree branch out of the way, then held it back so she could pass. Doing so meant he dropped her hand.

She wished he was still holding it.

"Back then, we were the only ones hanging out there. Everyone else went around to the other side," she said.

Ilya shot her a grin. "Yeah, where the shop is. Easier access there. Maybe I should've made more of a beach, you know? I thought about it. Bringing in a couple tons of sand. Setting up a hot-dog stand. Maybe if I had, it would've worked out better."

"Things work out how they're supposed to."

Ahead she glimpsed something looming. It turned out to be a fence, not the rusted, sagging chain-link fence she remembered but something newer, with a gate secured with a heavy padlock. Ilya pulled a key from his pocket to open it.

"I wanted to keep people out," he said, although she hadn't asked him or even said a word about it. He pushed open the gate and stepped aside for her to walk through, then followed. "I tore down the old equipment shed, too. It was a hazard. And . . . bad things happened there."

It was her turn to reach for his hand, and she barely snagged his fingers, because he was moving away. She managed to catch him, though. She waited until he'd paused to look at her.

"I do remember that," she said.

Ilya nodded. "If anyone remembers anything about her, it's usually that."

She was quiet after that. They reached the smooth, flat area and the rocky outcrop a few minutes after that. It hadn't changed. The moon glinted off the water that rippled in a faint breeze. Her toe caught a rock, which leaped across the ledge and through the air to the water beyond. She waited for the sound of it hitting. Ilya had moved on ahead of her to stand at the edge.

"Funny how it never freaked me out how high this was, back then," he said quietly. "We'd jump off it like it was nothing."

"That's what you do when you're young. You jump without thinking. When you get older, you start to be afraid of breaking something."

Theresa stood beside him, looking down into the water. It was going to be cold, she thought. And there was no way she was jumping from here.

"The rope's gone." He jerked a thumb back toward the closest tree. "But you can still get down the path there to the water. If you don't want to jump from the ledge, I mean."

She looked at him. "Do you want to?"

"It's dangerous," Ilya said.

"Yes." She waited for him to continue and, when he didn't, added, "but we've come all this way."

"That doesn't mean we can't change our minds."

She thought about the truth of that for a few seconds before she answered. "Are you saying this because you're afraid I'm going to laugh at your junk?"

"Because I'm . . . damn, woman. Again with the jabs about what I've got going on in my jeans. If you're not careful, I'm going to start thinking you're dying to find out."

She laughed at that. "Dream on."

Staring her down, Ilya stripped off his shirt and let it fall to the ground. She wanted to look away but refused to give him the satisfaction. His gaze stabbing hers, he undid the button of his jeans and pushed them over his hips to stand in front of her in a pair of tight red briefs.

"What?" Ilya said, throwing out his hands and giving her a head wag. "What, you can't handle it?"

Without a word, Theresa unzipped the hoodie to reveal the thin tank top she'd been wearing as pajamas. The night air was much warmer than it had been for months, but nevertheless her nipples peaked against the soft fabric. Ilya was no longer snaring her gaze; he was checking out the front of her shirt. More warmth flooded her, even as gooseflesh rose along her arms and the fine hairs at the back of her neck. She hooked her thumbs into the waistband of her pajama bottoms, then slipped them over her thighs and stepped out of them to stand, clad in only the tiny lace panties she'd been wearing when he texted her.

"Are we doing this?" she asked him. "Or are we just talking about it?"

Ilya looked toward the water. The moon at this point had risen high enough so that their shadows stretched out long and dark in front of them. It cast a shimmer on the rippling waters below.

"If we're doing it, we're doing it together."

"Deal." Theresa moved to the edge and held out her hand for him to take. He did, standing beside her with his fingers squeezing hers. Together, they peered over the edge.

She did not want to jump.

She could think of at least a hundred things she'd rather do than leap off this ledge and plunge herself into the frigid quarry waters. Yet here she was, and she was the one who'd urged him to do it. The same way she'd convinced him to sell the quarry to begin with, then had led him toward buying the diner. She wasn't going to back out now.

"Are you scared, Theresa?"

"Yes."

"You never liked to jump," Ilya said. "You always went down the hill."

She straightened, lifting her chin. "So tonight'll be a first."

"Your first time," Ilya said with a lilt in his voice, laughter that faded into a smile. "I'm honored."

"Let's go," Theresa said. Before she lost her nerve.

They put their toes over the edge, looking down.

"One," Ilya said. "Two . . ."

"Three!" They both cried at the same time, leaping together.

Hurtling through the air, Theresa was convinced she'd made the wrong choice. She would bounce off the rocks, break her bones. She would drown and die here in the same spot Jenni had so many years ago, but this would not be an accident. She'd done this to herself, her own bad decisions . . .

Somehow, she hadn't let go of Ilya's hand. When they hit the water, Theresa tried to scream, but nothing came out beyond a startled squawk. She'd forgotten to hold her nose, and grabbed for it at the last second as the water engulfed her and everything went dark. She'd closed her eyes but opened them as she kicked, frantic to get herself to the surface. Panicking a little.

She broke the water with a gasp that became a delighted shout. "Yeah-h-h-h!"

Beside her, Ilya surfaced. He sprayed a long blast of water and kicked to end up on his back, arms spread. "Nice."

Theresa treaded water, pushing the hair out of her face. Her teeth started to chatter, chipping her laughter into tiny shards like crushed ice. She splashed at him. He splashed back.

"We didn't bring any towels," Theresa said.

There was no question of them lingering in the water. In the hottest days of August, the temperature would've been barely tolerable for a long period of time. In late April, even after a mild winter, the water was already turning her toes numb. She struck out for the shore, finding her rhythm after a moment or so. It had been a long time since she'd gone swimming.

They made it up the hill to the ledge, where she grabbed up her hoodie and slipped into it with a grateful sigh. Her pj bottoms next, though the fabric clung to her wet legs and made it hard to get them on without a struggle.

Ilya was having similar problems with his jeans, but finally they managed to get dressed. He sat with his legs over the edge, and after a minute, Theresa joined him. Hip to hip, shoulder to shoulder. She was far from dry, but her teeth had stopped chattering.

"I haven't done that in a long time," Ilya said after a while. He shrugged, not looking at her. "I've been in this water thousands of times since . . . then. But never from here. Never off the ledge like this. I've come out here so many times, but I was never able to do it."

The hitch in his breath alarmed her. When he bowed his head, shoulders hunched, and let out a long, low sigh, she did the first thing she thought of—she put her arm around his shoulders. Ilya pressed his face against her shoulder.

"I loved her so much, Theresa."

Her throat closed, hot tears sparking the backs of her eyes. She blinked them away fiercely and half turned to press her lips to his wet hair. "I know you did. She was easy to love."

He laughed hoarsely. "No. She was fucking hard to love, Theresa. Nobody else seemed to think that. Only me. And by the time I figured out that it didn't have to be so hard, it was too late."

Theresa stroked a hand over his hand and the back of his neck. She let her hand settle between his shoulder blades. His shirt was damp, but the heat from his body came through it. She listened to the sound of him breathing.

"I thought for a while that it was my fault. That she'd done it, you know, on purpose. To herself. Because of me."

"Ilya . . ."

He shook his head, sitting up but not moving away. He swiped at his face angrily, perhaps ashamed of the tears that glittered on his cheeks in the moon's fierce white glow. "I thought I'd done something to her to make her hate her life so much that she wanted to end it."

Theresa had never heard even a rumor that Jenni had committed suicide. "I always thought it was an accident. Nobody ever said otherwise."

"That's what they determined. That she was high and drunk and she came out here." He slapped at the stone beneath them. "Here, right here, and she fell. She broke her neck, did you know that? She didn't drown. They found drugs and booze in her blood, but I guess they can tell if you're already dead before you hit the water."

"If her neck broke and she didn't drown," Theresa said carefully, "then at least she didn't feel anything."

Ilya barked out a humorless, harsh laugh. "She didn't feel anything, anyway. She was doped up and shithammered drunk. She was stupid. And it killed her."

"It wasn't your fault, Ilya."

He looked at her. "It will always feel like my fault. No matter what. Because I loved her, and she needed me, and I didn't see whatever was going on with her. I failed her, and she died."

Theresa didn't know what to say to that. There could be no convincing him he was wrong, because she wasn't totally sure he was. Jenni had needed someone, and Ilya had not been able to figure out what to do for her. Theresa didn't think that meant he needed to take the blame for her death, but she knew better than most how it felt to bear the burden of guilt for someone else's problems. Especially about addiction.

"My dad could never get his act together," she said after a moment. "He's been an addict for a long time. He couldn't ever quite commit to one thing. Sometimes it was alcohol. Most often it was pills, though not always the same ones. He'd take whatever he could get."

Ilya looked at her. "For how long? Back then, too?"

"I'm sure. Definitely before he met your mom. It was better when they got together, believe it or not."

Ilya shook his head. "That might be the first time my mother was ever a good influence on anyone."

"I don't know if she was a good influence." Theresa gave a rueful laugh. "But they were better together, at least until things ended up going so bad."

He nudged against her. "You know, I was never that nice to you. Back then."

"You were okay." She nudged him back.

"It wasn't because I didn't like you. I mean . . . I didn't think anything about you. Back then."

Theresa laughed. "You weren't supposed to, I guess. I was just some kid that came in and kicked Niko out of his room."

"He got the attic. That was way better." Ilya looked at her. "He still has it, now that I think about it. The bastard."

"Not for much longer." She paused, thinking about whether to tell him about what Alicia had shared with her about moving in with Niko. It wasn't her news to share, and it had already been a tiny bit of a shitshow night.

Ilya shrugged. "He's going to move in with Alicia. I guess that means she'll sell the house. Where does that leave you?"

Theresa shrugged, relieved she hadn't been the one to spill the beans. "I'll be okay. She said it'll be months before she's ready to even put the house on the market, and they plan to travel a bit in the meantime. That'll give me enough time to work on some things. She's not pulling the rug out from under me or anything like that."

"I want to be happy for them," Ilya said.

She pursed her lips. "I'm sure you do."

"He's my brother. I mean, he's the only one I have."

She thought about this for a second. "Yes."

"I'm not trying to be a dick about it," Ilya said sincerely, twisting to face her. "Galina seems to think we should all become one big happy family again, including you, apparently. But I don't think of you as my sister."

There didn't seem to be a good answer to that. He was looking at her like he thought she might be insulted, but there wasn't anything to be offended by. There might've been a hot second or so years ago when she'd viewed him as her brother, but that time had come and gone.

They sat in silence, both of them swinging their feet and looking out across the water. She was grateful for his warmth against her. The night was cooling as the moon moved across the sky and moved on toward morning. She could no longer hold back a yawn.

"I want to buy the diner," Ilya said. "I want you to help me run it. Will you, Theresa?"

Maybe it was the lateness of the hour, her brain fuzzy with the desire for sleep, but she turned to him with a smile. "Yes. Okay. Fine. Let's do it."

CHAPTER TWENTY-FOUR

Then

There was shouting going on, muffled behind his mother's bedroom door. Galina and Barry had been going at it, on and off, every day since the funeral. Ilya didn't care what was going on with them; he didn't care if they were breaking down or angry or grieving or in the depths of despair or anything else.

His whole world went dark, and nothing else mattered.

Still, the constant rise and fall of their angry voices drifting through the wall between their two bedrooms made it hard to sleep, and that was all he wanted. To sink into oblivion. He would get drunk again, if the thought of taking even a single sip of booze didn't make his throat convulse and sour spittle fill his mouth. He wouldn't be able to drink a sip without puking at the reminder of how hungover he'd been. Not enough to get a buzz, much less hammered the way he wanted.

That left sleep, and he couldn't find it. He put the pillow over his head, crushing it against his ears, but that didn't help. Tossing and turning, sweating as though he had a fever, Ilya clutched at his head and considered gouging his thumbs into his ears. He pressed them against his closed eyes instead, seeing the bursts and pinwheels of color.

Another rolling rumble of furious noise drifted toward him, and he swung his legs out of bed to get up. In the kitchen, he got a glass and opened the fridge, but nothing inside appealed to him, so he settled for a glass of tepid water from the faucet. It turned his stomach. At the sound of footfalls behind him, he put the glass on the counter and rested both his hands on it. Shoulders hunching. If it was Barry, Ilya would fucking punch him right in the throat. If it was his mother . . .

"Hey." It was Theresa.

Ilya turned. "What."

"I can't sleep, either."

"They should shut the hell up."

Theresa moved toward him hesitantly. "They've been fighting for days. They're not going to stop just because we can't sleep."

"We have school in the morning," he hissed after a second, the horror of this truth twisting his mouth and making him spit the words. His fists clenched. How could he go to school tomorrow or any day after that? How could he do anything for the rest of his life?

Jenni was dead.

She was going to be dead forever. He could do nothing about it. It would never change. How could school matter? How could anything?

"I just want to sleep," he said. "I want to sleep and not wake up. Okay? That's all I want right now. I just want to sleep."

His voice broke, and he turned away to hide the fact that he was about to break down in tears like a baby. Behind him, he heard Theresa leaving the kitchen. He considered gripping his glass hard enough to break, or tossing it into the sink to watch it shatter. Instead, he left it carefully on the counter, knowing it would make his mother lose her mind to find it there instead of the dishwasher.

Upstairs, the sound of the argument had faded, at least until he got back into bed. Then it started again, a rolling rise and fall of shouting and weeping. So far there'd been no sounds of anything breaking, no crack of flesh on flesh. If Barry hit Galina, Ilya would have to consider defending her. He wouldn't put it past her to take a crack at Barry, though, and then what?

"Ugh," he muttered. "Just shut up. Shut up, shut up, shut the hell up—"

"Ilya?" Theresa rapped on his door frame. "Can I come in?"

He gestured. She moved forward, holding out her hand, her fingers clenched around something. She turned her palm up and showed him the small oblong pill. She offered it to him.

"What's that?" Ilya asked suspiciously.

Theresa lifted her chin. "It will help you sleep."

"Yeah, but what is it?" He didn't take it.

"I don't know," Theresa said. "I got it from my dad's . . . drawer. But I know it'll help you sleep."

He sat. "Did you take any?"

"No. I'll be okay. You should have it. At least you'll be able to sleep." She offered it again, though she hadn't moved any closer.

Ilya had done his share of drinking and smoking a little weed now and then, but he'd never gotten into pills. You could get seriously messed up with pills, like long-term shit. "Nah. I'm good."

"Are you sure?" Theresa closed her fingers around the pill in her hand.

"You shouldn't be stealing your dad's meds," he said, aware that he sounded snotty about it. It wasn't like he even really cared.

She laughed. "He won't notice. Trust me."

"Thanks," Ilya said. "But no thanks. I don't want to get messed up in any of that. You shouldn't, either."

He wasn't sure why this made her look so stricken, why her eyes glistened with tears and she swallowed hard against an obvious lump in her throat. Her voice was cracked and shaky when she answered. "No. I'm not. I don't want to be. I didn't mean that you should be. I just wanted to help."

Ilya settled onto his pillow with his hands folded on his chest, staring at the ceiling. The noise from his mother's room had gone silent, finally. "Thanks."

"It'll be okay," Theresa whispered.

He didn't look at her. "No, I don't think so. Just leave me alone."

And, after a few seconds of silence, she did.

CHAPTER TWENTY-FIVE

Theresa's father didn't look good. Pasty. Circles under his eyes. He'd lost weight. Still, his gaze was clear, and he met hers unflinchingly as she took the seat across from him at the coffee-shop table. She hadn't hugged him when she came in.

"It's good to see you, Ter."

Her father was the only one who'd ever called her that, and she'd never liked it much. Theresa flashed back to how different it had felt when Babulya had called her Titi, an endearment, a nickname born of affection and not simply a truncating of her name for the sake of convenience. She'd never told her dad not to call her that, though, so it was her own fault that he still did.

"Thanks for coming," she said.

Her dad looked faintly surprised. "Of course. Why wouldn't I?"

The last time she'd seen him had been at Babulya's funeral, when it would've been out of line for her to cause a scene. Before that, though, the last time had been brutal. Her father had wept in a way she hadn't seen him do since Jenni's funeral. It had been one of the ugliest moments of her life, and although she doubted there were many people who would have blamed her for the things she said, guilt still managed to linger with her.

"I need to talk to you about . . . what happened," Theresa began, and held up her hand to silence him before he could speak. "I need you to sit there and listen, Dad. I'm not in the mood for your excuses."

He nodded, leaning back in the chair, and gave her his silence.

"I'm going into business with Ilya Stern." Again, she waved at him to be quiet when he opened his mouth to speak. "We're buying Zimmerman's Diner together. I've already told him I can't cosign anything with him, that I'm going to be a liability and not an asset. I have some cash I can put up toward the down payment, and we're working out the details of what that all means. I have a friend who's a lawyer, and it looks like we're going to be putting together something similar to a rent-to-own agreement. I'll promise to make payments toward my share of the property, along with some other things, and eventually I'll be a part owner. But I need to know from you, Dad, that everything's on track with you. So that I don't end up in the same situation I did last year."

He frowned. "This doesn't sound like a good idea, Ter. Ilya Stern? Rent to own?"

"It's unconventional, but it allows us both to participate in the project without my full initial financial contribution. Something I can't possibly make," she added sharply, "because you've basically put me into debt and ruined my credit."

"Believe me, honey, I never meant to put you in that situation," her father began, but trailed off, perhaps at the sight of her expression.

She lifted her chin, lips pressing together, not caring if she looked pissed off. "You didn't mean to, but you did. And it's going to take a long, long time to get out of it."

"I understand."

She was not convinced he did. Her father had not seemed to understand much beyond himself, his needs. His addictions. What he understood was that he'd been caught.

"How's it going in the program?" she asked.

Ah. There it was. The first cut of his gaze. The shift in his chair. Her father coughed into his hand.

"Good, good," he said.

"You haven't been going," she countered flatly. Not a question.

He licked his lips. "I missed a few meetings. No big deal. I'm not using, Ter. I promise you that."

"You seemed out of control at the Sterns', after Babulya's funeral. You want to tell me that you weren't even drinking?" She wished she'd grabbed a coffee before this all began, if only so she'd have something to do with her hands. She put them on the table, fingers linked, to keep herself from twisting them in her lap.

"I'm not an alcoholic."

"You know that doesn't matter. You're not supposed to be using anything while you're in the program. You promised me you'd clean yourself up. It was our agreement."

So that she wouldn't take this to the police. That he wouldn't be arrested for identity theft. So they could both pretend they were able to maintain a semblance of a relationship with each other, no matter how strained and terrible it might be.

His gaze turned steely, his jaw clenched, and that old familiar expression settled on his face. "Missing a meeting or two isn't going to make a difference, Ter. I'm on track. I'm in a good place. I got a new job. It's a shitty job, but it's better than going to jail, I guess, huh?"

She didn't laugh at this attempt at what she assumed was humor. "Where?"

"Doing janitorial for the school district. It's at night, which is why it's been hard for me to make the meetings. The ones I started off with are all in the evening, and sometimes I sleep through the ones in the morning." He shrugged. "It happens. I'm doing the best I can. You don't have to beat me up over it."

There were so many harsher ways she could've responded to him, but his defensiveness was typical. She wished she could stop letting it bother her, that niggling sense of doubt, like she was the one in the wrong. Like she was making it somehow hard for him.

"You promised me, Dad." She did not enjoy the way this simple statement seemed to break him, but she fought against feeling bad about it.

"I know I did. And I told you I'm doing the best I can. Okay?" His tone softened, his expression shifting to match. He reached across the table to cover her hand with his, an embrace she allowed for a few seconds before she pulled away. "I've told you I'm sorry."

He had, indeed. Made amends, early on, when he'd begun working the steps. As far as Theresa was concerned, it had placed the onus of forgiveness on her without any real signs of changes in his behavior. Her father had apologized to her plenty of times over the years, in many ways. Then he'd ended up taking out a dozen different credit cards in her name and racking up thousands upon thousands of dollars in debt.

"I want to know that you're on track," she repeated, stone-voiced. "Before I commit to this project, I need to be sure that I'm not going to end up fending off collection agencies or trying to get an apartment or a new car only to discover that my credit rating is so low again that I can't get approved for anything. You promised me you'd quit the pills, you'd get some kind of help, and that you would never, never—"

"I told you I'd never do that again, and I won't! Okay?" He ran both his hands through his hair, shaking his head. "I'm getting help."

"Maybe you need rehab," she told him. "Instead of convincing yourself that none of this was really your fault, and it's all going to be okay so long as you say you're sorry."

"How would you expect me to pay for it?" her father shot back.

"Right," Theresa said. "Because unless you're using my name to run up your bills, you have no way to pay for anything."

Too far.

She got up. "I want this to work out for me, Dad. I have the chance to be part of something fun that I also feel will be successful—"

That earned a caustic laugh from him. "Right. With Ilya Stern? That kid isn't going to make anything work."

"He's not a kid. He's almost forty years old."

"He had that dive shop for years and barely managed to make a go of it. What makes you think he could do any better with this?"

"Because I'm involved," Theresa said evenly, "and I *do* know how to make things work. I can be a success. I . . . Dad, I just need this chance to get back on my feet."

"And you think that somehow I'm going to mess it up for you?" He sounded weary. Resigned. Yet also a little resentful.

"You did mess things up for me," she said.

"You act like I ruined your entire life."

She felt like crying but would not do that here. They'd already earned enough attention from the people at the tables around them. More than that, she'd decided long ago not to waste her tears on him.

"I'm going," she said. "You've been late on the past two payments to me. I need to know that I can count on you to come through."

He shook his head. "I got a little behind. I'm sorry."

"Sorry doesn't pay my bills."

Again, she'd been too harsh. Too fierce. And again, Theresa fought not to feel bad about this. He didn't deserve softness from her, not after everything he'd done.

"You never lacked for anything, Theresa. You know that? You had a roof over your head. Clothes on your back. You never went hungry. And I was there for you," her father said. Affronted. Desperate. Throwing stones.

"And I ended up sleeping in my car!" She spat the words, hating the taste of them, a secret she'd been determined she would keep from him. Yet she couldn't stop herself from taking a sick and twisted joy in the surprise on his face, or the dismay in his expression a few seconds after that.

"Why didn't you come home, Ter? You could've just come home. I'd always make a place for you. You know that."

"You made me a promise," was all she said again. "I need you to keep it. For once, Dad. Just keep the promise."

She walked out on him without another word.

CHAPTER TWENTY-SIX

Ilya hadn't been this nervous about meeting a woman in a long time, and the fact that it was Theresa Malone meant his anxiety made no sense. Still, he paced. If he'd been a smoker, he'd have gone through a pack already.

She'd said she wanted to go in on the diner with him, but that she had to work out some things first. He knew that meant something with money. She'd been up front about not being able to cosign a mortgage with him, that she'd be a liability, and although it had been obvious there was way more to the story than she was telling him, he wasn't worried about that. Or about getting a mortgage. With the money he had from selling the quarry, even after paying off his portion of the debts, he had plenty to put down on the diner, and despite years of skating on the edge of losing everything, he and Alicia had always paid their bills on time. He'd get a loan, no problem.

He could do it without any help from Theresa, if he had to. He didn't want to, and he couldn't be sure why. All he knew was that it felt right to ask her. Felt right to imagine the two of them revitalizing something, making it new.

Maybe he was simply being an idiot.

Or maybe he was nervous because this felt nothing like a business meeting and everything like a date.

He hadn't been on an actual date in so long he was hard-pressed to recall exactly whom he'd been on a date with. He'd been more likely to go out and find an FWB for the night than make any kinds of plans in advance. "Once and done." That had been his motto. Sure, it had made him an asshole. He'd never cared.

She was late. Shit, she'd changed her mind. She wasn't going to buy the diner with him. Worse, she was going to stand him up.

At the sight of her car pulling into the lot on the far side, Ilya let out a long, slow breath. He stopped pacing. He smoothed his hair and adjusted his shirt. He should've worn a tie. Something nicer than these khakis and the button-down Oxford he'd snagged from Niko's closet.

Even from this distance, he could see that Theresa wore a dress. Low heels, but sexy with a pointed toe. He was a sucker for women in sexy shoes. She'd pulled the masses of her dark, curly hair on top of her head, a few tendrils escaping to fall around her face. She was smiling as she made her way toward him.

"Hey, you," she said. "Am I late?"

"No, no. I was early. Shall we go in?" His hand naturally fell to the small of her back as he opened the door for her. Inside, the maître d' took them to the table he'd requested toward the back of the restaurant. Someplace quiet, he'd said, so they could talk business.

This was totally a date.

It couldn't be, though, for so many reasons that he wasn't able to list them all on his fingers. Their convoluted family history. This pending business deal. His inability to make things work, romantically, with anyone long term.

"Ilya," she said, and he realized she'd been speaking to him.

"Huh? Sorry. I was . . . I didn't hear what you said. Um, yeah," he said to the server who showed up at the table like a rabbit popping out of a hat. "A glass of the Crane Lake Merlot. No, you know what? Bring the bottle."

Theresa's brows rose slightly before her expression settled. "Unsweetened iced tea for me, please. No lemon."

"So, you were saying?" Ilya reached for the small basket of rolls in the center of the table, offering it first to her before taking one for himself.

"I said I put some things together with a friend who specializes in things like this, so I'm . . ." Again she paused. "Are you all right? What's going on? You were staring."

He hadn't meant to, but he'd been caught trying to figure out if the dress, the shoes, the hair, if it all meant that Theresa had been thinking of this as more than a simple business dinner between friends and potential business partners. He tore the roll into several pieces and made a show of looking for the butter. "Nope, I'm good."

"So I put it all together, and I brought along all the points she made and an outline of the agreement. We can change things if you want to. It's a little unorthodox." Theresa slid a few papers across the table toward him.

Ilya looked at the papers, then at her. "Am I going to need an interpreter to understand this?"

"I don't think so. It lays out our individual responsibilities, both financial and otherwise. For example"—she leaned a little to point at an item lower down on the page—"it lays out how much I can contribute to the down payment and allows for me to make payments toward co-ownership. It covers what happens if either of us defaults. It has a sample schedule in there for work that might come up, along with a list of things we'd divide between us based on what I think works best with our strengths . . . you're staring again."

He'd never thought he'd be turned on by a woman's organizational skills, but watching her so carefully outline everything, he was definitely impressed. And aroused. He cleared his throat. "You put a lot of work into this."

"I think it's important," she said. "So that we go into this thing with clear heads and make it as easy as possible to keep ourselves on track."

"So you're really going to do it? For real?"

"Yes. For real." She grinned. "We have an appointment with my friend tomorrow afternoon at three in her office. Can you make it?"

He made a show of pulling out his phone to look at his calendar. "Oh, I don't know, let me check my busy social schedule. I think I can pencil you in between my polo match and that custom tux fitting. Yes, yes, of course I can. Tomorrow."

Theresa laughed, her head tipping back, and in that moment Ilya thought how he would gladly make a jester of himself every single day, if only to make her laugh.

This was dangerous. He didn't like it. He didn't want it. He didn't know how to stop it, but on the other hand, Ilya was positive he wouldn't know how to keep it going, either.

Theresa looked up as the waiter brought their drinks. "You know what? Pour two glasses, please."

"But you don't—" Ilya began, but cut himself off when Theresa lifted her glass of crimson liquid.

She nodded. "I don't. But it's not because I can't. I usually prefer not to, that's all."

He lifted his own glass to clink against hers. "Cheers."

They both sipped. She grimaced a little. Then laughed.

"I haven't had a glass of wine since my second year of college," she said. "I didn't like it then. This is better."

Ilya took up the menu to keep his attention on *it* and not the faint pink blush rising in her cheeks or the way her eyes sparkled or the white glint of her teeth. "So, what looks good? Steak? Shrimp? Lobster?"

"All of the above. I'm starving. But I want to save room for dessert. Hey," she added quietly, waiting until he looked up at her, "are you changing your mind? Because if you're having second thoughts, you should tell me now. I can call Rita, cancel the meeting. No problem."

"No. The diner's a great opportunity. And I do want you to help me with Babulya's recipes. I need you . . . for that part."

He did not want to need her for anything.

This date shouldn't be a date. The flirting, as lighthearted as it had been, should never have happened. No more kissing. No more midnight swims. They couldn't do any of that for so many reasons, but mostly because Ilya knew all too well that he would only end up ruining all this, and her, and he simply . . . could . . . not.

"I'm not changing my mind," he said.

◆　◆　◆

The wine had been a mistake. After the first few sips, a warmth had spread through her. At least that was what Theresa told herself. That it was the wine, and nothing at all to do with the man across the table from her.

The conversation at dinner had started off all right, then had become a little strained, but she'd kept it on track by focusing on their upcoming business partnership. Ilya had been enthusiastic about it, once she'd managed to get him talking. The menu, a liquor license, how they would decorate. So long as she kept the conversation aimed at the decisions they'd have to make for the business, he seemed happy.

Yet even so, it seemed like he had trouble meeting her gaze. The easy familiarity they'd shared the past few times they'd been together wasn't there. He kept looking over her shoulder or around the room.

"Are you . . . waiting for someone?" she finally asked over dessert, a thick wedge of chocolate cheesecake she hadn't left room for but was going to try to eat anyway. She dug in her fork and, at the first taste, let out a small noise of appreciation.

Ilya had ordered cherry pie with a side of vanilla ice cream, but he hadn't so much as picked up his fork. "No."

"You seem distracted." Theresa licked the tines of her fork, savoring the dessert.

Ilya grimaced. "Nah. It's late, that's all."

"It's Friday night. You can sleep in tomorrow," she began, meaning to tease him since, of course, he could sleep in late any day. At least for now. She watched him look past her to the room beyond, and her smile faded. "Did you have plans?"

Ilya pressed his phone to light the screen, checking the time. There was a text alert. She couldn't see whom it was from, not that she was trying to be nosy, but at the sight of it, he picked up his phone to swipe away the lock screen and type an answer. "Yeah, maybe. Something might be going on."

"Oh." She nodded at the server who'd come over to ask her if she wanted a box for the rest of the cheesecake. She shook her head at the offer of more coffee. "I guess we should get the check and get out of here, then. So you can go and do . . . whatever it is you wanted to do."

"Yeah, yeah." He nodded, focused on his phone, but he did give her a glance. "Meeting a . . . friend."

"I see." Theresa watched the server set the check on the table, midway between them, but she didn't reach for it. Picking up the tab or even offering to pay her part of it had been a long-ingrained habit, but she'd also had her share of business meetings in which she'd allowed herself to be treated.

And dates, too.

Ilya hadn't reached for the check at once, but when he slipped his phone into his pocket, he noticed the small faux-leather binder with the receipt sticking up. His eyes met hers for almost the first time the entire night as he took it and flipped it open to scan the numbers. "I got this."

Yes, you do, Theresa thought somewhat coldly, forcing a distance she didn't really feel but wanted to. He must've seen something in her expression, because Ilya frowned as he pulled out a wad of cash and tucked it into the binder. His brow furrowed for a moment before he smoothed his face.

"So, I'll see you tomorrow at three?" he asked. "Should we drive together?"

She frowned, thinking about being forced to spend what was now looking like it could be an awkward twenty minutes in the car together. "I have some errands I need to run in the morning, so no. I'll meet you there."

She didn't imagine the look of relief on his face, and it stung. She had time to back out of this, even though it had taken a lot of effort and thought on her part to commit to it in the first place. She could change her mind. Right now. Watching Ilya check his phone again, his smile grim but still a smile for someone other than her, Theresa thought ahead to the time they'd have to spend together. How uncomfortable it could become, if they let it.

She wasn't going to let it.

She wasn't going in on the diner with Ilya because she wanted *him*. She wanted work. Success. A career. She wanted to be part of something she believed in, something that would bring her joy the way cooking had always done.

"This might be a stupid idea," she said aloud. "It's going to be a lot of work and frustration. It won't be easy at all."

"I know," Ilya said.

They both got up. He didn't try to hug her, and she was glad of that. Whatever was going to happen now, she told herself, it was going to be strictly business. She could handle that.

She took a detour to the restroom before leaving, and by the time she got out, Ilya had already settled at the bar next to a tall blonde who was laughing at something he'd said. Watching them, Theresa's stomach twisted. She lifted her chin.

Next to them both, she paused, aware of how the Styrofoam box of leftover cheesecake was shaking in her hand. "See you tomorrow, Ilya."

The blonde assessed her with a glance and must've found no threat. "Hi, I'm Amber."

"Theresa. Three o'clock," she added, looking at him even though he was definitely not looking at her.

She didn't look back when she left, although the temptation to was strong. Outside the front doors of the restaurant, Theresa dumped the leftover container into the trash. She no longer had an appetite for dessert.

CHAPTER TWENTY-SEVEN

Ilya wasn't late to the meeting with the lawyer, although waking up this morning had been hell. He'd tried to get drunk last night and hadn't been able to stomach more than a single glass of whiskey. He'd tried to get laid, too—something that should've been even easier than getting hammered. When it came right down to it, though, Amber's blatant invitation had left him unsettled instead of turned on.

"Let's go back to your place," she'd offered first, and Ilya had told her they could not. His mother was there, and his brother. It would've been weird, he said. By the way she wrinkled her nose, he could tell that Amber agreed. She made another offer. "My place?"

At that point, after a few hours of his hand on the small of her back, her shoulder, his fingers trailing down her bare arm to settle on her wrist, a casual tug of that spiraling lock of hair tumbling so artfully over her breast . . . after all that, he was sure that he could take her into the backseat of his car, if he wanted. In the past, he would've wanted. Earlier tonight, he'd thought he wanted.

But now Ilya didn't want.

Not Amber, anyway. It wasn't her fault. She was as beautiful and charming and funny as he remembered from the last time they'd hooked up. He still liked her well enough, especially since he knew that whatever happened between them tonight was unlikely to lead to desperate-sounding texts or calls. Amber wasn't the sort of girl who would ever show up on his doorstep with her makeup smeared all over her face, asking him why he couldn't just love her.

It would've been sex, not too plain, and if he managed to be good at it, not very simple, but also far from complicated. Instead, he found himself alone in his own bed before two in the morning, his head clear from the blur of alcohol but nowhere near unjumbled in his thoughts. Sleep had come only when the first light filtered through his window, and he'd woken only an hour or so before it was time for the meeting.

He'd made it, though. Shaved, showered, even wearing a suit. It felt right, even though the last time he'd put this suit on had been to attend Babulya's funeral. It was the only one he owned. He'd never had a suit-wearing job.

"It's not like Theresa to be late." Rita looked pointedly at her gold watch. "Are you sure she's coming?"

"She said she would be." Ilya's palms itched with sweat, and so did the back of his neck. Rita didn't seem to think much of him, which irritated him, since he was getting ready to write a check for a lot of money, a nice portion of which would go to her if this all went through.

Rita looked at her watch again with a frown. "It's my understanding that you'll be the one making the offer? Theresa's not actually going to be on the paperwork for the offer, per the agreement between the two of you? That one is separate. You could get started on signing."

"Yeah, but I'd really like to wait for her." Ilya flashed the woman his best, most charming smile, but it didn't seem to work. Probably because he looked like hammered shit, as evidenced by the mirror this morning that had shown off the glints of gray at his temples and the bags under his eyes.

"I have another appointment at four. If she's not here soon, I'm going to have to ask that we get started." Rita tapped the thick folder of papers with her very expensive pen. She managed a smile. It didn't seem very sincere.

He was saved from further comment because Theresa came through the door. She took the seat next to his without the apology for being late that Rita was clearly expecting. Ilya wanted to kiss her for that reason alone.

"Are we ready?" Theresa smiled at him. "Let's do this."

It took a good twenty minutes of listening to Rita drone on while he signed page after page and then wrote the check, but while Ilya had thought he'd feel some kind of anxiety about that amount of money he was both offering to spend and what he was putting down as a deposit, all he felt was anticipation. The good kind: the sort that had him grinning and finding it hard to sit still. After hands were shaken all around, Rita packed up her files with the check, escorted him and Theresa out to the front of the office, and that was it.

"Signed, sealed, and soon to be delivered," he said. "And in three days we'll know if we have it or not, just like an STD test."

Theresa recoiled with a grimace. "Oh, brother."

"Sorry. Too crude?" She'd parked beside him, he saw, and the two of them walked toward their cars.

"I've had STD testing," she told him smoothly. "It can take longer than three days."

Ilya had also made that awkward, anxious visit to the clinic once or twice, though he'd been lucky enough for it to be a false alarm. "Sorry. I was trying to make a joke."

Theresa unlocked her car door. "Chlamydia is not a flower, according to the pamphlet they gave me. It could've been worse. I could've not found out, gone untreated. It could've been something permanent."

"No kidding." He shuddered at the thought. "Sorry, though. I didn't mean to make fun of it."

"It happens." She opened the door but didn't get into her car. "If you're going to sleep around, it's the chance you take."

Something in the way she said it sounded like a pointed jab at him. He wanted to tell her that he hadn't gone to bed with Amber last night, but saying it out loud would've seemed strange, a defensive response to an accusation it wasn't even clear she was making. When he didn't answer, Theresa started to get in her car.

"Wait a second. Theresa, hold on." He put a hand on her car door to keep her from closing it. "We should . . ."

"Celebrate? We did that last night, didn't we?"

"That was before we signed the paperwork."

She smiled; at least there was that. "We can celebrate again when they take your offer, okay?"

"Sure. That sounds good." He stepped out of the way so she could close the door.

She didn't. She fixed him with a steady look that felt like it was peeling him away, layer by layer. Like she was looking right into the heart of him.

"We're going to make this work, Ilya. It won't be easy, but I'm trusting you to put your all into it."

Somehow this didn't seem like a compliment. More like a challenge. Almost a threat. Irritated by the subtle implication that he couldn't be trusted to come through, Ilya frowned.

"Since I'm the only one of us with anything really to risk," he said shortly, "I think you don't need to worry about me screwing it up. You're just along for the ride, right?"

His words had hit home. He saw it in her eyes and the way her smile became a humorless line. He would've regretted it if he hadn't been pissed off.

"You don't know me," Ilya added when Theresa didn't reply. "You think you do, but you don't."

In lieu of an answer, Theresa turned the key in the ignition. Ilya closed her car door for her. She didn't peal out with squealing tires and a spray of gravel, or a flip of her middle finger, but the tiny wave she gave with only the tips of her fingers and the thin-pressed line of her smile was as much of a "Fuck you" as any of that would've been.

CHAPTER TWENTY-EIGHT

Niko had taken his lunch to eat at the café table in what had once passed for the backyard garden but had now become a patch of scrubby grass littered with weeds. The garden shed had never been in good repair, but over time the roof had partially collapsed, and the door hung on one hinge. If it were his decision, the whole thing would come down, but he wasn't up to the task right now. He'd have to get Ilya out here with a couple of sledgehammers. It would be fun, the brothers knocking down the rotten wood.

For now, though, he was content to sit in the warming spring sunshine and enjoy a thick sandwich of sweet Lebanon bologna on white bread slathered with mayo. The combination was as disgusting and delicious as he'd fondly remembered from childhood. He'd traveled around the world and eaten meals ranging from basic to gourmet, but nothing had ever matched the satisfaction of the local delicacy.

He hadn't been looking for his mother, but she was there. Incredibly, because she'd always been the sort to flip through gossip magazines but never to spend much time with novels, Galina was already at the table reading an oversize hardcover book.

She closed it when she saw him, and bent to tuck it into the giant tote bag on the ground by her feet. "Kolya, my heart. What are you eating?"

He showed her as he took the seat across from her. The chair wobbled, but so did the table. Everything around this place was falling apart. "What are you doing?"

She stretched and closed her eyes, leaning back to let the sun cover her face. "Enjoying the day. I'm not used to being cold anymore."

"Weather's better in South Carolina, huh?" He'd cut the sandwich in half, but it was still a mess to bite. Mayonnaise squirted. He offered her the other half, but she made a face and shook her head.

His mother made a tut-tutting noise and dug in her bag for a crumpled tissue, which she handed him. "Here."

Niko supposed he should be glad she hadn't licked her thumb and used it to swipe away the mess the way she'd done many a time when he was kid. He eyed the tissue before he used it, but it seemed clean enough. He wiped his lips and chewed slowly with a long sigh of delight.

"I missed Lebanon bologna like you wouldn't believe. Scrapple and souse I could do without," he said, naming a couple of other local favorite foods. "Shoofly pie I could go either way on. But, man, there's nothing quite like a good, sweet bologna sandwich on white bread with some mayo."

Galina wrinkled her nose. "I missed fresh corn on the cob. Nothing better than a crisp ear of corn covered in melted butter, with salt and pepper."

"They don't have corn on the cob in South Carolina? That's weird."

For a moment, Galina gave a soft, embarrassed laugh and shook her head. "Of course they did. I just . . . well, I didn't realize until just now how much I was looking forward to having some. The roadside stands will be opening soon. I'll get some then."

Niko took another bite and pulled out his phone to check his messages. There were a few from friends back in Israel, but when he looked up as he was replying, his mother's expression stopped him. "What?"

"I thought we could sit and talk, that's all. Put your phone away."

He hesitated, thinking of how he'd been looking forward to a simple lunch in the sunshine while he checked e-mails and followed up on some possible job leads. He set the phone on the table. "What's on your mind?"

"Do I need to have something on my mind?" She reached into her bag and pulled out a package of cigarettes, lit up, and blew the smoke off to the side. "Can't I just enjoy some time with you?"

"I guess so. Sure." He concentrated on his sandwich, anticipating that whatever his mother had to say, she was going to get around to it no matter what he wanted, anyway.

"You could put some hives back here."

He paused. "What?"

"You could put some hives back here." Galina gestured at the yard. "Nobody would be bothered. Nobody would know."

"First of all, it wouldn't matter if anyone knew. Beekeeping isn't illegal. But, second of all, I don't want to add any hives here," Niko said. "What made you think of that?"

"You spoke so fondly of your bees, that's all. I thought you'd want some here at home."

"They weren't pets." He *had* liked beekeeping, at least more than he'd liked any of the jobs he'd cycled through on the kibbutz until being assigned to the apiary. "You can't just toss up some boxes and throw some bees into them. It's more work than that. And here, the winters get cold, which makes it even harder to keep them alive from season to season."

"Oh. I thought they just did their own thing."

He laughed. "No, they definitely don't just do their own thing. Not in man-made hives, anyway. And what would happen to them when I'm not here anymore?"

"Where do you plan to go?" his mother asked.

"First, Alicia and I are going to do some traveling. After that, she's going to put her house on the market, and we're going to look for a place together."

"Ah." She nodded as though she wasn't surprised, but her fleeting look of disappointment made Niko give an inward sigh. "So it's like that with her."

Niko wiped his mouth once more with the crumpled, shredded napkin. "Yes, it's like that with her."

"After all this time I've been gone, and now when I come home you want to leave?"

"You can't expect that I'd live here forever," Niko said. "And let's face it. You didn't move back here so you could suddenly play house with me and Ilya."

Galina frowned. "Have you ever thought that I might be trying to make up for lost time?"

"You can't make up for lost time. It's lost. There's nothing you can do about it." Niko stood and took his plate, going back into the kitchen to put it in the dishwasher.

Of course she followed him. Once his mother had something in her head, she was never likely to let it go. She went to the freezer and began rustling around inside it, shifting the many frozen casseroles left over from Babulya's shiva.

Niko put his hands on his hips, watching her pull out several storage containers with labels, look at each one, and put them back. "What are you doing?"

"I thought I would make a nice dinner. You could invite Alicia if you wanted. Theresa, too. She's staying next door now. We'll tell your brother to join us. It could be a nice night," Galina said, but wistfully, as though she already knew it was unlikely to happen. She closed the freezer and settled two containers on the counter, then put a third in the microwave. She pushed a few buttons. "Like when you were kids."

The funny thing was that Niko could remember lots of good times spent with Alicia and Ilya and Jennilynn and, for a short time, Theresa, too. But most of them had never included his mother, who'd almost always been at work or, if she wasn't working, sleeping. There'd been few family moments, at least not ones he thought of fondly. Their family dinners had been set around the table with meals his grandmother had cooked. If Galina was there, arguments had often erupted between her and her mother, or between Galina and Ilya. Ilya and Barry had sometimes clashed, too. Family dinners at the Sterns had definitely been more of a dysfunctional family drama and not a sitcom.

"How about you be up front with me," Niko asked. "What's going on with you?"

"I don't know what you mean."

"You come back from South Carolina and tell us you quit your job at the hospital to get one at a diner—"

"What's this about a diner?" Ilya had come in from the front door, wearing a bright, broad grin.

Galina waved a hand. "Your brother is grilling me. Yes, yes, Kolya, I quit my nursing job to work in a diner. What's the problem?"

"Oh, yeah. I forgot." Ilya pushed past Niko to get at the fridge, where he bent to pull out three beers. He handed one out to each of them and lifted his. "Cheers. I have news."

Niko cracked the top on his bottle and drank, watching his brother. "Yeah? What's that?"

"I bought Zimmerman's."

"The diner?" Galina had set her bottle on the counter and looked at Ilya now, her face a mask of surprise. "What on earth? You don't know anything about running a diner, Ilya." Galina shot Niko a glance. "Tell him."

Niko clinked his bottle to his brother's and grinned. "I'm not going to tell him anything. If he wants to buy a diner, let him. Hey, maybe you can work there."

"Bite your tongue," Galina said with a frown.

"I thought you liked working for the diner," Ilya put in. "But, relax, I'm not going to ask you to work for me."

"Thank God," their mother said.

Ilya's look turned serious. "I might ask you to help us figure some things out, though. If you worked at a diner, then you'd have a better idea of how it all works than I do. Or Theresa."

"Theresa?" Galina asked, tone sharp. "What does she have to do with it?"

"She's going in on it with me. Kind of a silent partner," Ilya said. "Sort of. Not silent. Just not half and half. But she's going to get us set up to serve good old-fashioned Babulya recipes."

Galina took a step back, clearly shocked, a hand over her heart. It was a reaction that seemed both feigned and forced. "What? My mother's recipes? Ilya, what are you talking about?"

"Good diners serve burgers, fries, open-faced turkey sandwiches. That sort of thing. Great diners," Ilya said with a grin so infectious Niko couldn't stop himself from grinning, too, "serve something special. Greek salads, gyros . . . well, my diner's going to serve the kind of food Babulya cooked for us."

"Nobody in this hick shitstain of a town is going to eat that," Galina said flatly. "You'll be out of business and broke within six months."

Ilya's grin faltered, then faded. "Wow, thanks for the vote of support."

"I'd eat there," Niko said. "Are you going to have matzoh-ball soup?"

"Absolutely."

"I'm in," Niko said. "Sold. Especially if it's from Babulya's recipe."

"How do you have my mother's recipes? You boys never bothered to learn to make anything more complicated than cold cereal or disgusting sandwiches."

Ilya shrugged. "Theresa says Babulya taught her how to make a number of things. I remember her in the kitchen a lot, cooking."

"I don't remember that at all," Galina said.

"Maybe that's because you weren't around," Ilya replied, but lightly, in the way he and Niko had both adopted over the years to keep from starting drama with her. "Almost every day after school, they'd be cooking something. Just because you weren't there doesn't mean it didn't happen."

"Because I wasn't here?" Galina's shriek rose up and up, her voice cracking. "You say that like I was out gallivanting around, whoring myself! I was working! To support the two of you! You think sports equipment was cheap? You think those new jeans and sneakers you always had to have just grew on trees? No! I had to work to pay for those things to support the two of you—and that old woman! You think I liked being gone so much? You think it was easy for me?"

The microwave beeped.

Nobody moved.

She turned to Niko. "Will there be a wedding, do you think?"

Niko frowned. "I have no idea. We haven't talked about it."

"I could get a mother-of-the-bride dress. I didn't have one the first time around. Same daughter-in-law, but this time with a dress. Unless you decide to run off and elope the way they did the first time." Galina gave him a small but vicious smile.

"How about," Ilya said conversationally, "you keep your damned mouth shut about anything that ever had to do with me and Alicia."

Galina threw the beer bottle into the sink where it shattered and fizzed. She turned on her heel and stalked out of the kitchen, leaving Niko and Ilya to stand in silence.

"Well, that went well," Niko said finally when Ilya didn't seem like he was going to say anything.

"She's crazy."

"You pushed her buttons."

Ilya rolled his eyes and took a drink from his beer. "Are you kidding me? She was acting like we were in a freaking elevator and she needed to stop on every single floor. Pushing buttons? Please, man. She's the queen of that. And *you* weren't going to say anything to her about it, because you never do."

"I don't need you to defend me," Niko said.

Ilya shrugged. "You haven't been here, Niko. You haven't had to deal with her, remember?"

"You haven't, either," Niko pointed out. "She's been gone, too."

"And now she's back."

The brothers looked at each other, both of them solemn.

"She was reading a book in the garden," Niko said.

Ilya made a face. "What kind of book?"

"I couldn't see, and she put it away when I came out. But something's going on with her, for sure," Niko said, and added after a few seconds, "We haven't talked about getting married. I want you to know that."

Ilya shrugged. "You're going to do what you want to do. So is Galina."

"And what about you?"

"I just bought a diner," Ilya answered with a grin.

"With Theresa Malone." Niko looked at his brother's expression, noticing the shift in his gaze. "What's up with that, anyway?"

Ilya muttered under his breath. "Nothing. She's pretty."

"Dude." Niko shook his head.

Ilya looked defensive, embarrassed, but not quite ashamed. "Don't worry. I'm not a total idiot."

"You into her like that?" Niko took a drink, relishing the crisp flavors of the craft beer but really using the drink as an excuse not to say more than he just had. When his brother didn't answer, Niko held out the bottle and frowned. "Dude!"

"No. That would be stupid, wouldn't it?"

Niko shook his head. "It wouldn't be smart, that's for sure."

"Don't worry. It's not like I'm going to be a dumbass and get myself into some weird situation with someone who's kind of related to us, sort of, like, oh, say . . . a *sisterish* sort of thing," Ilya said sarcastically. "That sure would be stupid."

Niko put down his bottle on the counter. Holding one hand out in front of him, middle finger pointing downward, he said as he twisted his wrist to reverse the gesture, "Oh, hey, is this too quiet for you? Do you need me to turn it up?"

"It's just a business thing," Ilya said when they'd stopped laughing. He looked serious. "She thinks I'll be good at it. It's been a long time since anyone thought I could be good at anything."

Niko lifted his drink. "All right, then. Mazel tov on your new adventure."

They clinked their bottles together.

"Hey," Niko said after a pause, "you want to help me tear down that garden shed?"

Ilya grinned. "You're on. Let's go."

CHAPTER TWENTY-NINE

She owned a diner.

Theresa grinned to herself as she pulled into the parking lot, then walked around the back and up to the kitchen doors, the ones not for public use. She could use them because she owned the diner. *Owned. The diner.* Well, she didn't actually *own* the diner. She'd simply agreed to help *run* this diner, with the potential to eventually own part of it, so long as she kept up her part of the payments they'd agreed on.

She and Ilya Stern: partners.

This thought sobered her a little, her smile fading. It had all happened so fast her head was still spinning a little. This was crazy. Beyond insane. Yet she'd couldn't remember the last time she'd felt so excited to be part of something. Maybe she never had.

The door creaked open before she could even knock, revealing Ilya. His grin was as broad as her own. "Hey."

He stepped aside to let her in, then danced beside her as she stepped all the way into the kitchen. Such a kid, she thought, but fondly, letting his blatant enthusiasm coax some from her. She watched him shimmy up and down between the gigantic industrial stove and the stainless-steel prep area. When he flipped her another one of those infectious grins, she gave in to laughter.

"We are going to kick *ass* with this," she said.

Ilya snorted laughter. "Sure, because owning a restaurant is notoriously one of the easiest and most profitable businesses to take on, right? Money's going to rain down from the heavens."

"Don't be a cynic. This is a diner with a long history in this town, and you're going to make it better than it ever was."

Ilya stopped his shuffling to spin slowly in a circle. He shoved his hands deep into the pockets of his jeans and rocked back and forth on his heels. "Not me. We. You're the one who got us into it. We're in this together, or not at all. Don't tell me you're backing out."

"If I didn't think we could, I wouldn't have agreed to it." She leaned against the prep counter, arms crossed. "I did all the numbers back and forth, sideways and upside down. Yes, I think *we* can make it work."

"There's my girl," Ilya said.

He'd tossed off the endearment like it meant nothing. He might as well have ruffled her hair and called her "champ," Theresa told herself, even as something tingled and buzzed inside her at the way he'd claimed her so casually.

"The kitchen's in great shape. Stove, fridge, freezer—all good. We'll need new dishes, flatware, glassware, pots, and pans. That sort of thing." She touched the pocket of her jacket, where she'd been keeping a list of things she'd jotted down as they came to her. "But, really, most of what we need to do here is going to be more cosmetic than anything else. The key's going to be the menu—"

"Which is going to kick ass."

"And hiring a competent staff." She waited to see if he was going to comment on that, and when he didn't, she added, "It's going to mean a lot of long hours, working very hard."

Ilya turned to twist the knob on the stove, waiting until the blue gas flame flared to life. He shot her another grin. "We should cook something."

"We don't have anything to cook." Theresa went around the counter to the rows of cabinets on the wall where the plates and glasses were stored. She took one out, eyeing the thick white porcelain. "I wonder how many people have eaten meals off these plates?"

"Millions," Ilya said at once. "Bazillions."

"Weirdo." Laughing, she put the plate back and turned. Ilya was staring at her. Not smiling. Her own smile faded.

"What's the matter?"

He put both his hands on the prep counter, leaning. "This is real. It's happening."

"Yes," she said. "It's really happening."

"I don't want to mess it up. That's all." Ilya shook his head, shoulders hunching.

Theresa went around the counter to stand in front of him. "I don't want you to mess it up, either."

"Thanks," he said dryly. "You're always so good to me. So positive. Such a cheerleader."

She punched him lightly on the arm. "Hey, someone has to keep that insane ego in check. If not me, who?"

"Good question." He slid a hand down her arm to let his fingers circle her wrist, tugging her a step closer.

She let him.

"I really need someone who's good at keeping me in hand," Ilya said in a low voice. His gaze met hers and lingered. His smile, small and tilted, made her think of secrets. "Someone who can keep me in line."

She must've been standing closer to him than she'd thought, because she could feel his heat. It sent an echoing rush of warmth through her, up her throat to paint her cheeks. When he tugged her wrist again, bringing her right up next to him, her lips were already parting in anticipation of the kiss that came a moment after.

She should never have told herself she could deny this, but there wasn't time to think about it now. As Ilya's kiss deepened, his free hand slid up her back, between her shoulder blades at first, and then higher to cup the back of her neck. His fingers twitched in the thickness of her hair, loose over her shoulders and down her back.

He kissed her long and hard, stealing her breath. His tongue swept hers, probing, and she opened more to give him every access to her. At the press of his hardness against her belly, Theresa gave a small, helpless groan.

"I love the way you taste," Ilya whispered into the kiss. "So damned sweet. I want to touch you. Let me touch you."

She tipped her head back to give him her throat. "You're touching me."

"I want to touch you here." He let go of her wrist to slide between her thighs, pressing her through the thin material of her dress and the soft cotton panties she wore beneath. "Say yes, Theresa."

She could not say yes. First of all because the way his knuckles rubbed against her had taken most of her voice, but also because to give him permission was going to send them both tumbling into a very dark rabbit hole she wasn't sure they'd ever be able to climb out of. Ilya buried his face in the curve of her neck. The press of his teeth made her squirm.

"I want to touch you," he murmured. The hand between her legs moved. Stroking. Pressing.

She shivered with the pleasure of it and said Ilya's name instead, her back arching. Her stance widening. One hand went to his shoulder, her fingers digging deep. She waited, breathless, for him to slide his fingers under her dress. Inside her panties. She waited for him to touch her, even though she had not said yes.

"Tell me yes," Ilya said. "Please. I need to touch you."

Say yes to danger. That was what she'd be agreeing to. No pleasure was worth that, she thought. They'd signed away their lives to buy this diner, he with the money up front, she with the commitment to follow through over time. She was going to let him take her right here in the kitchen, and when it ended between them, as it certainly would, she would end up like Alicia had, working alongside him for years and watching him drift from woman to woman, never able to escape him because they owned a business together.

"Yes," Theresa whispered. "Yes, touch me."

His groan tightened her nipples and sent another slow roll of tingling heat through her. He inched up the fabric of her dress and slipped a hand along her belly, bared above the panties. His fingertips skated along the lacy waistband before dipping inside to find more heat there. He found her sweet spot effortlessly, circling, sending waves of desire flooding her.

When Ilya dropped to his knees in front of her, Theresa's first instinct was to slide her fingers into his hair—but to hold him back or pull him closer against her, she wasn't sure. The feeling of his tongue on her made it almost impossible to think straight. His hands gripped the backs of her thighs, sliding up to cup her ass, pulling her close against his mouth so he could feast on her.

"Wait, wait," she cried breathlessly, although she didn't actually have any idea what she wanted him to wait for.

She looked down at him. He looked up. His eyes gleamed. She shivered again with pleasure when he swept his tongue over his lips and gave her that specifically knowing grin she had not yet been able to resist. In seconds, Ilya was on his feet, turning her to face the prep counter. She looked over her shoulder at the sound of his zipper coming down.

"Wait," she said again, but he was already pulling something out of his pocket to hold up to her.

Theresa groaned at the sight of the small square. She had condoms in her bag, always. She'd decided she'd never again go through the embarrassment of visiting the clinic. He must have planned this, she thought, and wondered if she ought to be offended or aroused by his consideration. Her fingers skidded on the prep counter's metal top as he pushed her shoulder gently to bend her over. Her eyes closed as her muscles tensed, waiting for him to fill her.

She should protest.

She didn't want to.

"Tell me you want this," Ilya said in a low voice. He pushed her skirt up to her hips and tugged her panties down.

She felt the brush of him, his heat against her bare skin. His foot knocked against the inside of hers, urging her to open for him, and she did. "I want this."

"Tell me you need this."

But she would not. It didn't matter. He groaned when he entered her, and so did she. Eyes still closed, Theresa bent to let her cheek press to the cool metal of the prep counter. Ilya moved inside her, slowly at first. Then faster. It wouldn't be enough, she thought, and it wouldn't matter, because casual sex was one of those things she most often simply did so she could think about it later, turning it over and over in her mind and getting off more on the memories than the event itself.

His hand slipped around to touch her, his fingers stroking in time to his thrusts. She tensed, pleasure sparking and crackling through her. What had been an uncertain thing was becoming rapidly more likely. Theresa breathed, letting the desire build. Riding it. Letting it overtake her.

There is always a moment when orgasm becomes an inevitability. Unstoppable. She'd raced lovers in the past to get there, desperate to get off before they finished. There was nothing of that sense of desperation now, nothing but slow and easy, rising ecstasy. She was on the edge before she knew it and lingered there, gasping with it, waiting to explode.

Ilya's mutter urged her closer. "Yeah . . . like that . . ."

Theresa let herself give in. The rush of climax overwhelmed her so that she shook with it, moaning. She opened her eyes. She hadn't seen their reflection before this, the two of them clearly outlined in the glass of the cabinet across from them. Shadow figures, transparent, but nonetheless clear. He was looking at her when he came, his lips pressed together in grim concentration. He closed his eyes in the last few seconds, slowing, and then at last burying himself all the way inside her with a long, low groan.

She'd caught her breath by the time he withdrew. She deliberately did not meet his gaze in their reflection and took her time rearranging her clothes while he took care of cleanup. She smoothed her hair. Ran her fingers over her lips, feeling them a little tender, a little bruised. She closed her eyes again for a second, drawing in a hitching breath, unable to stop the smile from twisting her mouth.

He came up behind her to nuzzle at her neck. "Better than popping a bottle of champagne, huh?"

"Yes." She relaxed for a second into his embrace because she could; it didn't have to mean anything.

She thought for sure that Ilya would pull away, but he held on to her for another half a minute until at last she was the one to twist from his grasp. He was smiling at her. She gave him an assessing look.

"You're so beautiful," Ilya said. "When did that happen?"

It had happened the moment it occurred to him that she was beautiful, Theresa thought. Before that, had it mattered about the shape of her face or the alignment of her eyes? If her mouth was lush and full and her hair luxurious? Beauty only mattered when it meant something to someone else.

"I bet you say that to all the girls," was her light reply.

It had been meant to put a little distance between them. To remind him she couldn't take him seriously. Ilya frowned, though, as if he were taking her words to heart.

"Only to the pretty ones," he said. "And aren't they all pretty?"

Stung, and knowing she had no right to be since she'd been the one to push away first, Theresa half turned. "We should start making some lists of things we're going to want to replace. Get moving on things. That's why we came here tonight, isn't it?"

"Sure. Of course." Ilya nodded. His fly was down, something he seemed to remember right in that moment because he zipped it, then stuck his hands in his pockets and looked around the kitchen. "I guess you have some ideas about that sort of thing already."

She pulled the list from her pocket to show him. "I started something, yeah."

"Yeah," he said. "We started something, all right. Hey. Theresa."

She looked at him.

"I didn't take her home. I didn't go home with her. Amber. We didn't . . ." He trailed off, shrugging, letting his expression finish the sentence for him.

"It's not any of my business."

"I wanted to tell you, anyway," he said.

"What makes you think I'd care?" Theresa said quietly.

"Maybe I want you to care."

Another few moments of silence passed with neither of them smiling. Then she held up the list. He leaned closer to look at it. They talked about that list for the rest of the night, and that was all they discussed.

CHAPTER THIRTY

Alicia had pulled up a website that offered home-away rentals in exotic locations. The trip she'd taken on her own had been spent in hotels, hostels, and bed-and-breakfasts. She'd spent no more than a few days in each place, eager to the point of excessiveness to experience as much as she possibly could. But now she wanted to spend some real time in one place, getting to know it.

"I like this one." She pointed at the picture of a stone cottage surrounded by a garden of wildflowers. "Scotland. Near Loch Ness. Have you been there?"

Nikolai leaned forward to look. "Nope."

"One of the few places you haven't been," she said. "It would be fun to explore someplace brand-new with you."

"I won't eat haggis," he warned.

Alicia made a face. "Yuck. Me neither. But . . . Scotland? Is that a yes? This says it's close enough to town to ride bikes. There's a pub there."

"I think that's a requirement, isn't it?" Nikolai shifted on the couch to let his arm run along the back of it so his fingers could tickle her nape. "Looks good to me. Let's book it."

"You sure?" Her fingers hesitated over the keyboard.

"Absolutely." Nikolai's fingers curled around the base of her neck, a touch that had her mind going swiftly to sexy places. "Admit it, this is just a way for you to get me into a kilt."

She laughed and leaned against him to offer her lips in a kiss he easily took. "With those legs? You know it."

Nikolai kissed her again, and Alicia put aside thoughts of planning their trip. There were other things to think about. Like sliding onto his lap and taking his face in her hands. Like kissing him long and slow and then faster, harder. Like feeling him get hard against her body as his hands roamed—

The sound of the front door opening had them both scrambling to settle on the couch as though nothing had been going on, although Alicia couldn't stop herself from giggling when Theresa walked in. Asking the other woman to be her roommate hadn't been the wrong decision, and it wasn't like she was regretting it, but it had certainly made things a little less . . . spontaneous.

"Hey," Theresa said, eyeing them both with a look that said she suspected she'd interrupted, "I'm going to bed. Carry on."

"I don't have hot dogs in my pants," Nikolai blurted, an homage to a show they'd all watched one afternoon a million years ago in which the cartoon character had been lying to his father about sneaking out to feed alligators.

Alicia burst into laughter, followed a moment later by Theresa, who shook her head and covered her eyes for a second.

"Okay, weirdo," she said. "I'd forgotten all about that."

Nikolai shrugged. "Me, too, until just now."

"How'd your meeting with Ilya go? Did you get things settled?" Alicia asked.

Theresa nodded. "Yep. We signed the papers and got the keys and it's going to happen."

"Exciting," Alicia said, watching Theresa's face carefully. She didn't look that excited. "Are you nervous?"

"I'm not putting too much of my money on the line, to be honest. I don't *have* any to put on the line," Theresa said with a rueful chuckle and seemed to relax a bit. "But, yeah, I am a little nervous. It's a big commitment. It's going to take a lot of work."

"The best things usually do," Nikolai said.

Theresa hadn't moved out of the doorway, though now she shrugged out of her lightweight coat. She'd dressed up for the meeting, Alicia noticed. Pretty dress. Heels. She'd done her hair a little differently.

Interesting.

"So, where are you two crazy kids off to next?" Theresa asked.

It was clear she wanted to change the subject, so Alicia let her. She turned the laptop on the coffee table toward Theresa. "We're thinking of renting this place for a month."

Theresa moved closer. "Looks great. Hey, Nikolai, I got a lead on something the other day you might be interested in. You know the Mutter Mansion north of town?"

"Is that the museum we all had to visit in high school? The one that's set up kind of like colonial Williamsburg?"

Theresa took off her heels and picked them up with a sigh of relief, wiggling her toes. "Yeah, the museum is the main house, the outbuildings and barn, and some part of the grounds. There's a winery there, too. The original owners kept the summer house for their own use, and guess what?"

Nikolai laughed. "I can't begin."

"They keep bees. Have for years. They sell the honey, and the museum makes candles, lotions, and stuff like that from the beeswax," Theresa said. "Mrs. Mutter is now in her nineties and needs to hire someone to look after the hives. She has about a hundred."

Alicia's eyebrows rose, and she turned to him. "Wow. How'd you find out about this?"

"I never knew how many different people I'd met and knew until I started doing this freelance stuff," Theresa said with a grin. "I met

Mrs. Mutter's son, Ron, a couple years ago because he was the guy who built that apartment complex over by where the drive-in used to be."

"The shoe factory," Alicia said, since it was unlikely Nikolai would know about it.

"Anyway, Mrs. Mutter has kept the bees for years, but had hired someone to handle them for the past decade or so. Her current guy is retiring, and she wants a new person to take over, or else she's going to just let them go." Theresa swung her shoes from the tips of her fingers and gave Nikolai a look. "I should mention that Mrs. Mutter has more money than she knows what to do with, not to mention that because the property is considered a historical site, it qualifies for different sort of grants and things to cover staffing expenses."

Alicia blew out a soft breath. "Do you think that's something you'd like to do again?"

"It could be." Nikolai laughed, shaking his head. "Never thought I'd come home to do the same thing I did on Beit Devorah, but . . . hey. It's something to start off with, right?"

"I can give Ron your name and number, if you want."

"It's work. Sure. I need a job."

"Don't we all." Alicia was strangely relieved that Theresa had been the one to bring it up. "I don't suppose you've heard of something magical that would suit me?"

Theresa laughed. "I'll keep my eyes and ears open for you. It's my favorite part of what I do, you know? Putting people together who will make a great team. Alicia, when you're ready to put the house on the market, if you want a Realtor recommendation, I can give you one."

"That'd be great, thanks." Alicia studied the other woman for a second. "Everything okay with you?"

"Tired. Ate too much dinner." Theresa made a show of patting her stomach with a frown. "I'm going to take a shower and hit the hay. 'Night, guys."

After she'd gone, Nikolai turned to Alicia with a sexy grin and grasping hands, but she fended him off gently with a laugh. "Wait a bit. She's not asleep yet."

"I can be quiet. You're the noisy one."

She poked him. "Uh-huh. Right. Hey, what do you really think about the possibility of a job like that?"

"I don't know. I can't really think about it unless I know what it entails, you know? Beekeeping isn't as easy as people seem to think. If she's willing to pay me a living for it, sure. But I'd think about it." Nikolai sat back against the couch. "It's been bothering you, huh?"

Alicia nodded. "A little bit. I'm a little more worried about what *I'm* going to do, honestly."

"You'll find something great." He stroked her hair and tugged her closer for a kiss. "We both will."

With an ear cocked toward the sound of the running shower from upstairs, Alicia slid onto Nikolai's lap again. "I've already found something great. Right here."

CHAPTER THIRTY-ONE

Theresa had always been good with lists. Checking items off a list had made her feel accomplished, in control, and confident. She wasn't sure a list was going to help with this—the crawl space in Alicia's house. It was first on the list of things to do in order to get the place in shape to be put on the market.

"This is that last thing I want to do right before I leave to go to the other side of the world, but it's not going to happen by itself. And I didn't want to wait until I sold the house to have to deal with all of this," Alicia said. "There's so much of it. The furniture and stuff like that I can handle. Some of it's going to go with me, and I'll sell the rest. But all of this . . ."

Theresa laughed as she peeked into the long, dusty corridor festooned with spiderwebs. Boxes, some labeled but most not, lined the space, along with odd things like an old laundry hamper, some ancient baby toys, and a high chair. Other things she couldn't identify in the shadows. "It's a lot of stuff."

"So-o-o-o-o much stuff," agreed Alicia with a sigh.

In preparation for cleaning out the crawl space, Theresa had tied her hair into twin braids. She tugged both of them now and looked again into the crawl space, judging how low she'd have to stoop to avoid hitting her head. "Lots of people hang on to things for a long time."

Alicia groan-laughed. "Yeah, thanks, Mom and Dad."

"My dad never kept anything, really. He was always selling stuff to make some extra money." Theresa moved into the crawl space, ducking to keep from hitting her head on the slanting beams. "And we moved a lot. I was always ready to go, ready to take only what was absolutely necessary. I got used to keeping only what seemed really important."

Alicia followed her. "That must've been hard."

Theresa had never spoken much about what it was like to live with her father back in the day, and definitely not to Alicia. They'd known each other for a long time, but only now was there the beginning of any closeness. Funny, she thought, how things could change.

"It was, sometimes. But it taught me the importance of figuring out what was really important and what wasn't. Now I think it's kind of nice." Theresa shot a glance over her shoulder as she pulled up a rickety stool painted in primary colors and decorated with the alphabet. Behind it was a stack of boxes. She touched the top one. "Almost losing all the stuff in my storage unit actually reminded me of what it was like not to hold on to anything so hard. You can't miss losing it if you're not that attached to it in the first place, you know?"

"Or if you don't know what it is, in the first place," Alicia added. "Maybe I should just toss all these boxes without even going through them. I mean, if I haven't missed anything in them for the past twenty years—and my parents sure haven't—that says a lot, doesn't it?"

"If that's what you want to do. It would be a lot less work, for sure." Theresa shrugged.

Alicia sighed and shook her head. "Nah, I should at least make sure there's nothing important. When I told my mom I was going to sell, she did remind me that all this junk was in here. She didn't ask me for any of it, specifically, but . . . I don't think she would. She's the one who packed it all away to begin with."

"It was hard for her," Theresa said.

Alicia gave her a look. "It was hard for all of us. It might've been easier if she'd been able to face it. She hasn't ever, I don't think. Not really."

Theresa had not been the one to lose a sister or a daughter. She could make no judgment about how Alicia's mom had reacted to Jenni's death, not without sounding like a jerk. She grabbed a box, instead, swiping at the top to see if there was a label or something to indicate what was in it. Nothing. The tape closing the top had gone brittle and crumbling. She sneezed a few times, her eyes watering and throat itching.

"Hey, at least they're not covered in mouse poop," she said lightly as she coughed a bit from the dust.

"Thank God."

Alicia grabbed the top box and started backing out of the crawl space. Theresa grabbed another and brought it out with her. They put both boxes on the floor next to the bed and sat. Alicia flipped open the lid of hers first, peering inside.

"Get the garbage bags ready," she said.

Theresa chuckled. "Uh-oh. What's in there?"

"Looks like old school artwork and report cards. My mom must've kept everything both of us ever brought home." Alicia twisted the box to look at the side. "She dated it. That's good. Doesn't say exactly what else is in here, but at least there's some idea of the time frame."

Alicia didn't pull anything out of the box, though. Just continued looking into it. Theresa studied her. "You okay?"

"Yeah. I'll be okay. It's Jenni's stuff. That's all." Alicia looked up with bright eyes and a pinched smile. She tugged out a piece of faded construction paper and held it up so Theresa could see the scrawled childish signature on the bottom.

Theresa wasn't sure what to say. Offering to simply toss everything didn't seem like the best suggestion. It would've made her seem cold in a way she wasn't, really, even if she could only imagine what it must be like for Alicia to come across these reminders.

"When I was younger, I was glad to be an only child. It seemed easier. Dad never had much money, and I feel like I was very aware that if I'd had to share anything—his finances, his time, or attention—it would've meant less for me. But after I moved across the street," Theresa said quietly, "I started to wish for a sister. I wasn't that keen on the brothers I got, but watching you and Jenni, I figured having a sister must be like having a built-in best friend."

Alicia's smile broadened. "Jenni and I were kind of awful to each other when you lived next door. We fought a lot."

"Awful in the way that sisters are to each other. I remember her being so angry because you'd borrowed her sweater," Theresa said, then paused. "She came running down the street toward the bus stop, screaming at you, and she chased you around in a circle until the bus came."

"She'd have punched me and ripped that sweater right off me, if she could've." Alicia laughed harshly, shaking her head at the memory. "Wow, I forgot about that. I loved that sweater, and I was mad because she got it for her birthday and never wore it. It didn't even fit her, but it looked great on me. She just didn't want me to have it. And that's what you wished for?"

"Not the fighting and the screaming, but she also French-braided your hair for you. I envied that. My dad was terrible with girlie hairstyles, and mine was always so curly it was impossible to do anything with." She flipped up the ends of her thick braids, which sported tiny springs and coils of hair escaping the plaits. "She offered to teach me how, once."

"She did? That was nice." Alicia smiled. "I thought we were kind of terrible to you, sometimes."

"You were?" Theresa's eyebrows lifted in surprise. "I never thought so."

"You were a Stern. We were kind of terrible to Ilya and Niko, so you got lumped in with them. You don't remember?"

"No."

Alicia gave an exaggerated wipe of her brow. "Phew. That's good. I felt bad about it, sometimes, later. After you'd moved away. Like we could've been nicer to you."

"I don't remember you not being nice, so don't worry about it." Theresa looked in the box she'd brought out. Hers was also stuffed with papers and folders. She glanced at Alicia. "All of that was a long time ago, anyway. But sometimes I do still wish I had a sister."

"I was lucky. We fought. Jenni could make me crazy. But she was a good sister. I miss her," Alicia added matter-of-factly. "I always think that one day I won't anymore. But I still do."

After a beat of solemn silence, Alicia leaned over to pull out a handful of papers and started sorting them. Theresa dug in to her own box and began sorting things quickly into piles. Artwork, report cards, handwritten notes, miscellany. She glanced up to see Alicia giving her a bemused look.

"You'll have to decide what stays and goes," Theresa explained with a gesture at the piles and another small sneeze. Her allergies were starting to act up. "But I can sort them into some kind of order for you."

Alicia looked impressed. "You're very efficient."

"One of my talents." Theresa grinned. "Or flaws, depending on how you look at it. I know it's been making Ilya kind of crazy."

The words hung between them. Awkward. Theresa cleared her throat, thinking she'd try to explain them away, but Alicia waved a hand.

"I believe it. He's never exactly been very organized." She tilted her head to look at Theresa. "Hey. How is it going, by the way? You can talk to me about it. It's not a secret."

Buying the diner wasn't, anyway, but there was a secret Theresa wasn't yet willing to reveal. It had been a week since Ilya had put her up against the prep counter. A week since he'd kissed her, been inside her. They hadn't talked about it since then. Only about the diner, the lists, the chores and tasks.

Theresa sat back, leaning against the bed. "It's going all right. He's full of big ideas about the business. I'm the one who makes the lists. Keeps it in line. But I think it's going to be great, actually. Kind of a checks-and-balances thing."

Alicia nodded. "That's good. I always loved the diner. I'm happy you guys bought it. I'm glad working with him is going all right. It can be frustrating. I know."

Theresa thought again of the night in the diner kitchen. Ilya's hands on her. His mouth. Heat flushed through her, and she sorted through some more papers so she wouldn't give any of that away. It wasn't going to happen again because she wouldn't let it, so it wasn't like she had to own up to anything. Not even to Alicia. *Especially* not to her.

"But when he really wants something, he can be focused. He will work hard, when he thinks it's worth it," Alicia said after a few minutes of silence while they sorted papers.

Theresa paused in sorting a file full of fourth-grade essays to nod thoughtfully. "Yeah. I see that in him."

"Ilya's worst enemy can be himself. He thinks he's a screwup, and don't get me wrong, he can be."

"We all can be," Theresa said.

Alicia laughed. "Truth. But Ilya does have the ability to pull things together. He's smarter than he wants to think he is. I think because he didn't go to college, he wants to pretend like he *couldn't* go. Not that he made some dumb choices and *didn't*."

"Going to college isn't my standard of excellence," Theresa said. "I went to college for accounting, and I've never been an accountant. Nor have I worked for one. All I did was spend a lot of money on a degree I've never used."

"I think about going back to school. Getting a degree in something. I just don't know what." Alicia shrugged, her hands full of more elementary-school artwork. "For now I'm going to focus on getting this house on the market and my trip to Scotland."

"Exciting," Theresa said. "Tell me all about it. You're going to Loch Ness, right?"

They spent the next hour or so chatting and sorting through the boxes, discarding years of old papers and keeping only the ones Alicia felt she couldn't part with. Most of the boxes were easily sorted, although some of them contained years of financial paperwork and things that Alicia said she'd need to clear with her parents before destroying. Overall, they managed to clear away ten whole boxes and fill four trash bags before Alicia declared they should quit.

"I need a shower, and then Niko and I are going out to dinner. You want to come along?" Alicia took a long gulp of water from her glass.

Theresa shook her head, which had started to throb a little bit with what felt like the beginnings of a sinus headache. "Oh, thanks, but no. I don't want to be the third wheel. And I told Ilya I'd meet him later tonight to go over some things for the diner."

"On a Saturday night?" Alicia made a face. "There's a shocker."

Theresa paused before saying, "Yeah, he's usually got something going on."

"He must really be into making this business a go. Saturday night I'd expect him to be out, that's all." Alicia shrugged and closed the lid on the single box they'd been using to store all the things she'd decided to keep. She glanced up.

Theresa kept her expression neutral. "Maybe he'll go out after."

"Probably. He's a revolving door." Alicia shook her head, but something in Theresa's face must've caught her attention. "Sorry, was that too rude? I sound like I care about his love life, but I really don't."

"Especially not since you're dating his brother," Theresa said lightly.

Alicia made a small noise. "Wow. Sheesh, Theresa."

"Sorry," Theresa said. "That came out wrong."

"No, you're right. I am with Niko. I shouldn't give a second thought to what Ilya does. You're right." Alicia clapped both her hands onto her thighs. "It's an old, bad habit, and I should quit it. It's not any of my business whose hoo-ha hole he puts his dingle in, as the saying goes."

Theresa forced a smile, wishing she could laugh at Alicia's deliberately silly choice of words. "Nope. Not mine, either."

"Hey, let's toss this garbage, and I'll get this box out of the way so you're not tripping over it." Alicia glanced at the wall clock. "I have to get moving. You sure you don't want to grab dinner with us? There's live music tonight at the Brewhaus."

"No, really. I'm fine. I've got that meeting at the diner, and I want to put together a few lists—" She broke off when Alicia laughed, then joined her. "Hey, I'm organized! There's a lot to do!"

Together, they cleaned up the mess, and each took two bags of trash out to the curb. Alicia went in to use the shower, while Theresa lingered, looking across the street. Ilya's car wasn't in the drive. Although it was nearly seven, dusk had not quite started to fall. The windows in the Stern house were dark.

She had her phone in her pocket, but she didn't pull it out. She wasn't going to text or call him to find out where he'd been. They'd agreed to meet at the diner at eight so they could go over some upcoming tasks, and he'd promised to bring takeout. There was nothing else she needed to know about where he was or what he was doing.

Maybe I want you to care.

His words poked at her as she went upstairs to the room that had not yet started to feel like her own, and now never would. She picked out a pair of jeans and a pretty top from the drawer as she listened for the sound of the shower shutting off. She glanced at her phone, telling herself it was to check the time, but really seeing if she'd somehow missed a text from Ilya.

"Do not do this," Theresa muttered as she searched for a pair of socks, clean panties, and matching bra. "You're not that girl."

And the thing of it was—the terrible, truthful thing was—Theresa was *not* that girl. She'd never been that girl. Even after three years of presumable happiness with Wayne, she hadn't so much as cast a second look over her shoulder when she left him. If she'd had regrets, it was that she'd hurt him enough to cause him to kick her out, not that she'd decided she couldn't marry him.

So why, then, did thinking about Ilya feel like regret?

A missed chance not taken, an inevitable desire to have another. Theresa had never seen the point of looking behind when all that mattered lay in front of her. So why, then, now?

Because people could change, she thought. But usually they didn't.

CHAPTER THIRTY-TWO

Then

Jenni hadn't said more than a word or two to him in two weeks. Ilya tried to act like he didn't give two shits about what she did or whom she did it with, but the truth was, he'd been going crazy. She knew it, he thought, watching her from the back booth in the diner while Jenni moved from table to table, refreshing coffee and taking orders. Maybe she didn't know he was there.

More likely, she was ignoring him on purpose.

It would be easier if they'd had a fight. Something he could blame this on, the slow but inexorable distance growing between them. It wasn't even a cold shoulder—*that* he could handle. He could think she was a bitch and blame her for pushing him away, but the truth was that Jenni hadn't been cold to him. Or mean. She'd simply been . . . gone.

Looking at her now, he studied the faint dark circles under her eyes. Her cheeks seemed hollower. Her blonde hair was tied in a high ponytail but looked messy, all the same. She looked tired, even when she smiled.

He was suddenly, achingly, desperate to figure out what was going on.

What had gone wrong between them? Was it that he hadn't made her his girlfriend, officially? That he hadn't told her he loved her, hadn't bought her flowers, hadn't given her his class ring to wear? All that stuff might've made a difference, or not, but it had never seemed to be their thing. She'd been the one to scoff when he suggested it, but Ilya knew that meant nothing.

Women, he thought.

When, finally, she looked at him, her eyes narrowed. Coffeepot held high, Jenni came to his table and stood with a hip cocked. She didn't pour him a cup, even when he shoved the plain, thick white mug toward her.

"What are you doing here?" Her demand was crisp. Cool. And dammit, so distant, it made every part of him cringe.

Ilya sat up straighter in the booth. "Getting something to eat, what does it look like?"

"Are you stalking me?"

He started to laugh until he saw that she was serious. "What? No!"

"Look, this is where I work. You can't just show up here. I don't have time for this."

"Time for what? I'm not doing anything." It wasn't the truth, and he knew it. She knew it. Still, he tried to charm her with a smile.

It didn't work.

"You're going to get me in trouble." Her frown was genuine. "Reggie doesn't like kids just hanging around. I can't give you anything for free. Don't even ask."

"I don't need free anything. I came to get a burger and fries." Ilya pointed across the room. "There are tons of kids from school here, and he doesn't seem to mind them hanging out."

Jenni fixed him with a long, stern look that dug right into him. "I don't need you checking up on me, Ilya."

"I'm not even . . ." Defeated, he tossed up his hands and shook his head. There was no talking to her, and if he made a scene, she'd get even angrier with him. That wasn't what he wanted. "Whatever. I'll just eat and go, okay? Sorry to cause you such *distress*."

For a second, he thought he might've earned a response, a softer one. Then, she didn't answer him but instead took her coffeepot and returned to her section of the diner. She didn't look at him again, and something about this was worse than if she'd continued to shoot him daggers. All he wanted was her attention, for them to fix whatever it was that had gone so spectacularly wrong, and she barely seemed to notice he existed.

The burger arrived overdone, the fries limp, but Ilya wasn't hungry anyway. He picked at it, forcing a smile when Lisa Morrow invited herself and her best friend, Deana, to sit in the booth with him. Lisa wanted him; he did not want Lisa. Wasn't that how it always went?

Sensing his distraction, Lisa put on more of a show, giggling and tossing her hair. Her laughter was loud and braying, determined to draw attention to the fact that they were sitting together. She was trying to mark a territory that was not hers, and he let her because maybe if Jenni saw them, she'd decide she missed him.

Over Lisa's shoulder, Ilya watched Jenni talking to a man in the diner's far, opposite corner. He had to be in his fifties, at least. Older than their parents. A trucker, by the looks of his stained ball cap, rough beard, and belly pushing at the front of his plaid lumberjack shirt.

The trucker slid a wad of money across the table to her—way more than it would take to pay for the eggs and pancakes he'd been shoveling in his mouth hole. Jenni tucked it into her apron pocket and counted out some change. She put it on the table. The trucker covered it with his hand, sliding it toward him. For a second, both of them seemed to fumble with something, a stray dime, perhaps, but it was too hard to see from this distance. The trucker slapped his hand on it. He said something to Jenni, who nodded and moved away without a backward glance. She took the money and the check to the cash register and rang him out. The trucker passed her on his way through the front door, and whatever he said to her this time earned a pale hint of a smile from her.

"Ilya?" Lisa leaned across the table to tap his hand. "Hey, I asked you a question."

He hadn't heard. Didn't care. Once, last year, Lisa had offered him a hand job at Ben Masterson's party, and maybe Ilya had let her. He couldn't remember now; it had been dark and he'd been drinking. By the way she looked at him, he was pretty sure he had.

"Sorry," he said. "I gotta go."

Out back, he waited in his car for Jenni's shift to end. When at last she came out through the kitchen door, untying her apron and balling it into her fist, he thought about driving away before she could see him. She was already pissed off that he came into the diner. What would she say about him lurking in the parking lot?

A soft drizzle fell, and Jenni tipped her face up toward it. She was so beautiful that every part of him thrummed and burned and hurt from looking at her. Ilya got out of the car.

Wasn't this love? This fire, this sting? It had to be, and he moved toward her, thinking he would just tell her. Anything she said in reply couldn't hurt him any worse than these past few weeks had.

"Jenni."

She twisted, surprised. "What the hell are you doing here?"

"I thought you might need a ride home." He moved closer. Love was on his lips. He meant to say it, no hesitation, but she wasn't giving him the chance.

"I have a ride home! Go away, Ilya! You need to go away right now!" Incredibly, she shoved him hard enough to make him skid on the parking-lot gravel. "Get out of here. I don't want you here! What is wrong with you?"

"I love you, that's what's wrong with me!" His shout was hoarse. His voice, cracked. Not the declaration he'd intended. He sounded like he might cry.

Jenni pushed him again. "I don't care. You can't be here. I don't want you here, okay? Just go."

"What did I do wrong?" he demanded, refusing to go. "Just tell me that."

She shook her head. "You didn't . . . nothing . . . it's just that I don't need you here. Okay?"

"It's not okay!"

"Leave me alone, Ilya!"

"Fine. If that's what you want. Fine. Fuck you, Jenni." Ilya backed away, turning from her. "Forget it."

By the time he got back to his car, Jenni had walked around the corner of the diner. Out of sight. The rain was really coming down now, and it spattered the roof of his car, streaked the windshield. He couldn't leave her out there, not even after what she'd said. But when he drove around the corner, there was no Jenni. There was the distant blink of some taillights, a car pulling out of the lot, but it was raining too hard and too dark for him to see what kind of car.

Jenni was gone, and that was the last time he ever saw her alive.

CHAPTER THIRTY-THREE

Theresa had been sorting through one of the crawl-space boxes when she found the pictures. The Harrisons had been big fans of their camera. She remembered every hallway in their house being lined with framed family portraits as well as candid snapshots. She'd been lucky if her dad remembered to send money in on picture day so that she could come home with a single eight-by-ten. And the wallet-size photos all the kids passed around like trading cards? Forget it.

The photos in her hand now had been tucked inside the original paper envelope, along with the negatives. Alicia had gone through them to pick out the ones she wanted to keep—only one, a snapshot of the five of them in the Sterns' backyard, sitting around the old picnic table with platters of hamburgers, hot dogs, and potato salad in front of them. The ones of her sister and Ilya she'd looked at without comment and tucked back into the envelope, then put them into the pile of stuff she planned to toss.

The idea of simply destroying the pictures had bothered Theresa enough that she'd pulled them from the discard pile when Alicia wasn't around. Other than that one Alicia had kept and promised to make a copy of, there were no good ones of Theresa, just a glimpse here and there of curly hair and a flash of a brace-faced grin off to the side. Most of the pictures were of Ilya, a few of him with Jennilynn, both of them looking into the camera in vintage selfie poses.

Jennilynn had taken these pictures; Theresa knew it. She vaguely remembered a small pink camera attached to the older girl's wrist, along with commands to "Smile." Of course it made sense Alicia wouldn't want to keep the pictures. It wasn't likely she needed any kind of reminder that the man she'd married had been in love with her sister first. Ilya, however, had the right to decide if he wanted these memories.

She hadn't texted him first, but his car was in the driveway. She did knock, though. There'd been a number of times, even recently, when she'd let herself into the house like family, not a guest, but it didn't feel right to do that now. She was smiling when the door opened, though it faded at the sight of Galina.

Galina looked surprised. "Hello, Theresa."

"Hi. Is Ilya here?"

"I don't know. He doesn't tell me when he comes and goes." Galina looked around Theresa to the car in the driveway. "His car's here."

"I saw that. Are you going to let me in?" she asked finally when Galina had made no move to step aside.

"Sure. Come in." Galina moved out of the way so Theresa could get through the door.

The older woman headed back toward the kitchen without even seeing if Theresa was going to follow. She was pulling out a kitchen chair when Theresa came in behind her. She gave Theresa a calm, bland look.

"Sit," Galina said.

Theresa might have been obedient at fifteen, but she'd grown out of it. "I'm all right, thanks. Can you please go see if he's upstairs? I have something for him."

"What did you bring?"

Theresa had the envelope in one hand, but she didn't show it off. "Some pictures. Can you please go see if he can come down?"

"What pictures?" Galina made no move to get up from the table. She had an array of books and papers spread out in front of her, which she began tidying, stacking the papers and tucking them inside the books.

"Some old pictures I found in Alicia's crawl space, that's all. Look, I could just go upstairs myself, but—"

"You could. You've certainly made yourself at home here often enough over the past few months." Galina looked up at her. "I have something for you, too."

Theresa eyed her warily. "What is it?"

Galina got up and went to the cupboard, where she pulled out a small green plastic box. Theresa hadn't seen it in years, but she knew what it was. Galina slid the plastic box halfway across the table, keeping one finger on it as she looked up at Theresa. "It was my mother's. I thought maybe since you and Ilya were going to be using her recipes for this new diner thing you have going on, you might want to have the actual recipes. Not just work from memory."

The older woman may have been poison wrapped in a candy shell, but Theresa was moved enough to reach for her offering. "Babulya's recipe box."

"She sometimes told me her best recipes were the ones she held in her heart," Galina said.

Theresa nodded, not yet flipping open the lid. "She told me that, too. It's why I tried so hard to memorize her recipes when she taught them to me."

She inched the box closer to open it, looking inside at the collection of various-size index cards. She looked at Galina without taking any of them out. The other woman's expression was neutral, although there might've been the faintest hint of grief in her gaze.

"Thank you, Galina. I'm not sure I can take this from you—"

"Oh, just take it," Galina said with a bit of snap in her tone. "I've no use for it, and it belongs to Ilya as much as anyone, now that my mother is dead."

"But you're not giving it to him," Theresa said quietly. "You're giving it to me."

Galina stood. "If you don't want it, then throw them away."

"You know, it might work on your sons and maybe all the men in your life, I don't know, but *that*?" Theresa gestured with her fingertips in Galina's direction. "That does not work with me. You brought me this box of recipes, and I'm happy to have them, but not if it means you're going to play some kind of head game with me about it."

"You're so much like your father. You have a nasty mouth."

Theresa sighed and angled her gaze upward, as though she could see through the ceiling. Her head had been aching for the past couple of days, typical for this time of year, and it didn't help the pain when she hollered, "Ilya!"

"And a loud one," Galina added.

Theresa pulled out her phone to thumb in a message, since there'd been no answer from upstairs. **I'm downstairs.**

"Keep the recipe box," Galina said. "I do want you to have it. I know it's hard for you to believe me, Theresa, but I've never wished you harm. If you want to hold what happened in the past against me forever, then you're the one who'll have to bear that burden."

"You kicked us out with only a few hours' notice! You married my father, told me I was the daughter you'd always wished for, and you booted us like neither of us meant a damned thing to you. I never heard a word from you after that. Do you think that somehow that wasn't supposed to hurt me? Whatever might've happened with my father, Galina, did it ever occur to you that a kindness from you might've made a big difference to me?" Theresa swallowed hard to keep her voice from shaking. Her throat itched with tears.

Galina stared at her. "You don't understand. You have no idea what happened. If you did—"

"I can't think of anything that could've made what you did all right," Theresa said. "No matter what my father did to you."

"It wasn't me," Galina began, but Theresa didn't let her finish.

"If it wasn't you, then who was it? Are you telling me that my dad made it up?" It wouldn't have been the first time her father had lied to make himself the victim of a story, but somehow Theresa couldn't believe it had happened in this case. The finer details, maybe. His responsibility in what had happened, yes. But not the bare truth: Galina had kicked them out.

Her phone buzzed.

Come up.

"I'm going upstairs," Theresa said. "Thank you for the recipes."

Galina didn't answer.

CHAPTER THIRTY-FOUR

Ilya had been looking up restaurant equipment on his laptop. He'd been surprised to find that the search for interesting items he could use to decorate the diner was not much different from the time he'd spent looking up quirky items to sink in the quarry. It required vision, he thought as he scrolled through several pages of vintage diner booths and neon signs that could be had for surprisingly reasonable prices.

At the soft knock on his door frame, he slid the laptop to the side and sat up. "Hey. What's up?"

It did not feel right for his heart to beat faster for a few seconds at the sight of Theresa's smile, but that didn't mean it felt . . . wrong. The waft of her fresh perfume sent a now-familiar tingle through him as she sat next to him on the bed. He stopped himself from leaning closer to sniff her. A flashing memory of her heat surrounding him sent a shiver through him. That had happened, he reminded himself sharply. But he didn't have to be stupid about it.

"I brought these for you." She handed him a small rectangular envelope. "And look what your mother gave me."

He glanced at the green plastic box as he took the paper envelope. "What is it?"

"Babulya's recipe box."

He paused before opening the envelope. "Oh, yeah? Is that what that is? It's been in the cupboard forever."

"Oh my God, Ilya, if it was a snake, it would have bitten you," Theresa said with the first two fingers on one hand curled, like fangs, as she imitated his grandmother. "Sss. Sss."

He peeked inside the box, feeling nostalgic and melancholy at the sight of Babulya's familiar handwriting. He flipped through the cards. Some of them were crisp and pristine white while others had been spattered with evidence of the cooking, bent and folded, the ink faded and in some places almost illegible. This was a treasure, for more reasons than its contents.

"Galina gave you this?"

"She said she wanted me to have it since we're going to be using the recipes in the diner. And I'm glad to have them. I'm sure what I can do from memory isn't always right." Theresa scooted back a little on the bed so she could crisscross her legs. "But see what I brought you."

He put the recipe box on his nightstand and opened the flap, pulling out a sheaf of pictures. It took him a few seconds to process what he was looking at, but once he did, all he could say was, "Wow. Where did you get these?"

"Alicia's crawl space."

He felt her moving closer to him to look over his shoulder at the pictures. He flipped through them slowly. "I remember this day. It was right before your dad and Galina got married."

"Was it?" She leaned her chin on his shoulder.

Ilya relished the weight of her body on his as he turned just enough to show her more of the pictures. Positioned this way, her hair tickled his cheek. He could easily kiss her, he thought, wanting to.

It was the wanting that kept him from it, because once he kissed her, this moment would end. She'd pull away from him, or she wouldn't, and both reactions were a problem. Besides, he told himself as he held up the photos so they could both look at them, he wasn't totally ruled by his dick. Not completely.

Theresa reached over him to tap the picture in his hand. "That's a good one of her. She was so beautiful."

Someone had captured Jenni laughing, head tossed back and eyes closed. Her blonde hair had glittered in the sunshine, something hard to see in this time-faded snapshot, but he remembered. "Do you think that's what I want to hear?"

"No. But she was, whether you want to hear it or not."

Ilya put all the pictures back in the envelope and tried to hand them back to her, but Theresa shook her head. Again he tried, but she moved away from him and refused. "Here."

"They're yours," she said. "You keep them. Or not. It's up to you. I thought you might like to have them, that's all. Alicia was going to toss them in the trash."

He leaned to open the drawer of his nightstand and put them inside it. "Thanks."

"Hey," she said quietly, so he turned, "I'm sorry if they upset you."

Had they? He couldn't be sure. Even a few weeks ago, the sight of those pictures would've sent him seeking refuge in the bottle or the arms of a one-night stand. Something had started shifting inside him. Something that had to do with Theresa.

"I know you loved her," Theresa continued. "I thought you'd like to see them."

"She never believed in me," Ilya said.

Theresa looked as though she meant to speak, then stopped herself. Tried again; stopped again. Instead of words, she spoke to him by taking his hand and linking their fingers together.

"It didn't matter if it was a chemistry test or remembering to be on time or if I could be the guy she took to the dances and showed off to her friends. Jenni didn't believe in me," he repeated, really feeling it for the first time. Admitting it. He looked down at his hand, fingers curling around Theresa's. "Alicia sure as hell never did. My mother. Feels like every woman in my life has no problem taking what she can get from me, but nobody has ever believed in me. Until you."

He thought for sure she'd recoil or cut her gaze from his or find an excuse to get up and leave. Theresa did none of those things. She tightened her fingers in his and leaned against him again, her cheek pressed to his shoulder. She sat there in silence for a few moments until he gave in to the urge he could no longer deny and pressed his lips to her temple.

She looked at him then. "I know you're going to make the diner a success, Ilya."

He wanted more from her than that. When he kissed her, lips parted, the sweet press of her tongue on his made him think that maybe Theresa wanted it, too. When he slid a hand up her back to cup her neck beneath the fall of her hair, though, she turned her face. She didn't pull away, but she murmured his name like either a warning or a plea; he couldn't be sure.

So he kissed her again, waiting for her to break it first. Neither of them did until, breathing hard, they eased apart to look into each other's eyes. She cupped his face with one hand, gaze searching his.

"This is crazy," she said. He was uncomfortably hard and tried to shift a little on the bed to ease the pressure of his erection against his jeans, but all that did was draw her attention to the bulge there. Theresa laughed. "Oh."

"Yeah," he said. "Oh."

"What is this?" she asked him.

Ilya hadn't spent a lot of his life honing honesty, but now all he felt he could say was the truth. "I don't know. Making a mistake?"

"Feels like that, doesn't it?"

It felt exactly the opposite of that to him, but he wasn't going to be the one to say so, not if she was having second thoughts. "We signed papers, Theresa."

She leaned to offer her mouth to him again, a simple, brushing kiss that lasted barely a second. "Is that what we're really talking about?"

"You tell me."

She sat back then, and he wished he'd said something else, if only so that she would kiss him again instead of putting distance between them. She gathered the thickness of her hair and pulled it on top of her head, securing it with an elastic band she pulled off her wrist in that magical way women did things. She used her thumb to wipe the corner of her mouth, her gaze contemplative.

"We had sex in the kitchen. You can't unring a bell, Ilya. We did that, and it changed things."

He knew that, but still frowned at her words. "Does it have to?"

"It almost always does," she said.

"You told me you . . ." He coughed lightly. "You slept with guys so you could have a place to stay."

"Or sometimes because I wanted to," she said, a little sharply. "It wasn't like I did it with guys I didn't like."

"No. No, I didn't mean that. I didn't do it with women I didn't like, either," Ilya said. "I mean, I always liked them at the time."

"I need to know that I can trust you, that's all," she said. "Sex is one thing. I think we both agree we're pretty good at that."

"Think how much better we'll get with practice," he said, rewarded by her laugh.

Theresa shook her head. "I believe you can do this. The diner. This thing with me, whatever it is now, whatever it might become. But I need to believe that you think you can do it, Ilya. And you've told me over and over again how you can't ever seem to make things work. Business, relationships, whatever it is. So it's not enough for *me* to believe that you can make any of this work. You need to believe it, too, and I need to trust that you do. I need to trust *you*."

"And you don't think you can?"

She shrugged. "With a business? Sure. I've already faced bad credit and debt and financial ruin. But with my heart . . . I don't know about that. I'm not quite as willing to risk that for someone who doesn't believe he's capable of keeping it safe."

Irritated because she'd hit close to home, he pulled away from her. "What are you saying? You need a commitment? You need me to—what?—sign a contract saying that I'll be faithful or that I'll marry you within a year or something like that?"

"Oh my God, no," she retorted, expression twisting. "Absolutely not."

"What, then? What do you want me to do?" he demanded.

"If it was that easy to figure it out," she shot back, "we'd be doing it already."

When Ilya looked back on his life, there weren't many moments he felt proud of. Most of them had been related to Go Deep; even if it had never been as financially successful as he'd wished, there'd been some damned fine things about it. He stood in front of another chance, now, to do something good with his life. To make something work.

It wasn't just the diner.

"I like you," Ilya said. "You're smart and we laugh together, and you have your shit together in a way I admire and envy and doubt I could ever live up to. You always did, even back then. The rest of us were running around like idiots, but you had yourself together."

Theresa was silent for a second or so. "That's what you see when you look at me?"

He shrugged, moving closer to her again. "Yes."

"I am the last person to have her shit together, Ilya."

"That's not what I see." He pushed a stray tendril of her hair over her shoulder. He didn't kiss her, even though he wanted to. He looked at her instead. Into her eyes. Seeing her. Really trying to see her. "You're beautiful."

Theresa gave her head the tiniest shake. Tears glinted but didn't fall. "I'm not asking you to promise me that it's all going to end up sunshine and flowers, Ilya. Nobody can know that. But I can't do . . . this . . . with you if I don't believe you think you're capable of it. That's all."

"I want to be," he said in a low voice. "Can that be good enough?"

She linked her fingers in his, letting their hands sit quietly together on his thigh. When she leaned to put her face against his shoulder again, the soft brush of her sweet-smelling hair tickled his face. He closed his eyes, breathing her in.

She shook her head again. "I don't know."

CHAPTER THIRTY-FIVE

With her trip to Scotland only a few days away, Alicia had gone a little into overdrive on cleaning out the crawl space. She didn't have a job to keep her occupied, and the more she got rid of or cleaned up, the better she felt about her decision to unload this house and start moving forward with her life . . . and Nikolai.

"I haven't even started looking for someplace new," she said as she and Theresa started tackling a new set of boxes. "Part of me thinks that if he doesn't take that job with the Mutters, we could end up traveling around the world or back on a kibbutz or something like that."

Theresa pulled a box closer to her, flipping open the lid. "Would you like that?"

"I don't know. I've only gone on one trip." Alicia shook her head with a laugh. "It seems like fun, doesn't it? Roaming the world, doing things . . . I don't know what I'd do for money, though. Teach English maybe? Dig wells? Cook dinner on a kibbutz? Hell, I have no idea. I'm just going to enjoy Scotland for a month with Nikolai, and if we come home still willing and able to talk to each other, then I'll figure out what to do from there."

Theresa nodded, then tilted her head to look at her. "Do you think you'll end up sick of each other?"

"It's possible. I hope not. But it could happen. I won't lie. This trip is sort of a test, I think. For both of us." Alicia pulled out a Raggedy

Ann doll she vaguely remembered getting for Christmas one year. It had always creeped her out, and she put it into a box marked for donations.

Theresa's box seemed to be full of baby clothes, and she shook out a little onesie and held it up. "What do you want to do with all of these?"

"Donate. I don't think I'm ever going to need them." Alicia dug out another couple of stuffed animals. "Why did my mom keep all of these things? The toys we really loved, we kept out and played with. But all this stuff . . ."

"Sentimental value?" Theresa closed the lid on the baby-clothes box and pushed it to the side. She opened another one to pull out some more papers that looked like schoolwork.

Alicia sat back with a small groan. "Ugh. I want to get rid of all of it. Everything. All of this stuff. It feels like it's weighing me down. I mean, seriously, I don't care about my second-grade report cards. I want to travel the world, Theresa! I want to get out there and be . . . unburdened!"

"Then you should be." Theresa slapped her hands together from the dust at the top of the box. "C'mon. Get this stuff. Let's take it out in the backyard and burn it."

"No." Half-horrified, Alicia put her hand over her mouth, then took it away. Put it back. "No, I couldn't. Could I? Oh my God. I could. I really could, right?"

"You totally could. You have the fire pit. We can haul this stuff down there. Light it up." Theresa grinned. "You have any marshmallows?"

"In the cupboard. Graham crackers and chocolate, too. Let's do it." Alicia felt like she'd slammed a couple of beers on an empty stomach. Giddy, dizzy, buzzed. Euphoric.

It took them only twenty minutes to haul all the boxes of papers to the backyard and pile them next to the fire pit. The items for donation had been settled into the trunk of Alicia's car and would be delivered to the thrift store tomorrow. The stuff she needed to send to her parents had been sealed up and addressed, and she'd take that to the post office tomorrow, too.

Now they would burn.

"Do you want to call the boys over?" Theresa asked as Alicia handed her one of the metal stakes they used to roast marshmallows.

She thought about it for a moment, then shook her head. "Nah. I'll hang out with Nikolai later, and to be honest, I don't really want Ilya to see all this stuff that was Jenni's. It might upset him."

"Are you sure it won't upset you?" Theresa asked.

Alicia shook her head. "Trust me, when I think about Jenni, the last thing I think about is her essay on how beavers build dams."

"And your parents?"

"My mom put all that stuff away because she couldn't stand to look at it." Alicia shrugged. "The things we really needed to hold on to, I think we did. I did, anyway."

Theresa looked solemn, then smiled. "Right. Let's light this up. What do you say?"

Alicia hadn't been able to find the bottle of lighter fluid, so they settled for twisting old papers and lighting them one at a time, then setting them on top of a small pile of papers in the fire pit. Slowly, the blaze grew, lighting the night and warming them against the balmy evening air. Pretty soon they were each gathering handfuls of papers and feeding them to the fire, gleeful at the way the flames rose.

She felt lighter with each handful. Letting go. Alicia tipped her head back to watch the ashes lifting on the breeze, like black lace edged with red and gold.

"This was a great idea," she murmured. "Thanks, Theresa."

"Anytime." Theresa stuck a marshmallow on the end of the metal spike and held it over the flames, turning it to get it evenly, goldenly toasted.

They made a few s'mores, then sat down on the telephone poles Alicia's father had sunk as seating around the fire pit. Theresa warmed her toes by pointing them toward the fire. Alicia pulled a box closer to her so she could add some more papers to the blaze. Her fingers brushed something hard. It rattled when she picked it up.

"Huh." Alicia held it to the light, turning it from side to side to try to read what it said. "It's a mint tin. Weird."

She shook it, listening to whatever was inside clatter against the metal. The contents confused her even more. "Aspirin?"

"Let me see." Theresa took the tin from her hands before Alicia could get a good look at it.

In the firelight, Theresa looked like she'd seen a ghost. She peered inside the small tin, then closed it. She clutched her fingers tight around it.

"What's wrong?" Alicia asked. "What is it?"

"They're not aspirin."

"No?" Alicia held out her hand to take the tin back, but Theresa didn't release it right away. "What is it?"

"Looks like pain pills." Theresa lifted one, held it up.

She tossed it into the fire before Alicia could stop her. "Hey! Are you sure?"

"Yes." Theresa made as though to toss the entire tin into the pit, but Alicia snagged it from her before she could.

"Don't. I want to see." She opened the tin to shake out a few of the dozen or so pills into her palm. She tried to see what was written on them, but the shifting firelight didn't give her good-enough light. "I'm going inside."

"Alicia . . ." Theresa followed her into the house. "Wait. What are you doing?"

Alicia had spilled the pills out onto the kitchen table and was carefully using her phone to figure out what they were. Not all of them were identifiable, but the ones she could figure out were definitely prescription pain meds. Something told her they weren't for her mom's infrequent but debilitating migraines. She pushed the pills back into the tin and closed it.

"They don't even make these kind of mints anymore," she said.

Theresa sat at the table across from her. "They probably don't make some of those pills, either."

"So they're vintage illegal pain pills." Alicia forced a laugh that twisted and faded into nothing. "They were Jenni's. She must've put them in the crawl space to hide them."

"I'm sorry, Alicia."

Alicia shrugged. "What do you have to be sorry for? You're not the one who got my sister hooked on pills."

Theresa blanched, a reaction that seemed extreme. "No, I didn't. I'm sorry you found them, though."

"I knew she was on something. More than booze or pot. I asked her, but she denied it. I knew, though." Alicia swallowed around the lump in her throat. "I wish I'd known then. It might've made a difference."

"It wouldn't have," Theresa said with conviction.

Alicia frowned. "You can't know that."

"You can't beat yourself up over it. I do know that. Whatever your sister was into back then, it wasn't anything to do with you. And if she didn't want your help, or she didn't want to get sober, then she wouldn't have, no matter what you said or did, or how many times you tried to help her. If you threw the pills away, she'd have found a way to get more." Theresa cut herself off abruptly, looking away. She shook her head. "It's what they do."

Alicia traced the letters on the lid of the tin. "I'm going to toss this in the fire."

"Good idea."

Out back, a shadowy figure standing by the fire pit startled them both. Alicia had gripped the tin in one fist but put both hands up in automatic reaction when Galina stepped out in front of her. Alicia yelped even as she recognized Nikolai's mother.

"I smelled smoke when I got home. I thought something might be going on over here. I had no idea you were having a weenie roast." Galina looked at the tin in Alicia's hand, and her expression tightened. "What are you doing? Burning papers? What's that?"

"I'm clearing out the crawl space so I can get the house ready to sell it. This is just some old junk I found in one of the boxes." Alicia tossed it into the fire pit, sending up a shower of sparks and ash into the night sky.

When she turned around, Galina and Theresa were staring at each other, neither of them moving. Theresa was the one who broke the gaze. She bent to grab one of the marshmallow sticks that she held out to Galina.

"Want a s'more?" Theresa asked.

"Yes, thank you. I wanted to be sure everything was all right over here. It's good to be neighborly, yes?" Galina smiled. "My girls. Sisters."

Alicia gave Theresa a surprised look. "Galina . . ."

The older woman clapped her hands together, with another look at the fire. "You might as well be, yes?"

It was an odd thing for her to say, but Galina had always been a little strange. Alicia looked at Theresa, who was making a weird face that she quickly smoothed when Galina turned to look at her. Galina tilted her head, her long dark hair falling over her face until she pushed it back.

"How's your father?"

Theresa's expression went completely flat. "I'm sure he's fine."

Galina looked over the graham crackers and chocolate bars Alicia had set on one of the wooden benches. She looked over her shoulder at Theresa. "Is he?"

"Let me make you a marshmallow," Theresa said.

Galina had never been mean to Alicia, not like in the horror stories she'd heard from some of her friends who'd had to put up with jealous, manipulative, or vindictive mothers-in-law. She'd been sometimes difficult to deal with in her erraticism. Kind and generous in one breath, spiteful and histrionic in the other. Still, Alicia had never had to actually live with her, and Theresa had. It seemed to have left a mark.

"So," Galina said when she'd piled together a gooey, melty s'more but had not yet bitten into it. "You girls. My boys."

Alicia smiled, a little self-conscious, noting Theresa's startled look. "What about us? And them?"

"I want to see them settled and happy. If you'd had children, you would understand."

It might not have been meant as a jab, but it probably had been. Alicia's smile became harder. "It would've been difficult to have children when I was married to one."

Theresa pressed her fingertips to her lips, holding back a tiny chuckle. It drew Galina's attention. The other woman licked some chocolate off the side of her s'more.

"You think what she said is funny? What about you? What do you think about my son?"

Theresa pulled a marshmallow from the bag and jabbed it onto the end of the metal spike. "I think we all need to acknowledge our flaws and grow from them."

"So many secrets," Galina said sharply.

Alicia looked from Nikolai's mother to Theresa and back again. "What's going on?"

Galina ignored her. "My mother was a good cook. Not terribly inspired, but consistent. She never taught me, you know. How to cook. It was a joke with my boys what an awful cook I am. But she taught you, and I don't even remember seeing the two of you in the kitchen."

"That doesn't make it a secret," Theresa snapped.

"She liked you, Theresa." Galina looked at Alicia. "She liked you, too."

"I loved Babulya," Alicia said.

Theresa nodded. "So did I."

"Well, of course I loved my mother, too," Galina said sharply. "We didn't always get along, but that doesn't mean I didn't *love* her."

"I never thought you didn't," Alicia said, wondering if this was the start of a Galina tantrum.

The older woman stared into the fire. "You're burning your past, Alicia. Too bad it's not so easy to do that with everything."

Neither Theresa nor Alicia responded to that with words; they shared a look between them of commiseration and bemusement. Galina tossed her s'more into the fire and got up. She gave them both a smile.

"Next time, invite Dina Guttridge so she doesn't have to peek out the windows and wonder what's going on," Galina said. "Good night, girls."

With that, she left by way of the side of the house, leaving Alicia and Theresa to sit and watch the burning-down fire. Alicia wanted to laugh but didn't. It wasn't terribly funny.

"What do you think she wanted, really?" Theresa asked finally.

Alicia shrugged and tossed another handful of papers into the fire. They were almost all gone. "I'm not sure. I'm not sure it matters."

"Right." Theresa coughed into her hand, shifting on the lawn chair. "Alicia. Look. Those pills . . ."

"It doesn't matter anymore. Jenni got herself into a bad place, and it ended up being bad for the rest of us, too." Alicia poked at the fire with a stick. "I don't really want to talk about it, okay? Knowing she was taking drugs doesn't change anything that happened. It can't bring her back. Nothing can do that. The best I can do, the best we all can do, is move on from it."

Together, they watched the fire for a few more minutes, until Theresa excused herself to go inside. "Will you be okay out here?"

"Yeah. I'm going to make sure the fire goes out. I'll be fine." Alicia smiled. "Thanks, Theresa. 'Night."

Alone, Alicia sat and studied the fire as it turned from tall orange flames to golden-and-red coals, then steadily became black. Clouds had covered the moon, so there was no light. She sat in the silence and the darkness until her eyes grew heavy; then she went inside to fill a pitcher with water, which she brought out to splash over the remains of the fire.

The tin had not burned. She heard the spatter of water on it, different from the soft sounds of it in the ashes. Using her phone, she shined a light into the fire pit. She used one of the sticks to shove ashes over it. It had not been destroyed, but that didn't matter. She didn't need to look at it anymore.

CHAPTER THIRTY-SIX

I believe you can do this.

Theresa's voice, quietly confident, echoed in Ilya's head every time he used his keys to open the diner doors. He had monthly payments to the bank, utilities set up in his name, new equipment ordered to replace the few things that had been bad, and a small construction crew taking care of the interior renovations.

He *was* doing this.

Alicia had been the one to handle the day-to-day crap at Go Deep. Ilya should've appreciated that way more than he had at the time. Now, faced with a shadowed and quiet diner left empty but smelling of sawdust and varnish, his head was bursting with plans and ideas he was discovering needed more than enthusiasm to implement.

He needed Theresa.

He hadn't seen her for the past few days. The last time, they'd argued lightly, over takeout food eaten at the prep counter, about whether they should even bother to try for a liquor license. Since the diner's original owners hadn't had one, Ilya had said they didn't need one. Theresa, surprisingly, had been in favor of getting one, because she thought it would give their new place an edge beyond the fresh menu and the nostalgia they were hoping to capitalize on. She agreed to research the possibilities and let him know what she discovered. He'd tossed a straw paper at her. She'd rolled her eyes. They'd shared a thick wedge of chocolate cake, with her feeding him bites off her fork, and when he kissed her good-bye, she'd let him.

He'd thought about trying to make more of it than that. Another round on the prep counter, maybe. Or he could've taken her into the dining room and made love to her there. Something in the way she'd responded to the kiss had told him Theresa would not have turned him down. So why hadn't he, then?

I need to know you believe you can do this. I need to be able to trust you, Ilya.

I want to. Is that good enough?

I don't know.

I don't know.

The trouble was, he didn't know, either. He wasn't convinced he could. So he'd left her hanging with a question in her eyes and the taste of chocolate cake and kisses in his mouth. He couldn't be sure which one of them had decided not to reach out, but it felt like they were both avoiding each other. He'd picked up his phone a dozen times to text her, to ask her out to dinner, or even just to get together at home to talk about the diner as though that was all they had in common, but he'd erased all the messages before hitting "Send." They did need to talk about the diner, but that had nothing to do with why he wanted to see her.

He'd spent a lot of time looking at the pictures she'd given him. He'd known then what love felt like. How it burned. He and Jenni had both been so young, but the difference was that now he'd grown older, and she would always be that laughing seventeen-year-old girl who'd insisted on breaking his heart.

He'd thought about throwing the pictures away but hadn't been able to. He'd satisfied himself with putting them in a cardboard shoe box on the top shelf of his closet, along with some old school medals and a few other mementos of his childhood. That's what Jennilynn

Harrison had become to him, Ilya thought. A memory to be put away in a box.

Yet it had still taken him four days of not hearing from Theresa before he could bring himself to go after her, and he was only doing it now because he could no longer stop himself. If she didn't want anything to do with him romantically, that was fine, but he did need her help with a bunch of stuff, and they would have to get through it, whether either of them liked it or not.

Steeling himself, he thumbed in her number and listened to the ring. She answered right before he expected to be sent to voice mail, her voice thick and rasping. She sounded groggy.

"What's the matter?" Ilya asked at once.

"I have the flu."

He frowned. "You okay?"

"No. Fever. Headache. Can't get out of bed." She coughed. "I e-mailed you with a list of things that needed to be taken care of and told you I wasn't going to be in for a few days."

"Oh."

She coughed again. "Let me guess, you didn't read the e-mail."

She'd set up a special e-mail account specifically for the diner, but he hadn't yet added it to his phone. "Is Alicia there? Is she helping you?"

Theresa gave a rough, rattling sigh. "She and Niko left for Scotland, remember?"

"Shit, I thought they weren't leaving until tomorrow. So you're alone? That's no good." He was already turning off the lights, locking the doors, and heading out to his car. "I'm on my way."

"You don't have to do that—"

"I'm on my way," Ilya said. "Don't argue."

He disconnected before she could protest more. He stopped at the pharmacy to pick up medicine, as many different kinds as he could find to cover all possible symptoms, along with a couple of boxes of tissues. He tossed a few gossip magazines into the basket in case she got bored with daytime TV. He stopped at the grocery store for chicken-noodle soup, juice, ginger ale, and saltines in case it turned into that sort of flu. He parked in Alicia's driveway and, laden with bags, went to the front door.

"Ilya! Hi!"

"Hey, Dina," he said as he put down some of the bags so he could test the front door. "How's it going?"

"I haven't seen you in a while."

Shit, she was actually coming over. Ilya tugged the front door, but it was locked. There was a spare key in the flowerpot on the railing, but he didn't have time to get it before Dina had crossed the lawn to the first porch stair.

"How's it going?" he asked again, lamely.

"I've missed you," Dina whispered with a shifty glance toward her own house. "Maybe you could come over later?"

"Oh, I'm busy later . . ."

"Sometime, then." She eyed him as he rang the doorbell. "You should come over sometime."

He heard the shuffle of something on the other side of the door. The click of the lock. He picked up the bags again and gave Dina a firm smile.

"I don't think so, Dina."

She sneered and crossed her arms. "Alicia isn't home, you know. She went on a trip with your brother. They're a couple now."

"I know that," Ilya said as the front door opened. "You think I don't? Jesus, Dina. Enough. Okay?"

Theresa, looking like death warmed over, peered through the crack in the door. "What the hell is going on?"

"You're here for her now?" Dina asked. "I get it. Boy, do I get it. You know what, Ilya, screw you!"

He pushed the door open wider, bags in hand. Theresa had already turned to shuffle away from him, toward the den. Ilya looked out the door, but Dina had already left, thank God. That was a mess he didn't want to deal with now. Or ever. He closed the front door and took the bags to the kitchen table, then went to the den.

"Hey. How are you feeling?"

Theresa had gone back to the couch, her head on a pillow in a brightly patterned case, and a bunch of knitted afghans on top of her. She made a small noise in answer, kind of like a whimper, half a moan. She put her hands to her head and squeezed.

"Hey," he said softly, as he sat on the edge of the couch near her knees. He put a hand on her, then withdrew it quickly. "Shit, babe, you're burning up."

She let out a small sigh and burrowed deeper into the pillow. "I took some medicine a few hours ago."

"You need more. I'll get it for you." In the kitchen, Ilya set some soup on the stove to heat, then shook a few acetaminophen tablets into his palm and took them to her with a glass of water. Her eyes were closed when he came back, her breathing raspy. She was shivering even under the pile of blankets. "Hey. Theresa? Here."

She sat up with a groan, her eyes ringed with dark circles and her hair stuck to her forehead and cheeks glistening with sweat. She took the glass and the pills from him but choked a little when she swallowed them. She clapped a hand over her mouth to hold back a gag, then shook her head with a grimace before sinking back onto the pillow.

Ilya rubbed her shoulder. "That's going to help. I've got some soup heating up for you."

"Not hungry."

"Well, when you are. Do you want something else? Something to drink?" Slowly, he let his hand move over her. She was so hot, almost scalding him even through the layers of clothing. He should get her a thermometer, he thought.

"No. I want to go up to my bed, though. The couch is lumpy." She sat up with one of those whimper moans and struggled with the blankets.

He was startled to see tears leaking from the corners of her eyes. "Let me help you. Hey, shhh."

"I haven't felt this terrible in . . . ever," she said with a small gasp.

"Let me help you," Ilya repeated, and slipped an arm beneath hers to help her up. She sagged against him, and without thinking, he bent to lift her. Her head nestled perfectly against his shoulder, and he thought for sure she'd protest, but she only made another small sound as he carried her toward the stairs.

By the time he got her to the bed, his arms were aching and legs trembling, but he managed to settle her carefully onto it. He helped her get beneath the blankets but realized the pillow she'd been using on the couch was meant for the bed. He ran downstairs, turned off the soup, grabbed the pillow, and went back up.

She looked like she was sleeping, at least until he carefully tried to lift her head to place the pillow beneath it. Then she opened her eyes, her gaze unfocused. She put her hand on his wrist. She barely squeezed him before letting go.

He stroked her hair off her forehead. "What can I do for you?"

"Let me sleep."

"Yeah. Okay." Still worried, he felt her forehead. He couldn't tell if it was cooler or not. "Are you sure I can't bring you something to drink?"

"Water." But when he tried to leave, she grabbed his wrist again. "Wait. Just sit with me for a minute."

"Okay." He did, watching while her eyelids drooped and her face went slack. The rise and fall of her shoulders slowed as her breathing did, too. He continued to watch her as she slept, making sure she looked comfortable, and then he went downstairs to put away the groceries he'd bought.

CHAPTER THIRTY-SEVEN

Theresa awoke in darkness, noticing for the first time that her head, which had felt like it was going to explode for the past two days, actually only ached a little bit. Her body still creaked with pain, but it felt more like she'd been run over by a bicycle than a tractor trailer. She felt sticky and gross from sweat, her pajamas clinging to her. For the first time in three days, she thought she might actually be able to take a shower.

It was a mistake. She'd eaten next to nothing since coming down with this, and as soon as she leaned over to turn on the hot water, the world spun as dizziness overwhelmed her. She sank onto her knees next to the claw-foot tub, knowing there was no way she was going to be able to get herself in and out of it without falling.

Theresa had not cried—really cried—for a long time. There'd been a few bouts of tears when things ended with Wayne—mostly of the self-castigating sort—because she'd allowed herself to get close enough to him for anything he ever did to bother her even for a second. Now, though, she couldn't stop herself from letting a frustrated sob slip out of her throat as scalding tears stung her eyes. She was on a bathroom floor clutching a bathtub while steam filled the air, her pajamas only half-off, and she wasn't going to be able to get herself under the water, which was the only place she wanted to be in that moment.

When the bathroom door creaked open, she managed to raise her head from its place on the tub's curved lip. So Ilya taking care of her had not been a fever dream, though it had seemed something like one.

"Theresa, shit, did you fall?" He knelt next to her, taking her hand.

She was aware that she was barely dressed but couldn't bring herself to care. It wasn't like he'd never seen her nearly naked. "No, I wanted to take a shower. I feel so gross, but I got dizzy."

"You should've called for me," he said. "C'mon, let me help you get back to bed."

"No," she muttered. More tears. She hated that she was crying but couldn't stop herself. "I want a shower . . . please . . . I just feel so sweaty and awful, Ilya."

She also hated the sound of pleading in her voice, hated being dependent on him, hated feeling this way. She did not hate that he was there; that was clear to her even through the again-rising ache in her head. She blinked, trying to force away the tears, but they wouldn't go.

"Okay. Sure. Shhh. Hey, it's fine." Ilya stroked the hair off her face, where it had stuck to her with sweat and tears and God knew what else. "I'll help you in the shower."

He got her up and tested the water as she struggled to tug at her pajamas. "No peeking," she managed to say, as ridiculous as it was.

"No," Ilya promised. "Not a single one."

He kept his back turned when she was naked, then his face as he gripped her arm to steady her as she put first one foot, then the other, in the tub. She sat at once, not daring to stand. With her knees pulled to her chest, head bowed to let the water pound away at the tension in the back of her neck and shoulders, Theresa let out a long, sobbing sigh of relief.

"I want to lie down," she said after a minute, certain Ilya was still there, although she hadn't raised her head to see him. "I want to sleep in here."

"Okay." She heard him tug the shower curtain all the way around the tub. "I'll wait here. The water's going to turn cold after a while. You'll need help getting out."

She slipped onto her side along the tub's curved bottom. It wasn't big enough to let her stretch out, but the warm water pattering all over her felt so good she didn't mind being a little cramped for now. She couldn't really sleep, but she could doze.

"You okay in there? Don't drown," Ilya said.

"'M okay . . ."

The curtain rattled a little. "I'm right here, if you need me."

She was feeling far from well, but she was starting to feel better. At least the stickiness of her fever sweats was washing away. The sound of the water thrumming on the tub soothed her, along with the warmth and the steam that relieved some of the pressure in her head. By the time the water began to cool, she felt ready to get out.

Ilya had a towel ready for her, and her robe. Wrapped up but with her hair still sopping wet, Theresa was steady enough to make it back to her room, where she sat on the edge of the bed and didn't feel like she was about to topple over.

"My hair," she said. "It's a mess. I need to comb it, and I don't think I can do it."

"Where's your comb?"

"You can't do it for me," she protested, but Ilya had already found it on her dresser and was sitting on the bed next to her. "Ilya, no."

He didn't argue with her, but he didn't stop, either. She thought mildly about fighting him off but didn't have the strength . . . and didn't really want to. He grasped her hair at the base of her neck and tugged the comb gently through from his fingers to the ends. She braced herself for pain, but his grip kept the comb from yanking.

"I haven't had anyone comb my hair for me in so long. I can't remember the last time. I must've been a kid." Her body sagged at the comfort of being pampered in this way. "Being taken care of."

"Had a . . . friend . . . who was a hairdresser. She told me the trick to combing out without hurting the person is to do it this way. I've never, um, you know, actually combed someone else's hair." He moved the comb higher to work on the tangles at the crown.

Theresa laughed, surprising herself that she was able to, at his use of the word "friend."

"Uh-huh. A friend. You've had a lot of friends."

"Nothing wrong with having a lot of friends." Using his fingers, he tugged them through her hair.

She shivered at the touch. "Sure."

"You okay? Fever coming back?" Ilya put a hand on her shoulder to turn her a bit toward him.

"No. I don't think so. I always shiver when someone touches my hair." She pulled her robe tighter around her throat, more aware that she was naked beneath it than she'd been in the bathroom.

"You should get some sleep."

She looked at him. "You don't have to take care of me. Thank you, but you don't need to."

"Someone needs to."

"Nobody," Theresa said more fiercely than she meant to, "needs to take care of me. I can take care of myself!"

The force of her words made her head hurt again. She shifted away from him, but his hand on her shoulder kept her still. His gaze bore into hers.

"You *deserve* to be taken care of, Theresa. I want to be here."

"And you're the one to do it?" Her voice roughened again, her throat aching not from her illness but from the effort of holding back the urge to cry again. "Am I another one of your . . . friends?"

Ilya shook his head. "Not like them. Shit, I don't know."

"Like Dina from next door?" Theresa whispered.

"Definitely not like her. Look, we don't have to talk about this now. You're sick. You should rest." He pushed her hair over her shoulder, and she shivered again.

They stared at each other.

"Why did you kiss me in the hall that night?" she asked.

Ilya's brow furrowed, then smoothed. "I wanted to. Why did you let me?"

"I wanted you to, I guess." Her head was really aching again now, not quite at the splitting level it had been, but enough to make her ready to lie down with her eyes closed. No more talking. She didn't have the energy.

"I'd kiss you right now if you weren't sick," he said.

Laughing hurt her head, but she couldn't stop herself. She closed her eyes against the throb of pain, but her smile remained. "Weirdo."

"Go to sleep. I'll bring you some soup when you want it."

Theresa opened her eyes. "What are we doing, Ilya? This is crazy."

"It's crazy," he agreed, and pressed a chaste kiss to her hand, which she had not realized he was holding. "So . . . maybe we can be a little crazy?"

It was the fever. She wasn't thinking straight. Maybe this was all a delusion, Theresa thought as she let him squeeze her fingers and press the back of her hand to his lips.

"You always got away with it. Whatever trouble you were getting into, you got away with it . . . are you going to get away with it this time?" She sounded a little drunk, her words slurring and voice rasping. She was so tired now, nothing much was making sense.

"Go to sleep. I'll be here when you wake up."

Unable to protest anymore, she let him tuck her into the blankets and press a kiss to her forehead. She let him sit with her until she drifted into sleep, and, when she woke up, she let him feed her soup while they both laughed at old Three Stooges movies he played on her laptop. Later still, she let him get into bed beside her to spoon until she slept again, then woke feeling almost normal.

Ilya snored lightly beside her, his head on the mattress because she only had one pillow. His face had turned away from her. He wore a pair of briefs, no shirt, and had pulled the sheet only up to just past his belly button. One hand curled on the center of his chest while the other rested above his head.

She didn't want to wake him. They would have to talk, again, about what was going on with them. Or what wasn't going to happen. She didn't want to talk about it, to make it real one way or another. She didn't want to have to decide.

This time, she made it into the shower all by herself without feeling like she might faint. She showered quickly, keeping her hair out of the water so she wouldn't have to deal with combing it again. She dressed quickly in fresh pajamas, not quite ready for "real" clothes. Ilya was still sleeping, his face now buried in her pillow, when she passed by the room's open door.

She made tea and toast, nibbling slowly to give her stomach time to adjust after days of eating next to nothing. The food settled her as the tea warmed her. She didn't feel like she had a fever, but she shook a couple of acetaminophen into her palm and swallowed them with swigs of tea, anyway, to fend off the slightest hint of a lingering headache.

"Hey." Ilya, hair sticking up all over and still bare-chested, came into the kitchen as easily as if he lived there.

He was used to doing that, Theresa thought suddenly. Of course he was. The thought of the reasons why should've bothered her more but somehow didn't. She watched him help himself to a mug and hot water, a tea bag. He turned to see her looking.

"You feeling better?" he asked. "You look better."

"If that's a nice way of saying I looked like death before, thanks." She sipped her tea.

Ilya smiled. "You could never look like death. But you do look much better now."

"Such a charmer," she said. "Thank you for being here. Thank you for taking care of me."

He pulled a face, looking as though he was going to make a joke. It was what she expected of him, anyway. Instead, his smile softened. When he crossed the room to her, she should have turned her face away, but he was too fast or she was too slow, because his lips brushed hers as one hand tipped her chin gently upward to allow him full access to her mouth. The kiss lasted only a second or so, barely long enough for her to even close her eyes. His touch on her face lingered a little longer, until he moved his hand around the back to comb through her hair.

She shivered.

"I wanted to be there for you. Even if you looked totally disgusting."

A rush of heat flooded her, but it had nothing to do with the return of a fever. She managed a whisper. "Thanks, Weirdo."

There seemed to be so much more to say, but she didn't have the strength for it right then. She needed to get back beneath a pile of blankets and watch some mindless television while she sipped at tea and dozed off this headache. She didn't have the strength to think about the possibilities of what any of this might mean . . . but it was clear the possibilities were there.

"I'm really tired," she said in a low voice. "My head's hurting a little again. I think I need to lie down."

"I could stay," Ilya whispered. "Hang out for a bit. Make sure you're okay."

Refusal rose to her lips, but the faint taste of him left from his kiss would not let the "no" escape. "I could eat some soup."

He smiled. Nodded. "Okay."

There it was: the crazy. And the crazier part of it was she couldn't make herself care.

CHAPTER THIRTY-EIGHT

"You're going next door again?" Galina looked up from her laptop, her reading glasses perched low on her nose. She'd been typing away there for an hour or so. Ilya hadn't asked her what she was doing. "She's still sick?"

"She's feeling better, but yeah, I'm going over." He held up a take-out rotisserie chicken and sides he'd picked up from the grocery store. "We're going over the menus. Talking about staffing. That sort of thing."

Galina made a noise low in her throat. "Hmm."

"Hey, Mom. You know, we could use your advice on some things. About the diner," Ilya said.

He wasn't expecting her to look so affronted, but she did. Deliberately, his mother removed her glasses and looked down her nose at him. She closed the laptop lid.

"The diner? Why on earth?"

"You've worked in one," he said.

Her scowl flashed into something else for a moment before she smoothed her expression. "I'm not going to come waitress for you, Ilya."

"I'm not asking you to be a waitress. I just thought you might have a decent idea about how some things are run. Forget I asked." He shook his head. "I'll see you later."

"Ilyushka. Wait."

He grimaced. "Don't call me that. You're not Babulya, and I'm too old for it."

Galina sighed and took off her glasses to pinch the bridge of her nose. "You're so sensitive."

"Hello," he said. "Pot, have you met kettle? I asked you a simple question, and you jumped down my throat."

"I'm sorry."

He'd had apologies from his mother in the past, plenty of times. Galina blew more hot and cold than March winds. He didn't trust her, so he'd been a little stupid to even ask her the question in the first place, but that was the thing about his relationship with his mother. He would probably always give her another chance, and she would probably always prove she couldn't be trusted.

"Look, I asked to be nice, and because I thought maybe you might want to help out. This is a big deal for me. It's a lot of work, and I'll be the first to admit I don't have the first idea how to run a restaurant. I've been going into this blind. I thought maybe for once, just once, you might want to do something to help me out." Before she could speak, he waved her to silence. "I'm going next door. Forget I asked. Keep on doing whatever it is you're doing."

He heard her calling out behind him, but he didn't stop. Crossing the street, he let himself into the Harrison house, calling out Theresa's name as he went into the kitchen. He found her there wearing soft pajama pants, a thin T-shirt, and a half-zipped hoodie. She'd pulled her hair into a messy tangle on top of her head, but several dark ringlets had sprung free to frame her face. She was still moving slow, recovering from being sick, but she smiled when she saw him, and that was all it took to make his heart do a slow barrel roll.

"I brought dinner." He held up the food.

Theresa rubbed her belly. "Yum. I was going to make tuna-fish sandwiches and macaroni and cheese, but that smells much better. I actually have a little bit of an appetite back."

"Tuna with mac 'n' cheese—damn, that is old school. I think that needs to be a menu item. On whole-wheat bread with the crusts off?"

"It'll be a top seller," she said. "Side of salt-and-vinegar chips, right?"

"That's how we always did it." He set the food on the table and moved closer to her so he could take her by the shoulders to study her face. "You think you'll be back to work soon? You look better."

"The Internet tells me this flu's been hitting everyone hard, that it takes about a week and a half to really get through it. I'll be okay." She tilted her head and gave him a faint smile. "I'm sorry I haven't been up to getting over to the diner. I know you've been busy. I really want to see everything that's been going on."

"When you feel up to it, that will be fine. I was over there today. The electrical guys finished up with everything, and the plumber will be there tomorrow, although he said he hadn't seen anything that needs to be replaced beyond a few washers in the sinks." He let his hands run down her arms to grip her above the elbows, reluctant to let her go.

"That's a relief," Theresa said.

The past week had seen them spending a good portion of every day and most evenings together. She hadn't felt up to driving anywhere but had been able to do some work from her laptop, including researching suppliers and getting quotes as well as arranging service appointments to take care of the few problems they'd known about before buying the place. Ilya had done the running around, meeting contractors and supervising deliveries.

The "them" part of all this had hovered between them, unspoken, since the night he'd slept over to take care of her. He'd thought about kissing her every single time they were together but hadn't. First, because although she'd been fever-free and the headaches and body soreness had passed, Theresa had still been feeling weak and easily worn out enough that by the end of the day, all she'd wanted to do was lie on the couch and watch funny movies. The fact that he'd been willing to do that and nothing more had told Ilya more about how he felt about her than anything else, but if Theresa had noticed it, she hadn't brought it up.

They were dancing around it, but it felt a little bit like Theresa might be doing a country line dance while Ilya was attempting a waltz. They were both moving, but not always in the same direction or to the same beat. Now he'd been holding on to her for too long that it was becoming awkward, so he made himself let her go.

She gave him that curious head tilt, studying his face. "Let's eat. I have some menu samples for us to look at. We'll need to get them printed soon to have them ready in time. Are we still aiming for the June opening date?"

"If everything goes as planned, yeah. I talked with the sign guys you hooked me up with. They can have it ready and installed, but we need to decide on the name." Ilya went to the cupboard to pull out some plates.

Theresa got silverware from the drawer and added it to the table. They settled in to eat, making lists on a pad of yellow paper she'd already filled most of. He got her laughing, and although the giggles trailed into a fit of light coughing, she was still grinning when she recovered.

"I love how you laugh with your whole body," he said abruptly.

Theresa had gone to the sink to wash her hands after coughing into them, and she turned with a look of surprise. "What?"

"You laugh with your mouth, your eyes—your shoulders shake. You vibrate with it. I can always tell when you're laughing for real or you're faking it," Ilya said.

"That's funny. Most men can't tell when a woman's faking it."

He groaned. "Nice."

She laughed—stopped as though in surprise to look down at herself—then laughed again, harder. "Oh, man. It's true!"

She shook with infectious guffaws that made him laugh, too. Their hilarity spiraled up and up. Every time there was a pause, their eyes met and it began again, until Ilya had to wipe his eyes against tears, and Theresa was clutching her belly and leaning on the counter like it was holding her up.

"Stop," she gasped. "Omigod, stop . . ."

He couldn't, not really. Laughing with her felt too good, too perfect. It felt right in that moment to get up from the table. To kiss her.

Hesitantly at first, the lightest brush of his lips on hers. Deeper in the next moment when she didn't pull away or push him off. She tasted of the sweet tea they'd been drinking, when his tongue slipped inside her mouth, and of her own unique flavor. Her hands went to his hips just above the waistband of his jeans.

"You're going to get sick," she murmured against his mouth.

"You're not contagious anymore. If I was going to get the flu from you, I'd already have it." He kissed her again.

It broke when she turned away, twisting out of his embrace to cough. "Ugh, sorry, sorry. So gross."

He squeezed her shoulder. "If you don't want me to kiss you, Theresa, all you have to do is say so."

He said it lightly. Teasing, the way they often did with each other. It earned him a nudge in the ribs and a roll of her eyes.

"I want to kiss you," she told him.

"You do?" Heat lit him from the inside, starting somewhere low in his gut and spreading upward. "I mean, yeah. Of course you do."

"We're doing this," Theresa said quietly, her gaze steady on his. "We're going to do this complicated thing."

She let her hands slide up the front of his shirt to tug the open collar, her body leaning naturally against his, a perfect fit. Without waiting for his answer, she pressed her face to his chest. Ilya ran a hand over her hair, feeling her shiver and hearing her laugh softly when she did.

"Yeah," he said. "We're doing this."

CHAPTER THIRTY-NINE

For the first time in nearly two weeks, Theresa felt good enough to put on clothes that were not pajamas and throw in a load of laundry, run the vacuum, and clean up the piles of books, magazines, and empty tissue boxes that littered the den near the couch where she'd been spending most of her time. Her in-box had been filling up with messages from her freelance clients, and while she'd been able to keep on top of a lot of it, there were some things only in-person meetings could handle. There were also the long lists she'd been making with Ilya to take care of.

There was also Ilya, in general.

She paused while stripping the sheets from her bed, her arms full of cotton, to bury her face in the pile and let out a muffled squeal. It did not turn into a bout of throat-ripping coughs, so that was a relief. It did end up with her turning to sit on the bare mattress to fend off a wave of dizziness that she had to admit had nothing to do with her recent illness. It was the thought of what she was getting herself into. A few deep breaths dispelled the spinning of her head, but not the squeezing feeling in her chest.

The summer Barry and Galina got married had been the first time Theresa ever went with the Stern boys and the Harrison girls to the quarry to swim. Ilya had been the one to invite her, last-minute, when they were already heading out. It had meant something to her back then, because she'd been struggling to find her place in the new family dynamic, and he'd made it seem like the most natural thing in the world for her to be included.

"Aren't you coming?" he'd asked, his towel hung over one shoulder. "C'mon, Malone."

She'd grabbed her suit and towel and a pair of sunglasses and hurried after them, following the sound of their voices because they hadn't waited for her to catch up. That had told her more than anything that she'd become a part of their group. No special treatment.

Niko had been the first to jump off the rock ledge and into the water, followed by Ilya and Jenni, while Alicia shook her head and refused. Nobody had bullied Theresa into following the other three. Her own desire to fit in with them had pushed her to the edge, her toes curling over the smooth limestone. She'd looked down to the water below, and her heart had seized, her vision had blurred a little in anticipatory fear, and she'd forgotten she was holding her breath until her ears began to ring.

"Jump, Malone!" Ilya had shouted from the water.

She had not jumped.

She'd gone swimming with all of them many times after that, but she'd never jumped off the ledge. Yet here she was, already on the way down, this time already knowing how it felt to leap and fall and have the quarry water close over her head. The cold had taken her breath away exactly the way Ilya's kisses did, except this time she was not going to do it only once.

The sound of her front doorbell ringing got her up and moving, and she paused to dump the sheets in the laundry room before she answered it. She wasn't expecting Dina Guttridge to be standing there with a bottle of wine in her hand. The other woman looked like she'd been crying.

Dina held up the bottle. "Can I come in?"

"I . . . sure." Theresa stepped aside, though not fast enough, because Dina was already shoving past her into the kitchen.

The wine was in a screw-top bottle, which meant Theresa didn't need to offer a corkscrew. Dina had already opened it and was looking at her with a sour expression. "Glasses?"

"Sure." Theresa pulled out a single glass and handed it to the other woman, who frowned. "I don't drink."

"Figures." Dina poured a glass and sipped it, then shuddered with distaste and put the bottle and glass on the table. "Yuck. I knew I should've gone with the Cab."

"What can I help you with?" Theresa eyed the other woman warily. She already had a suspicion about why Dina was there, and she didn't particularly want to deal with it.

"Are you fucking him?"

Theresa leaned against the counter. "That's none of your business, Dina."

"I knew it. Dammit." Dina wiped the back of her hand across her mouth, cutting her gaze to the side before fixing it on Theresa's. "You know he can't be trusted."

If there'd been any suspicion that Ilya and Dina had done any fooling around, it dissipated under those words. Theresa would have laughed, if that hadn't felt so terribly cruel. Instead, she said nothing.

Dina's laugh had little humor in it. "You're already in deep, huh? He does that to you. Makes you think you're something special. Gets close to you. Then . . . nothing."

"Whatever happened between the two of you is none of my business." Theresa kept her tone neutral. "And whatever is going on with me and Ilya is none of yours."

Dina sagged. "Yeah. Right."

"I think you should go," Theresa said, but gently.

"Don't you even care? I'm trying to warn you."

Theresa wanted to laugh again, not because there was anything funny about what Dina had said but because the warning was all too legitimate. "I can take care of myself."

"You think I'm a terrible person, don't you?"

"It's not my place to judge you," Theresa said.

"But you are! I would be," Dina added.

There was no way she and Dina were ever going to be friends, but in that moment Theresa had at least the tiniest shred of sympathy for her. "People make mistakes. It happens. You either learn from it or you don't, I guess."

"Oh, I learned from it," Dina said bitterly. "I'm trying to make sure you don't make the same mistakes."

"I'm not married," Theresa said coldly, getting tired of Dina's insistences and the conversation in general. "Whatever happens between me and Ilya is only going to affect me, and I already told you I can take care of myself."

Dina winced. She nodded. "Fine. I guess I should go."

"Please. And take the wine."

"You can keep it. I'm done with it, and you're welcome to take my leftovers." If Dina's tone and snide words had been meant to make Theresa feel bad, they missed the mark. Without waiting for an answer, the other woman turned on her heel and stalked out of the kitchen. The front door slammed a minute or so later.

CHAPTER FORTY

"So, we need to have a little talk."

Those were never the words a guy liked to hear from the woman he was dating. Or maybe dating. Or wanted to date.

Theresa smiled at him from across the kitchen table. "Ilya?"

"Not about the diner, huh?"

"It's about us. And Dina Guttridge."

He groaned. "Shit. Look, it was a stupid thing that happened once, two years ago. You can't get more stereotypical than that whole thing. I delivered a package to her that they'd dropped off by accident at my house, she invited me in for an iced tea . . ."

"Spare me the details, please." Theresa held up a hand. "I don't care."

"No?" He wanted to be relieved but eyed her cautiously.

"I don't care about your previous poor judgment. No."

Ilya blew out a small breath. "Okay . . . ?"

"She came over here earlier, warning me off you. Because you were not to be trusted." Theresa raised an eyebrow and leaned back in her chair.

God, she looked gorgeous. Hair pulled up, minimal makeup, tight T-shirt, and jeans. Bare feet. Her toes had killed him a little when he came in the front door and saw her, and he'd never even been a foot guy.

Everything about her seemed to affect him, though. Even the haughty look she was giving him. Maybe especially that.

"You've said something along those lines already," Ilya said. "More than once."

She nodded. "Yeah. I know."

Ilya leaned across the table to take her hands, his thumbs rubbing gently across the backs. "I'm not saying you don't have a point."

He'd been hoping to make her laugh, and she did. He'd have kissed her except for the distance between them. He settled for linking their fingers.

Theresa looked down at their hands. "So here's the thing, Ilya. I'm not sure I do trust you. But I want to. Okay? I want to try. This thing between us that we've been pretending didn't mean anything for months, I want to give it a try."

"Me, too. You can trust me on that." This time, he did get up from his seat to lean across the table for a kiss.

"I'm going to try," Theresa said, and took a deep breath as though her words had taken a lot of courage to say.

Ilya knew how that felt. He sat back in his chair. "I want you to be able to trust me. I believe you can."

She smiled.

This time when he got up, he knocked the chair over in order to get to her. His mouth found hers. His fingers sank into her hair. He kissed her like a promise.

"I love the way you taste," he told her.

Theresa laughed into his open mouth, then let her tongue slip along his as she drew him closer. Her chair creaked. His back and neck ached a little from the awkward position, but he couldn't bring himself to stop kissing her. He slipped an arm behind her shoulders to get her up and out of the chair. He turned her until she sat on the edge of the table. He eased between her knees, his hands roaming over her back until one anchored at the nape of her neck. He kissed her as hard as he'd wanted to do the past couple of weeks while the flu had cock blocked him, and she kissed him with as much fierce hunger.

When she cupped him through his jeans, Ilya groaned her name. Her soft laughter sent another surge of arousal through him. He pushed into her touch, already aching from wanting her.

They hadn't done more than kiss since the sex in the diner, and that had been before they'd had any sort of discussion or agreement about where they were going with all this. He didn't want the second time to be on a kitchen table. "Wait . . ."

Theresa broke their kiss, her expression almost comical with surprise. "What?"

"Not here. I want this time to be . . . slower." He kissed her until she responded and then withdrew to tease her with only the brush of his breath on her face. "I want to take my time. I want to make you crazy . . ."

"I'm already crazy," she said in a rough voice.

"I want to make you lose your mind."

She laughed huskily. "I have a bed upstairs, you know. You could take me up there. It has fresh sheets and everything."

He cupped her face in his hands, searching her gaze. "You want this, Theresa?"

"Yes. Of course." A shadow drifted across her expression. "Do you?"

He did, more than anything, but somehow it was going to be different this time. No hasty, furtive coupling, with both of them pretending it meant nothing. The idea of it, that they might be getting ready to make love instead of fuck, sent a series of tingling chills, sharp as shattered glass, up and down his spine.

He wanted this time to matter. More than that, he needed to be worth mattering to her. He kissed her again, softer this time.

"Yeah. I want to make love to you, Theresa. But upstairs. In a bed."

She noticed his deliberate turn of phrase. He saw it in her eyes and the curve of her smile; he felt it in the way she kissed him slowly but without lingering. She pushed him gently away from her so she could get off the table, and then she took him by the hand and led him upstairs.

◆ ◆ ◆

Ilya touched her with reverent hands. Not hesitant or uncertain, not fumbling, and not even particularly gentle, which Theresa loved, because the harder he held her, the better it felt. He touched her as though she were precious. He excavated her a layer at a time until she was revealed to him, nothing left to hide, but so much left to discover.

She murmured his name when he moved his mouth over her collarbone, the syllables of it hissing into a sigh at the nip of his teeth. She arched under the delicious sting, and he cupped her breasts so that he could kiss the nipples, one at a time. When he drew one into his mouth, sucking gently, Theresa cried out. Her hands were over her head, gripping the spindles of the creaking headboard.

"Make that noise again," Ilya said as he slipped a hand between her legs to toy with her there. "Aah, God, babe, you're so wet."

She made the noise again, helpless to stop herself at the stroke of his fingers on her and the sound of aching desire in his voice. Ilya had promised her he was going to make her lose her mind, and she was well on her way. At the teasing pinch of his fingers between her legs, she let go of the headboard to dig her hands into his hair. She hadn't meant for it to be a command, but she didn't complain when he moved down her body, his mouth skimming over her bare flesh, to settle between her legs.

"Tell me you want this." His breath gusted against her heat, making her incredibly aware of her arousal.

She licked her lips, forcing herself to make words. "You love that, don't you? Making me say it."

"I do." He gave her a slow, exploratory lick and chuckled at her gasp, then muttered a cry when her fingers twisted in his hair. "Tell me you want my mouth on you."

"I want . . . your mouth . . ." It was too much, trying to speak around the urge to moan.

He gave her what she'd asked for. Teasing flicks of his tongue that sent her close to the edge but not over it, then the slow, steady pressure of his lips. She was mindless with it, muscles tensing and the world going away until there was nothing but Ilya and the pleasure he was giving her. He was talking to her, words muffled as he brought her ever closer to climax with his mouth. She could not hear what he was saying, could not make sense of it, nor could she answer him with anything but the low, rasping noises that forced their way out of her throat.

She came, finally, in a series of pulses so strong the pleasure bordered on the edge of pain. She heard herself crying out, but it was the sound of Ilya's answering muttered moans that tipped her into another wave of orgasm that hit hard on the heels of the first. It left her plundered.

She tasted herself on his kiss when he moved up her body, and she managed to open her eyes. His hardness rubbed her belly, and she shifted, meaning for him to slide inside her. Ready for it.

"Tell me that you want me," he breathed.

She tipped her face to kiss him, adding a nibble on his chin. "I want you."

Still, he hesitated, a confusing array of emotions moving over his face. Theresa frowned. "What?"

"I don't have anything."

She laughed, softly at first, then louder and louder until she bit off the giggles so she could kiss him again. Her hand moved between them, stroking, until he shook and groaned and pushed into her grip. She looked at him.

"I know it's important to you," Ilya began, his voice breaking as her hand moved.

"We've both had all the tests, right? We established that." He nodded, and she kept her hand moving. It was her turn to tease him, and she reveled in it. "I'm on birth control, and I haven't been with anyone since I got the all clear. You?"

"No . . . damn, babe, I'm not going to last long enough if you keep doing that."

All it took was another shift of her body, a slight press on his shoulder, a wiggle, and he was inside her as easily as taking a breath. Ilya shuddered again, pushing deep. He buried his face against the side of her neck, and she felt his gasp and the press of his teeth on her.

"I want you," she told him, urging him to move with her hands and the lift of her hips and the way she hooked her heels behind his calves. "I want you, I want you, I want you . . ."

Ilya pushed up on his hands, his thrusts getting deeper. Faster. His expression turned grim at first, but then he smiled as he looked down into her face. When she dug her nails into his ass, he gave a low groan, shaking, but never looked away from her eyes. She watched his pupils dilate. She felt him surge inside her.

"I want you," Theresa whispered as Ilya slowed and finally stopped with a gasping breath.

"You have me," he said.

CHAPTER FORTY-ONE

It had been months since he'd lived in this house alone, and it still startled him a little to walk into the living room to find the television on and his mother on the couch. Most of the time she also had her laptop with her, typing away at whatever it was she'd found to keep herself occupied. Tonight she had the sound turned down low enough that she couldn't have been paying much attention to the black-and-white movie scrolling across the screen.

"I heard from your brother. He sent pictures," she said without looking up.

"Yeah. I got them, too. Looks like they're having fun." It had been a little hard to see Alicia's smile, his brother's arm around her. She'd never looked that happy with him, not that he could ever remember. It bothered him, although he didn't want it to.

His mother tipped her head to look at him over the rims of her reading glasses. "Where've you been off to all day long?"

"Working."

She laughed softly. "It's good for you, to have something to do. Keeps you out of trouble."

"I'm not in high school."

"No, you're a grown man who spent a lot of his time drifting," she said.

Ilya's lip curled. "I wouldn't call spending most of my adult life running my own business *drifting*."

"There are lots of ways for a man to drift. Some do it all over the world. Some do it all in one place." She closed the laptop lid. "I never figured you for a restaurant owner."

"Me neither. But I'm doing the best I can." He paused, unsure if he wanted to bring it up. Asking for her help before had been a mistake, but talking with his mother so often led to him tripping over land mines. "So, we're having this thing. A soft opening."

"Sure, sure. A trial run. That makes sense." She nodded.

"I want to invite you," Ilya said.

Galina smiled. "Of course you do. I'm your mother. I should be there."

Her calm assumption that she deserved a place witnessing his success—or failure, as the case might be—was typical Galina. Still, Ilya couldn't be sure he disagreed. She might have her quirks, and his dislike was certainly more deep-seated than his fondness for her, but she still *was* his mother.

"It's going to be a big deal. Lots of people there. It can really help get the word out about the place, get people excited about the changes we're making. So I want to make sure it goes off without a hitch."

"What night is it?"

"June fifth. It's a Thursday. If everything goes all right, we'll open on Sunday."

Galina looked stricken. "Oh . . . I have a conflict that night."

She'd missed baseball games and school concerts and birthdays and holidays, so he shouldn't have been surprised she would miss this, too. He shrugged it off. "Okay."

"No, wait . . . what time? I'll try. Okay? Thank you for inviting me."

"Of course I invited you," Ilya said wearily. "You're my mother. And it's better than simply having you show up angry at not being asked. You know, like the wicked fairy in 'Sleeping Beauty.'"

"I said I'll try to be there, Ilya. You don't have to be cruel about it. Believe me, if I could be there for sure, I would tell you."

"So be there," he said. "To be honest, what could you possibly have going on that would be more important than this? Why does it have to be so hard?"

"It's my final exam," she snapped suddenly. Fiercely. Tears glittered in her eyes, and for once he didn't feel like she was putting them on for show.

"Final exam for what?"

"I've been taking a class," she said.

Ilya shook his head. "Obviously, but in what?"

"Microsoft Office."

This stumped him. Seriously set him back. "Why?"

"Because I don't know how to use any of the programs, and I need to," Galina said with an angry swipe at her eyes.

He frowned. "Why do you suddenly need to know how to use Microsoft Office so bad you have to take an actual class?"

He saw her struggle with an answer, but in the end, she chose to keep her secrets, and he let her.

CHAPTER FORTY-TWO

The notice came in Theresa's e-mail from the credit reporting company she'd been subscribing to. A credit inquiry, made in her name, had triggered it. It had been refused, thank God, although that only reminded her of how long it would be until she could get credit on her own.

"If *I* can't get a credit card because of this mess you put me in, what made you think you could get one? What made you think it would be anything close to okay for you to pull this shit again, Dad? Why would you do this?" Theresa tossed the printout she'd made of the message onto his shabby kitchen table, highlighting the part pointing out that her score had dipped once more.

Her father gave her a pleading look. "I was behind on some bills—"

"Join the club!" She whirled on him, sick with fury. Devastated. Hating him but not enough. Not quite enough. "I told you. If you ever pulled this again, I would report you. I would turn you in to the police."

"No, no, honey, I'm sorry." He held up his hands, helpless.

She shook her head. "I mean it, Dad."

"You can't do that. I'm trying hard, I'm getting clean. It was a slipup. That's all. I promise you."

"You know something, Dad? You're the reason I hold back from everyone, even the ones I could love. How does that make you feel?" She wanted to sound angry but was unable to manage it. She sounded only sad.

"You can't blame me forever, Theresa. I know I've messed up, and I've made my amends to you—"

"It's no amends if you do the same thing over and over again!"

He was silent for a moment, then nodded. "Fair enough. I was wrong. I had a lack of judgment."

"Were you stoned when you did it?"

The look on his face told her the answer. That was it. She was done with this. With him. With everything that had happened.

"Theresa. Honey. Listen . . ."

"No. No more, Dad. No more excuses, no more apologies, no more forgiveness. I don't want to hear from you or see you. Don't call me. Don't e-mail me. Do you understand?" He didn't reply, and she stood in front of him deliberately until he had to look at her. "If you ever use my name to steal from me again, I will do everything I possibly can to make you accountable for it. Do you understand?"

In a querulous voice, her father agreed. "I'm sorry. What else can I do?"

"You can stay out of my life. That's what you can do." There was no more to say after that, and she left his apartment without another word.

By the time she got to the diner, her hands had stopped shaking and she was able to breathe a little easier. She took a minute to freshen her lipstick in the rearview mirror, making sure her face showed no signs of her recent distress. She counted to ten with her eyes closed, pushing away the anger.

In the diner's small office, she found Ilya at the desk with a small sheaf of papers in front of him. He held one up. "Hey, babe. Look at what I got. It's fancy stationery with our logo on it. B's Diner. See, there's a bee? I'm going to use it to print the invitations for the soft opening. Do you think it's too much to invite the mayor?"

She laughed, loving his enthusiasm. She loved watching him get excited about all the small details they'd been working so hard on. She loved *him*.

The realization set her back a mental step, but Ilya was looking at her expectantly. "No. I think it's great to invite the mayor. Did you get the name of the woman from the paper I sent you?"

"Yep, yep, she's on the list. Hey, come here." He gestured for her to come around the desk and take a place on his lap. "Mmm. Hi."

"Hi." She kissed him. The kiss deepened. His hands moved up her thigh. Theresa laughed and put her hand over his to keep it from moving higher. "Don't get distracted."

"Can't help it." He grinned against her lips but pulled away a little to shift them both on the chair. He tilted the laptop screen toward her so she could see. "Okay, so, here's the list I've been working on. I asked my mother, but she says she has something else to do and she might not be able to make it."

"What's going on with her?" Theresa leaned against him, running her fingers through his hair while she looked over the list. "Oh, you can take my father off there."

"Huh? Why?"

It was all there, ready to spill out of her. The credit cards, the debt, the truth behind her months of living in her car and crashing on couches. She meant to tell him. She wanted to. Unburdening herself of it all was going to be a relief. Yet at the last second, she changed her mind. If things didn't work out with Ilya, and it was still entirely possible that they would not, she didn't want him to know all this about her.

"He's not speaking to me," she said.

It wasn't a lie. Not really. If her father wasn't speaking to her, it was because she'd demanded that he stay out of her life. Ilya frowned, so she kissed him as a distraction. His hands settled on her hips, but he didn't seem properly distracted.

"You could send him an invitation, leave it up to him if he wants to come or not," he said. "I mean, don't get me wrong. I never really liked your dad that much. But he should be there to support you."

Theresa smiled and ran her fingers through his hair. "No. Don't. We're having a rough patch. So promise you won't invite him."

Ilya frowned, clearly uncertain about this. Her fingers tightened in his hair to tip his head back so she could nuzzle him. At the nip of her teeth on his chin, he wriggled, pinning her arms against her sides so he could hold her still and duck away from her mouth.

"I just want it to be the best night, for both of us, but especially for you," he said. "We've worked really hard on this, and if not for you, most of it wouldn't have come together."

"You did it," she started to say, but Ilya shook his head.

"No. You're the one with the lists and the contacts. You brought everything together and kept me on track. I never would've thought to do this in the first place, and I never would've done it without you. I wrote the checks, but you're the glue that's holding this entire project together."

She shook her head, moved by his declaration but even more by the look in his eyes. "We make a good team."

"Better than anyone could've guessed, especially me. You were right, Theresa. I did need this." He tugged her down so her mouth met his. "You sure you don't want me to invite him?"

"Promise me you won't," she said, too sharply. Too harsh. It confused him—she saw that—but in the end he must've thought about his own problems with his mother, because Ilya nodded and kissed her again.

"Okay. I promise."

CHAPTER FORTY-THREE

All their hard work had—well, perhaps *not*—come to fruition. Not yet. But they were well on the way. The staff had been hired, the menu perfected, the diner redecorated. There were a few glitches to work out, but that was the purpose of the soft opening. Theresa bent over the desk in the tiny diner office to go over her checklist. She was going to forget something, she knew it.

"You okay?" Ilya came up behind her to press a kiss to the nape of her neck in the spot guaranteed to send a thrill all through her. "Nervous?"

Theresa turned to kiss his mouth, her fingers linked loosely behind his neck. "A little. Not too much."

"You don't look nervous. You look gorgeous. Like you should be on the menu under dessert." He nibbled at her neck, making her giggle and twist away from him.

"We're not alone," she said. "And, hey, only dessert? I thought I would at least be a full entrée with two sides, including your choice of soup or salad."

"Super salad. Comes with a cape." Ilya snorted soft laughter against her skin, but he let her go.

She saw something in his eyes and gave him another kiss. "You're nervous."

He broke away from her to pace. "Nah. No need to be nervous. What's the worst that could happen? We could get a bad review on an Internet site."

"Hey." She snagged his elbow until he stopped and faced her. "It's going to be fine. We got this."

"I know dick-all about running a diner, Theresa. What the hell made me think I could do this?"

"I did," she told him honestly. "I made you think you could do this."

Solemnly, Ilya pulled her closer. "It's going to be all right. Right?"

"Absolutely." At the knock on the door, they both turned. "Come in!"

Niko poked his head around the door. "Hey, guys! We're a little early. Is that cool? We came in the back. The front's still locked, and the girl out there wouldn't open up."

"That's Britney, and we told her not to open until we gave her the okay. So far, so good." Theresa eased herself out of Ilya's embrace to give Niko a hug. "Hey, Alicia. Thanks for coming."

Alicia had come through after him, and she hugged Theresa, too. After a moment's hesitation, she also hugged Ilya, but briefly. She looked down at her dress, then laughed. "I was worried I'd be overdressed."

Theresa did a small twirl to show off her black cocktail gown and heels. "Hey, this is as fancy as this joint might ever get. Might as well do it up for tonight, at least."

Alicia laughed. "You look great. Are you guys excited? Big night."

"Big night," Theresa agreed.

Ilya and Niko, heads together, had gone out of the office already. Alicia and Theresa followed, through the kitchen where Billy, the cook, and his assistant, Hank, were ready in their whites. In the dining room, the new servers, Britney and Sam, waited with order pads in hand, while Betty, who'd been a waitress at the diner for the past thirty years, lounged against the counter and typed on her phone. She was probably the only person here tonight who wasn't at least a little nervous.

Beyond the glass front doors, Ilya had spread a narrow red carpet. A red velvet rope hung in front of the doors. Beyond that—

"Oh, shit," Ilya said aloud. "People."

"Shh. You invited them," Theresa said. "It's friends and family, and they're going to come in here, order some food, and celebrate with us. It's all going to be great. Deep breath."

He kissed her. "Let's do it."

So, they did it.

Britney, given permission, went ahead and opened the doors. People came in and were handed a hundred dollars in B's Diner Bucks, fake cash Ilya had printed up for use tonight since all the meals were going to be on the house. Sam, acting as host, asked everyone if they had a reservation and checked their names in the book where Theresa had listed a random selection of their guests in order to simulate a regular night at the diner. Finally, everyone was seated with brand-new menus in front of them, ready to get started.

"It's all going fine," Theresa said from behind the lunch counter as Ilya studied the room. "See?"

"My mother's not here."

"You invited her, she'll be here. Do you really think she'd miss it?" Theresa took his hand to squeeze it.

Ilya attempted a smile that didn't come out looking sincere. "I'm thinking maybe I'm hoping she will."

"I'm going to check the kitchen, make sure Billy's got it all under control. It's unlikely that anyone ordered the liver pudding, but you never know." It had been one of the more obscure items in Babulya's recipe box, not particularly Russian and not exactly Jewish, but Ilya had insisted on including it on the menu.

Billy, as it turned out, had everything completely under control, including the liver pudding, which one person had indeed ordered. Theresa checked a few of the steaming pots and gave Hank a thumbs-up at his place on the grill. She'd only been gone a few minutes and pushed out through the swinging doors, expecting to find Ilya just beyond them where she'd left him.

"You'll never believe it. Someone ordered it. I bet it was . . . Niko . . ."

"Hi, kiddo."

Theresa stopped, stunned. "Dad. What are you doing here?"

"Ilya invited me," her father said with a sheepish grin, holding out his hands. "I wanted to be here for your big night."

CHAPTER FORTY-FOUR

Galina and Barry had shown up at the same time. Ilya had seen them come through the front doors together. They didn't look like they were making this a date, and so long as neither of them made a scene, he wasn't going to complain. He was more relieved than he realized he'd be to see her.

"Mom." He kissed her cheek, noting the faint scent of perfume and the lipstick she wore. She'd dressed up, and he wasn't sure why that made him feel sentimental, that she'd made an effort for him, but it did. He shook Barry's hand. "Glad you could make it."

Ilya took his mother to Niko and Alicia's table to take a seat, and Barry excused himself to use the restroom. Ilya, relaxing a little as he looked around at everyone enjoying themselves, decided to play the part of restaurant owner and walk around to make sure everything was all right.

"I don't want you here!"

Theresa's voice rang out, turning heads. Ilya's stomach sank as he turned, already knowing what he'd see. He hadn't expected Barry to be yanking Theresa's arm, though, and there was no way he was going to allow that. He crossed the room at a half run to grab the older man's shoulder and turn him.

"Hey," Ilya said evenly, "not cool."

Ilya remembered Barry as a bit of a bully, a hard talker, rough with his words, though not ever his hands. And, like most bullies, when confronted, Barry folded. Now he held up his hands, backing off.

"Sorry, I didn't know you didn't tell her I was going to be here. I thought the invitation came from both of you," Barry said.

Theresa's head swiveled, her gaze boring into Ilya's. "I told you," she said from clenched jaws. "I told you, Ilya. I did not want him here tonight."

The diner had been filled with the sound of silverware clinking on plates and the low hum of voices, but some of that had silenced at the sound of Theresa's shout. More became quiet as people noticed the turning stares of those who'd heard her and were looking. Not everyone inside the diner was paying attention, but most of them were.

"Theresa," Ilya said.

She looked at him, but he wasn't sure she really saw him. Her gaze was unfocused, bright and hard, and glinting, but it shifted beyond him. She shook her head and tossed up her hands, then turned and went into the kitchen.

"I'll go," Barry said.

"Yeah. Go, man. Just go." Ilya kept his voice low, aware of the curious looks and mutters.

Across the room, he saw his mother standing, looking their way, her expression twisted. Niko was saying something to her while Alicia had put a hand on Galina's wrist. To keep her still or urge her forward, Ilya couldn't tell. He didn't much care, not in that moment, when everything he'd been working so hard for during the past few months, both in his career and in his life, looked as if it was going to go swirling down the drain. And why? Because he'd told Theresa she could count on him and trust him, and when it came right down to it, he'd fallen short.

Time slowed. In that moment, Ilya knew he'd fucked up. Worse than big time. Maybe for *all* time.

"Go," he repeated to Barry, and left everything behind to follow Theresa into the kitchen.

"She went out the back." Billy jerked a thumb.

Ilya pushed through the back door, searching for her and not finding her immediately. His heart sank, but then a figure shifted in the shadows, and he stepped forward. Reaching, but not quite grasping.

"I told you," Theresa said. "I told you, Ilya."

"I thought . . ."

She whirled to face him. It would've been easier, somehow, if she'd been crying. Instead, Theresa's expression was blank. "I trusted you." The words came out in a low hiss.

Ilya had done his share of hurting women in the past. He'd been on the receiving end of vitriol and accusations. He could not recall ever being on the other end of such a simply perfect expression of disgust.

"I told you I didn't want him here," Theresa said in that same low, fiercely contemptuous tone. "I told you not to invite him. You promised me, Ilya. You promised, and I believed you, but you went and did it anyway. And you have no idea what it means. What is going to happen now. What I have to do, Ilya! You have completely fucked with my life!"

He reeled, understanding that he'd messed up, but not the extent of her fury. "He's your father. I thought he should be here to celebrate with us, Theresa. I'm sorry."

She didn't answer him at first. When she did, her voice was so cold and distant that he was shot right back to the past and every other woman he'd loved who'd turned away from him. Ilya squared his shoulders, tightened his jaw. Knowing it was a reaction to what had happened in his past didn't make a difference.

"You have no idea."

"So tell me," he said, desperate. Feeling this could be the end of everything they'd built, all of it turned to ashes with nothing more than a few wrong words.

"I have nothing to say to you right now. Nothing." She pushed past him and back inside.

She avoided him for the rest of the night, a smile on her face that would have looked natural to everyone else but didn't fool him. By the time everyone started leaving, shaking his hand and clapping him on the back in congratulations, Ilya's jaw ached from clenching his teeth, and he'd never wanted a drink more in his life. He had a bottle in the back he'd been saving for after closing, but he no longer felt much like celebrating.

"Mazel tov, as Babulya would've said." Galina hugged him, to Ilya's surprise. "You did a wonderful job."

"Thanks." He looked across the room to where Alicia and Niko were chatting with Theresa. The rest of the staff had been excused. It was time to go home.

"You should not have invited her father."

Ilya snapped his head around to look at her. "You think?"

"To be honest, I was surprised you wanted *me* to come. But I was glad to be here. Theresa and her father are estranged, Ilya." Galina tilted her head, brow furrowing.

"Well, how the hell was I supposed to know that?"

Galina hesitated, opening her mouth to speak but closing it without saying anything. She shook her head. Ilya moved closer to her.

"What happened with them?"

"You should ask her that question, not me. It's not my place to say." His mother's glance flicked over his shoulder, and she closed her mouth again.

"No, it's not your place, Galina," Theresa said from behind them.

He turned. "Just tell me what the hell's going on. I'm sorry I invited him. I didn't know it was going to be such a huge deal."

He was aware of Niko and Alicia standing behind Theresa, watching. Neither of them looked confused. Alicia, in fact, leaned to murmur something into his brother's ear, and Niko nodded as though he knew exactly what was going on.

"Her father got her into financial trouble," Galina said.

Theresa scowled. "This is not your business, Galina!"

"If you won't tell him, I'm going to. He's my son!"

"Mom—" Niko began, and was cut off by Ilya saying, "Galina, enough."

Theresa advanced on his mother, jabbing a finger. "You can shut up. Right now."

"I won't shut up! You want to be involved with my son? You have to deal with me! What? You think I don't know? You might be keeping it a secret from everyone else, but I know." Galina sneered. "Oh, I see it."

Ilya caught sight of Alicia's surprised expression, then her narrow-eyed look from Theresa to him and back again. This wasn't the way he'd wanted her to find out, but it wasn't exactly like she had room to judge, he thought. Still, he was ready to shut down Galina's smug grin.

"Mom, shut up," Ilya snapped. "Back off."

Theresa sneered. "Mother of the goddamned year, right? You want me to tell him all about how my father stole my identity so he could open a bunch of credit cards in my name, the debt he ran up so I ended up having to live in my car?"

It all began to fall into place, piece by terrible piece.

"That's why you were so insistent about making that deal happen, right? The sale. You needed the money," Ilya accused. He ran a hand through his hair, pacing one step, then another and back. "That's why you came back around?"

"I came because your grandmother had been good to me, and I wanted to pay my respects when she was passing away." Theresa's voice was thick with tears, but she wasn't crying.

"Sure. Right. That's why you kept at me to sell. It was all about the money, right? That's why you stuck around, too. It had nothing to do with . . . with me." He swallowed hard against the rush of anger and betrayal choking him. Her look of guilt proved him right, and he turned away so he didn't have to see it again.

"I asked you not to invite him, Ilya, and you did anyway. I thought I could trust you."

"You want to talk about trust, when you had all this going on, and you never said a word about it to me?" He refused to look at her.

"Why did my dad need that money, Galina? Can you tell me that? Could it have been because he kept sending you money for all these years?"

Ilya tensed. The check from Barry, his mother's casual dismissal of it. He took a step or two back. "Yeah. That. Why *was* Barry still sending you money?"

"It was to keep her quiet, wasn't it? You want to spill some truth tea all over the place, Galina, why don't we start with that," Theresa said coldly. "Why don't you tell everyone exactly why my father ruined my life. For you."

Ilya had seen his mother in a rage many times, but he couldn't remember ever seeing her afraid. She shook her head and crossed her arms, but she didn't speak. Theresa let out a long, low, and humorless laugh that Ilya hated the sound of.

"It was to keep you quiet, wasn't it," Theresa said.

Everyone was quiet when she said that.

Ilya broke it. "Quiet about what?"

Galina waved a hand, refusing to speak. Behind him, he heard the murmur of Niko and Alicia muttering something, but he didn't turn. He didn't look at Theresa, either.

"What was Barry paying you to keep quiet about, Galina?"

"It was about the pills. It had to be about the pills, right?" Theresa's voice tore like wet paper.

Alicia stepped up. "Answer her!"

With everyone staring at her, Galina finally looked up, her gaze going to each of their faces while her own expression remained a mixture of defensiveness and guilt. Ilya had never seen his mother look like that. For as long as he could remember, Galina had never looked guilty about anything, not even when she was allegedly admitting she was wrong.

"What about the pills?" Alicia demanded, her voice low but fierce. She looked at Theresa. "The ones in the tin that Jenni hid in the crawl space?"

"My father kept his in a tin like that. He probably still does, although he says he's off them, but I don't believe him, because that's what addicts do. They lie. They lie and cheat and steal to cover up their tracks," Theresa said. "I knew as soon as I saw that tin where she got them."

"I'm not an addict," Galina retorted finally. "That was all him, always."

Ilya shook his head. "What does this have to do with Jenni? What the hell is going on here?"

"Barry got my sister hooked on pain pills, is that what happened? Oh my God, is that why she . . . oh my God." Alicia's voice broke, and she buried her face against Niko's chest.

"Your sister was only supposed to sell them, the stupid little girl! Nobody got her hooked on anything. She did that all by herself. She was only supposed to sell them . . ." Galina let her words trail off.

"To the truckers. Here in the diner. Right here," Ilya muttered, thinking back to the last night he'd seen Jenni alive. Alicia looked sick to her stomach, and he knew exactly how she felt. "In this fucking diner."

Galina squared her shoulders and gave each of them a defiant yet somehow weary look. "I would take the pills from the patients in the surgical recovery room. One here, one there. The doctors would prescribe them two pain pills, and I would give them one. Nobody paid attention, and when they were transferred to the floor, they had a whole different schedule for meds. A pill here or there, nothing big, but enough to sell. Barry was in charge of that. He recruited Jenni, a pretty face, all that blonde hair. The truck drivers loved her. They'd pay twice as much for a couple of pills that came from Jenni's hand."

"She was on drugs the night she died," Ilya said. "Because of you. Because of him."

"I don't know what happened the night she died. She was asking for more money. Some of the product had gone missing. I don't know. She was seeing one of the guys who bought from us, and he'd been rough with her," Galina said in a voice that sounded like she was telling the truth. "Barry was supposed to handle it. I know they argued."

Theresa made a low, strangled noise. "Did my father . . . kill her? Is that why he's been paying you off all this time? To keep quiet because he killed her?"

Ilya felt as though he'd stumbled, but he was standing still. His fists tightened. He had to swallow fiercely against the swell of bile in his throat.

"My God, Theresa, no. He didn't kill her, nobody killed her. They argued, and he left her alone. Whatever she did after that was all on her own."

"How can we believe a word out of your mouth?" Ilya asked her through gritted teeth.

Galina looked at him without flinching. "Because it's the truth. He didn't kill her. But I did have him send me money so I would never tell anyone that he was the last person to see her. It would have implicated him."

"And you, too," Theresa said. "Anything you said would've gotten you into just as much trouble. He didn't have to pay you off."

"No, he didn't. He did that because he loves me." Galina shrugged, any trace of her earlier guilt gone and replaced with an almost fierce pride.

"I should turn you in to the police," Alicia said.

Galina shrugged. "It won't bring your sister back, and I had nothing to do with her accident. You can go to them, I'm sure, but the case was closed a long time ago, and they determined there was no foul play. It won't make you feel better to go telling anyone."

"It might make me feel better to have you go to prison," Alicia said.

Galina laughed, then sighed. Still no look of shame, but Ilya wasn't surprised by that. Whatever fleeting sense of responsibility his mother had felt would've been suppressed by her consistent selfishness.

"Oh, my dear," she said, "I've already been."

CHAPTER FORTY-FIVE

"We had a nice little thing going, Barry and I. I took the pills. He sold them. Eventually, he recruited that girl to help him. I told him it was a bad idea," Galina added with a weary wave of her hand.

All of them were hovering in a combination of exhaustion, rage, grief, and another entire collection of emotions Niko couldn't begin to describe. The staff had been sent home. The doors locked. Ilya had broken out a bottle of champagne, but the rest of them had switched to coffee or nothing at all.

"He didn't tell me, by the way, when she started skimming the money, either. I didn't find out any of that until after she died, and by then he owed me thousands. So I kicked him out. And you," she added, to Theresa. "But honestly, what else could I have done? Kept you? You weren't mine."

"You made that abundantly clear," Theresa said in a cold voice.

Galina gave each of them a harried, defensive stare. "None of you can understand what it was like. Struggling the way I did. The money I made from those pills—drugs those patients didn't need, by the way, so it's not like I was taking something away from them. That money bought your sneakers and sent you to camp. It paid for the pizzas you ordered on a Saturday night. I did what I had to do. That's all."

Niko rubbed at his eyes. "And it caught up to you, huh?"

"I moved to South Carolina, and I'm not proud, but yes, I ran into some trouble."

"You didn't quit your job at the hospital down there. You were fired," Ilya said. He looked like shit, and Niko couldn't blame him.

"I *quit*. But I was named in part of a roundup. I got five years. It would've been more, but I gave up some other names. You do what you have to do," Galina said.

"How could you have gone to prison without telling us?" Alicia asked.

Galina scowled. "I think that's a question you all should answer for yourselves. How could I, indeed? How could I be essentially missing for years, not a damned word from any one of you. You never bothered to find out where I was, what I was doing. I could've been dead!"

"You weren't dead. We got your Christmas cards," Ilya said.

Niko wanted to give his brother a high five in that moment but refrained. It felt irreverent and wrong, especially in the face of Alicia's obvious red-eyed grief. "How'd you manage that?"

"I sent them to a friend, who mailed them for me without a prison stamp. I didn't want you to know, any of you. I didn't want you to worry."

Ilya's lip curled. "Or you were ashamed?"

"Of course I was ashamed!" Galina shouted.

Silence. Painful, awkward, broken only by the sputter of the coffeepot on the counter behind Theresa. Ilya let out a strangled laugh, though his expression was humorless. Niko put an arm around Alicia, pulling her closer, offering what comfort he could. It wasn't much. It might not have been enough, in fact, but he was grateful she let him.

"My driver's license lapsed. I lost my medical license. I couldn't work in my career any longer, and what else could I do? I got word my mother was dying. I came home, thinking at least I have a place to stay and people who will love me. My family. I should have known better." Galina shook her head, then put her face in her hands and started to cry.

Niko had seen those sorts of tears too many times to be truly sympathetic, although his instinct was, and maybe would always be, to try to defuse the situation with her. This time he managed to keep his mouth shut. It was Ilya who stepped up and put a hand on her shoulder.

Galina looked up with a hopeful expression. "Ilya. Believe me, I'm so very sorry. I'm so proud of you and what you've accomplished here tonight. The last thing in the world I wanted was for tonight to be ruined."

"Then you should've told us all of this a long time ago," he said without a shred of sympathy in his tone. "When I get home tonight, I want you gone."

More silence, and this time it was fierce. Beneath his arm, Alicia's entire body tensed. Niko thought she might say something, but what could she do? Defend Galina?

Not a single one of them did.

She stood, slowly, stiffly. Her shoulders squared. Chin lifted.

"A thankless child is sharper than a fang," she said, misquoting Shakespeare. "All of you. I may not have been the best mother—"

"No," Ilya said. "No, you were never even close."

Galina continued as though he hadn't interrupted. "But I love you. All of you. Yes, Theresa, even you. And I wanted nothing more than to come home and have us all be a family again. I'm sorry that none of you can appreciate that."

"Be gone when I get home," Ilya said again.

"It's still my house," Galina whispered finally in a broken voice. She looked at Niko, her gaze pleading. She held out a hand, clearly expecting him to take her side. "Where on earth do you expect me to go?"

Niko was done placating and making excuses for her. "You'll find a place. You always do."

"Fine." She gathered herself and gave them each another long, hard look before she let herself out the front door.

From the parking lot came the flash of lights and the sound of tires on the gravel. None of them said anything for a few seconds. Theresa turned on her heel and went into the kitchen, and after a second, Ilya followed her. Alicia turned to look up at Niko. She wasn't crying, but it was clear she was barely hanging on.

"I want to go home. Please, take me home," she said.

"Anything," Niko promised. "Anything you need."

CHAPTER FORTY-SIX

"We need to talk about this!"

Theresa frowned. "Don't shout at me, Ilya."

He held up the second bottle of champagne he'd been holding back for all of them to share after the other guests left, but Niko and Alicia had taken Galina out of there, and Barry, thank God, had gone and not come back. Ilya popped the cork, spraying foam, then splashed a glass full. Only one.

He lifted it. "Cheers. What a goddamned mess of a night."

Her phone had buzzed four times in the past forty minutes, and she didn't have to look to see that it was her father calling. She watched Ilya down the glass of champagne and pour another, again without offering her some. It would've been a kind gesture, if it was because he remembered her preferences instead of blatantly trying to deny her something that had been meant to be shared in celebration. She thought about reaching for him but didn't.

"You broke a promise to me, Ilya."

He faced her with a sneer. "Yeah, I broke a promise. Make this my fault, okay? Sure. It has nothing to do with the fact that all this time you never once told me what had been going on with you. For months, Theresa, and you just kept all your secrets."

"Because they were mine to keep!" she cried, advancing on him. "Would it have made a difference to you, in the beginning? If I had come to you and said that my dad had stolen my identity, run up debt, caused me financial ruin, that my entire life was in shambles because of it?"

"Maybe I—"

She laughed harshly. "Sure. You'd have sold your share of the quarry right away, right? To help me out? C'mon, Ilya, I came back into your life after twenty-some years gone. We were strangers with the barest thread of a relationship, and, yeah, I needed that deal. I needed the money, and I pushed you for it so that I could maybe try to get out from under that crushing debt."

"You made me want you!" he shouted. His voice cracked. "All along, right, you just made me want you so I'd help you out. Because that's what you do, right? You get men to take you to dinner or to bed. Why not get me to sell my business?"

"No. Oh my God. No . . ."

He threw the champagne glass into the industrial-size sink, where it shattered. Theresa's mouth opened, but nothing came out. All she could do was take a step back in the face of his clear fury.

Ilya gripped the edges of the sink, shoulders hunched. He didn't look at her. "All you've done is keep your secrets from me, Theresa. All this time when I thought you . . . that we . . . shit. Never mind. Forget it."

"Ilya, I'm sorry. I never meant for it to go this way. My troubles with my dad were mine, and I was ashamed. I didn't want to tell anyone what had happened, because how could I have been so stupid to not see it for so long, to let it get so bad? I didn't want to tell you because . . ."

"Because what?" He turned, leaning against the sink with his arms crossed. Mouth grim. Eyes narrowed.

"Because you had this idea of me as being smart and capable and someone you could maybe l-love." She stumbled on the last word but put it out there. "I guess I didn't want you to find out you were wrong."

When she moved toward him, Ilya held up a hand. "You want to talk about trust, Theresa, and you're right. I shouldn't have invited your dad when I'd promised you I wouldn't. But you should've told me the truth, and you didn't because you didn't trust me with it. So the way I see it is that I can't stand to be with someone who keeps secrets from me, and you can't share your secrets because you can't trust me. We're both screwed."

"Ilya."

He shook his head. "No, Theresa. That's the way it is. I fell in love with a woman once who kept everything that was important hidden away from me, and you know what? It wrecked me."

"That was a long time ago. Maybe you need to be able to get past that," Theresa snapped. "Using Jenni as an excuse about why you can't love me is pretty cheap."

Ilya's lip curled. "You never even gave me a chance, so don't you talk to me about cheap excuses not to love someone."

"But I do—" she began, hating the desperation in her voice and cutting off the words before they could escape and become real.

"You can't even say it out loud, huh? What? I guess that's a secret, too?"

When she tried to speak, he waved her away, dismissing her. It was more than Theresa could take, so she left.

CHAPTER FORTY-SEVEN

Alicia had stopped crying an hour or so ago, but her eyes still ached and her throat itched. Beside her, Nikolai's slow breathing soothed her, though not toward sleep. It was going to take her a long time before she'd be able to do that.

He hadn't said much, but now he stirred to press his lips to her hair. "You okay?"

"I don't know." She'd already told him she'd found the tin of pills in the crawl space and how Theresa's reaction to the sight of it had made so much sense once Galina had spilled the truth. Alicia closed her eyes and let herself nestle into the curve of his shoulder. "I keep thinking how I knew something was wrong with her. I knew that she'd been getting into things over her head. I had no idea . . ."

"You couldn't have. None of us did."

She pushed up on her hand to look at his face. "Are you okay?"

"Because I found out that instead of quitting her job at the hospital, I found out my mother was fired and sent to prison in South Carolina for stealing narcotics? And that she learned to cook in the prison kitchen, not in a diner?" He rubbed his fingertips up and down her arm. "I'm about as okay as you can expect. To be honest, I can't say I'm that surprised. It wasn't anything I ever suspected, but it all makes sense."

"What do we do from here?" Alicia asked.

"What do you want to do?"

"I want . . ." Frustrated and angry now rather than grieving, she got out of bed to pace. "I want them both to be punished for what they did."

Nikolai sat up to rest against the headboard. "Take it to the police?"

"What will they do about it?" She sagged, and when he reached for her hand, she let him take it and draw her to the bed. She sat. "Nothing. Do I want to stir it all up again for my parents?"

"Only you can answer that." He pulled her close so she could cuddle against him. "But whatever you want to do, I'm on board."

Alicia sighed, then kissed him. "I love you."

"Love you, too," he answered. "I'm here for you. I know she's my mother, but if you think you need to pursue this . . ."

"I don't know. Galina said Barry was the one who gave Jenni the pills, and that makes sense. But they never declared anything about her death being suspicious, and she says Barry wasn't with her when she died."

"Do you believe her?"

Alicia clenched her fists, fruitlessly angry. "I don't want to. I want there to be some reason, a goddamned reason that my sister is dead, and not just that she made some bad choices and fell off the ledge, all on her own. I want to blame someone for it, Nikolai! I want . . . justice."

More tears came, when she thought they'd all gone dry. She punched one fist into the opposite palm, but it gave her no satisfaction. She swiped furiously at her eyes, wanting to clear her vision.

His face was there when she did. The face of the man she loved. Their paths to each other had been full of complications, yet here they were. Together.

"I'll never get it, will I?" she asked him.

Nikolai took her hand to kiss the back of it. "No. Probably not."

"Do I have to just let it go?" she asked him quietly.

"I don't know," Nikolai said. "Do you think you can?"

She had no answer for that. Some days she'd wanted to scream and fight the universe and demand it bring her sister back; some days she'd quietly yearned and mourned and wished that Jenni hadn't died. Except she had, and nothing would ever change that or bring her back.

"I don't know," Alicia said.

It was the best answer she could find within herself to give.

CHAPTER FORTY-EIGHT

Barry Malone was one pathetic son of a bitch. The moment he'd opened the door to see Ilya standing on the other side, he'd burst into blubbering, terrified gasps and pleas, begging Ilya not to kill him.

"I'm not a murderer, Barry."

Ilya pushed past Theresa's father and through the doorway into the dank apartment. It smelled like cat piss and sour milk. Light came in through the broken blinds in stripes like bars on a prison cell. The kitchen looked clean enough, but it didn't take a detective to spot the garbage pail overflowing with beer cans and empty wine bottles. The guy couldn't even be bothered to recycle.

"No, no, of course not. I just meant, please don't hurt me." Barry closed the door behind them and followed so close on Ilya's heels that his toe kicked Ilya's boot when he stopped and turned. Barry put his hands up at once, flinching.

"Like you hurt Jenni?" Ilya shoved his hands in his pockets, his fists aching to connect with Barry's face.

"I didn't. I never! What did your bitch of a mother tell you? Because she's a goddamned liar."

Barry shook his head, his expression smoothing. He swiped angrily at his red-rimmed eyes and straightened his shoulders. His finger stabbed the air, swiping so close to Ilya's face he felt the swish of air as it passed his nose. On instinct, Ilya grabbed Barry's wrist, twisting the older man's arm until he felt he could break it with the tiniest bit of extra pressure.

Breathing hard, Barry let out a cry of despair. "Stop! Jesus, I said stop."

Ilya didn't let him go. He wanted to break this asshole's arm. He wanted to do more than that. Instead, he released Barry with a shove so the old man stumbled a few steps away.

"My mother said you were the last person to see Jenni alive. She also said you didn't hurt her," Ilya added in a shaking voice, "but we both know the truth. My mother is a liar. So if she says you didn't do anything to Jenni, maybe I don't believe her. Maybe I think you were the last one to see her, and maybe I think you fucking hurt her, and I'm here to find out what exactly happened. And then I'm going to maybe beat the shit out of you. Or drag your sorry piece-of-shit ass down to the police station and turn you in. Or both."

Barry coughed, long and hard, as though Ilya's accusations had surprised him. "I didn't hurt her. I swear to God. Not that night."

"Other nights?" Ilya grabbed the front of Barry's shirt and yanked him closer. "If you ever put your fucking hands on her—"

"Just once, just the once!" Barry shouted, cringing away from Ilya. "She came on to me—"

"Jenni would never have come on to you," Ilya said, disgusted and recoiling from the idea. "She thought you were a creep, and she was right."

"You think I don't know that? You think I believed a girl like her would have the hots for me, for real? It was because of the money she owed me," Barry said. "She owed me a lot. She told me that instead of paying me back, she'd . . . do things. Stuff she learned from that trucker she went with."

Ilya went cold first, then hot, then cold again. "The fuck you say?"

"Yeah. Bet you didn't know that, did you?" Ilya's clear shock seemed to give Barry courage. His sneer twisted. "Your girl was no angel."

That's when Ilya finally punched him in the mouth. He pulled it at the last second, so at least the old man would be able to keep his rotten teeth, but the blow still landed with enough force to send Barry tottering back against the counter. It split one of Ilya's knuckles, and a few fat drops of blood spattered onto the stained linoleum.

"You shut up," Ilya said.

Barry smeared his palm across his lips, spreading the crimson stain. "You said you wanted to know what happened? Are you really sure? Because it's not something you can forget about, you little punk. Once you know it, you're going to have to know it for the rest of your life."

Ilya had always known Jennilynn was no angel, but Barry's words still hit him hard. He'd spent decades without knowing what had happened to Jenni in the months leading up to the night she died. He'd spent as many years being uncertain of what had caused her death.

"Tell me," he said.

Before he answered, Barry went to the cupboard and pulled out a bottle of wine, the screw-top kind, and filled two mugs. He handed one to Ilya, who took it but didn't drink. The other, Barry held in both his hands as though he was afraid their shaking would spill the liquid. Barry also didn't drink, although he looked into the mug's depths as though he wanted to drown inside them.

"She was the perfect salesgirl. She wanted the money, was crazy for it—"

"She had a job at the diner," Ilya cut in.

Barry frowned. "Yeah? So? You know women. Always needed money for new shoes, get their hair done, whatever. Once she told me she needed cash so she could run away."

Ilya flinched at that, not because he hated the words but because immediately upon hearing them, he knew they were true. "So you got her pushing your pills. What then?"

"She took to it. I figured she liked getting the guys hooked. She had that way about her, you know? Like she really got off on making people want something she had, just so she could keep it from you." Barry tipped the mug to his lips but then took it away without drinking. "Shit. I promised Theresa I wouldn't. Dammit."

Yes. Jenni had been that way. Holding out the promise of something always forever slightly out of reach. Shaking, Ilya turned away from the old man.

"That night," he said.

Barry was quiet for so long Ilya became convinced he wasn't going to speak. In that moment, it would have been so easy for Ilya to walk away. More of his life had been haunted by the memories of Jennilynn Harrison than he'd ever spent making them. She'd become a fantasy. He didn't want that anymore.

"That night," he repeated when Barry still said nothing. "Tell me what happened."

"She was working her shift at the diner. She was supposed to be making a payment to me that night, but I was suspicious that she was going to run off with the cash *and* the pills."

Ilya remembered that night. Watching Jenni and the trucker. The fight Ilya'd had with her, after, in the parking lot.

"So you picked her up?"

Barry looked surprised. "No."

"Who did?"

"I don't know." Barry shrugged and tipped the mug to his lips again. "One of her boyfriends, if you can call a guy twenty years older than her a *boy*friend."

Ilya frowned. "I saw her at the diner that night. She got picked up by somebody."

"Well, whoever it was, she ended up with a black eye and a bloody nose," Barry said in a clipped tone. "And she didn't seem to mind it, if you know what I mean."

Ilya's lip curled. "I don't know what you mean, and if you don't stop fucking around with me, you're going to get the same as she had. And you *will* fucking mind."

"It means she was into rough trade," Barry said. "She liked it."

Ilya shook his head. "What are you talking about?"

"She liked it when guys hurt her." As soon as he said it, Barry put up a hand as though Ilya was going to hit him again.

"No . . ." Ilya shook his head again. "That's . . ."

"Look, you don't have to believe it. I didn't want to. But the time she was . . . with . . . me . . ." Barry paused. "She wanted me to choke her."

Sickness flooded him. "Did you?"

"No!" Barry shouted, but weakly. "Hell, no. Hey, there's no doubt I was enough of a piece of shit to cheat on your mother with a teenage girl who came on to me, yeah, but me and a hundred other middle-aged guys would do the same thing."

"You were the piece of shit who got her hooked on pills—"

"She was never," Barry put in, "supposed to be taking them. Only selling."

Ilya paced in Barry's narrow galley kitchen, clenching and unclenching his fists to keep himself from hitting something. Anything. Punching a hole in the damned wall or beating Barry to a pulp. Hitting himself in the face so he wouldn't have to listen to this anymore.

"She came to the house. What then?"

"We met at the old equipment shed, not the house. There was no way I could risk that. I demanded my money. She said she didn't have it, or the pills, and she wasn't going to give it to me anyway. She threatened to tell Galina about us if I tried to come after her for it. She told me she was only a few days away from running off. I asked her with who, but she wouldn't tell me."

Ilya's shoulders hunched, and he spun on one heel to face Barry. "You're lying."

"I'm not. She was already drunk when we were in the shed. High, too. She said otherwise, but . . ." Barry looked truly shamefaced for the first time as he lifted the mug. "I knew. I could tell."

"So you left her there?"

"What did you want me to do? She was threatening to ruin the rest of my life! And shit," Barry added, "she did. Didn't she? She ruined all our lives."

"Do you think . . . whoever it was she was with . . . do you think he killed her?"

Barry put the mug on the counter and linked his hands together in front of him. Again, he didn't speak right away, and when he finally did, his voice was low and rasping. "I've wondered. If maybe, yeah. All I can tell you for sure is she was totally shitfaced when I left her, and it makes total sense that she might've tried to go swimming and fallen by accident. She didn't say anything about meeting anyone else there. So far as I know, she had no reason to. I don't know, Ilya. I've thought over the years about it, if I could go to the police and tell them what I knew, see if they could connect anything. Because, sure, yeah, I wanted to know what happened, the way all of you did. If it was somebody who did it, wouldn't it be a relief to know, so they could be punished?"

Yes. So they could be punished the way Ilya had come here tonight in order to bring some justice down on Barry. "But you never said anything. You never went to the police."

Barry frowned. "I'd have been implicated."

"You're a hypocrite and a coward," Ilya said with a sneer.

"Yes." Barry nodded. "Yeah, I am."

"I should still go. Tell them what I know."

"You won't," Barry said. "Because of Theresa."

It was Ilya's turn for silence.

"I've put her through a lot. I know it. I've been a shit father, and I want to change that, but it doesn't seem like she's going to give me the chance. Can't say I blame her. But you don't want to do anything that's going to cause her more pain, do you? If it gets out that I was in any way tied up in your sister's death, think about what that would do to Theresa."

"She already knows."

"But nobody else does in this buttstain of a town," Barry said. "Think of what it would do to her, now when she's trying to make something of herself . . ."

"Theresa doesn't have to make something of herself. She's already something. She's good at what she does, and she's going to continue to be a success, because that's who she is. She doesn't need you in her life," Ilya retorted.

Barry gave him a weary smile. "Like I said, she doesn't need to be caught up in any of that drama, either."

"You're a self-serving son of a bitch, you know that?"

"Yes," Barry said. "But if you love my daughter the way I think you do, you're going to keep letting me be."

Ilya's invitation to meet at the diner had taken Alicia by surprise, but she'd agreed. She probably always would, she thought as she slid into the booth in the back, with him across from her. They had a history that could never be erased.

It didn't have to be, she realized as she looked him over. The tie, the pressed shirt, his face freshly shaved, and his hair combed. They could both have their own futures, and nothing in their shared past had to keep them from it.

"I wanted to tell you that I'm sorry," Ilya said without bothering to start off with small talk. "For everything."

Alicia chewed on her answer before she gave it, wanting to be certain of her words. "I'm not sure I need you to apologize, Ilya. But thanks."

"I was not a good husband," he said. "I could lie and tell you that I wanted to be or that I tried, but the truth was I never really did. You deserved better than I ever gave you, Alicia. So I'm sorry for that."

Her throat closed. She warmed her hands on the mug of coffee. "You deserved better, too, Ilya, than being my reason to never leave. I held on to that for a long time, making you the bad guy, even if I didn't say it out loud—"

"Oh," he interrupted, "I think there were plenty of times you said it out loud."

They both laughed. Loud. She covered her mouth with her hand and shook her head but looked at him fondly.

"I'm proud of you, Ilya. You know I want nothing but the best for you. And for Theresa."

He smiled, but it faded into a more serious expression. "I want you to know something. I confronted Barry about what happened that night."

Her stomach fell. The coffee she'd drunk threatened to come back up. "Oh God. Oh God, please don't tell me he did something to her—"

"He says no—"

"I can't bear to think she was murdered," Alicia blurted. "It's bad enough it was an accident. Worse to find out she was into the pills, and that whole business with Theresa's father—it's so gross, Ilya. I loved my sister, but I knew she wasn't perfect. Still, I just don't think I could handle knowing that something that bad happened to her."

Ilya's lips pressed together, and his brow furrowed. He looked away from her in his classic manner. He was about to be untruthful with her.

"Was it Barry?" she whispered, horrified, waiting to learn the worst.

"He says no, and I believe him," Ilya told her and met her gaze. "He's an addict and an asshole, but I believe what he told me. It matches what Galina said, and besides that, I just . . . I believe him."

Relief flooded her, even as she wondered what he'd been lying to her about. It didn't matter, Alicia decided as Ilya sat back in the diner booth. The truth about Jenni's death wouldn't change the fact she was gone and would never come back.

"I already started making my peace with it," Alicia said. "For the first time since it happened, maybe, I think I've started finding a way to put it to rest."

"I'm glad," Ilya answered. "Good. We all need that."

She reached across the table to take his hand. Their fingers linked. She squeezed. He squeezed back.

"Yeah," Alicia said. "We all do."

CHAPTER FORTY-NINE

There'd been no further confrontation with her father. Theresa had refused to see him or to answer his calls, and he'd left close to a dozen. She hadn't bothered to listen to the messages. They'd all be the same, she thought. First, he'd beg her to forgive him. Eventually he'd start to accuse her of being in the wrong, and finally, at the end, he would cry that she hated him, and there would be no good answer for that. She probably did hate him.

She had not spoken to Ilya for two days. She had left him a single voice mail, which he hadn't answered, and one text he hadn't replied to. She'd been careful to spend as much time away from the house as possible, leaving Alicia and Niko their space. In the aftermath of the huge reveal, Theresa had tried to talk to her, but Alicia had refused. Politely, with tears thick in her throat, but making it clear she was not going to discuss anything with Theresa, at least not right away. Theresa wasn't sure where it left their friendship, but she could respect Alicia's reluctance.

Today was the B's Diner grand opening, and Theresa could not miss it. No matter what had happened, or how terrible she was at apologies and trust, or that Ilya had broken his promise to her, she had to be there. Not because she'd put her time and effort and, yes, her future financial security into it. She had to be there because this was the work they'd done together, and she believed in him, and she wasn't going to give up.

Not on him.

Not on them.

By the time she got to the diner, the lot was full. A good sign, but one that gave her an anxious stomach and sweaty palms. The soft opening had gone off basically without more than a few hitches, but today was full staff, regular operating hours, and all the problems that could come along with it. She took the time to check her lipstick and hair in the rearview mirror and smoothed the front of her summer dress.

The back door was unlocked, and she went inside to be greeted with the delicious smells of breakfast and the bustle of a kitchen running at top speed. She wasn't too worried—a number of the full-time staff they'd hired had worked for the Zimmermans and had a lot of experience. Even so, new menu items, new policies . . . she greeted everyone, making sure to stay out of the way and leave them to their work.

She found Ilya in the tiny office, where he was fixing his tie in a small mirror. He didn't turn when she came in, but he looked at her in the reflection. For a moment, Theresa froze, waiting for him to tell her to get out.

Ilya smiled.

"You made it," he said.

Then he faced her, and she was crossing the room to push his hands gently away from the mess he'd made of his tie. She fixed it for him, loosening the knot first, then smoothing and tightening it. She ran her hands over the front of his suit.

"There," Theresa said. "Gorgeous."

Ilya put his hands on her hips and waited until she was looking into his eyes before he said, "Let's do this thing."

"A lot of people showed up," she said.

He shook his head. "Not the diner. Let's face it. We're still going to screw up some things, but we hired good people, and you're smart and organized, and I come up with crazy, brilliant ideas. But I don't mean the diner. I mean us. Let's do this thing, Theresa. Okay? No more back and forth, no more keeping secrets."

"You think it'll be that easy, huh?" She let her hands slide up his chest to rest on his shoulders so she could curl her fingers around the back of his neck.

"Hell, no. I think it's going to be harder than anything I've ever done, that's for sure. But if you'll let me, I'll try. I can't promise you I won't be an asshole sometimes—"

She kissed him. "I wouldn't expect anything else. And I'll do my best, but I'm sure there are times when it will be hard for me to share things with you, because that's my damage."

"I have no idea what I'm doing. You know that, right?" His hands anchored on her hips, pulling her a little closer.

"Oh, believe me, I know."

This time, he kissed her. A knock on the door interrupted them. They both turned.

"Hey," Betty said, "I have a customer out here who wants to know about catering. Can you come talk to her?"

"Sure. Be right there." Ilya waited until Betty had closed the door, then added, "You ready for this?"

Theresa drew in a deep breath. "Yeah. Let's do it."

◆ ◆ ◆

"What a day." Ilya couldn't remember ever being so exhausted or exhilarated in his life.

Theresa yawned and stretched as she kicked off her shoes and fell onto the couch. "No kidding. I'm not sure my feet will ever recover."

They'd left B's Diner in the hopefully capable hands of Matt, the night manager. With takeout packages of liver pudding, potato salad, matzoh-ball soup, roasted chicken, and challah so they could test out the kitchen's prowess in reproducing Babulya's recipes, as well as feed themselves after a day of nonstop working, they'd come back to Ilya's house. The food was warming in the oven. He had some other things on his mind.

"Hey." He slid onto the couch next to her. "We made it."

She chuckled and leaned against him. "Yeah. The first day. You know how many days we still have to get through?"

"All of them, I'd say." He grinned.

"If we're lucky." Theresa's expression turned solemn. "It was a good day, wasn't it? Tell me I'm not just imagining it. People were having a good time, right? They liked the food."

"Patty said she'd never had a better day, with tips," Ilya said. "I think that says a lot, doesn't it?"

Theresa shifted to sit up straighter, facing him. "I had fun, too. Did you?"

"You know what? I did." He shook his head. "I didn't think I would, you know? I thought I'd be stressed about everything. I thought I wouldn't be able to handle it."

"I knew you'd be able to handle it," she said.

"I love you," Ilya said.

It came up and out of him as easily as any words ever had in his entire life. Stranger still, he didn't regret saying them. If anything, the relief of finally admitting it to her had him breathing a deep-seated sigh.

"I . . . oh my God," Theresa said. "Wow."

Ilya leaned closer. "Don't say it back or anything, it's not like I care. I'm going to love you whether you love me back. I'm all in it, and there's nothing I can do about it now."

"I love you, too," Theresa whispered into his kiss. "Weirdo."

CHAPTER FIFTY

Theresa would always remember the quarry best in the early autumn, when the leaves had started to change color but had not yet begun to fall. They'd been a quintet all those years ago, and now were only four, but they were good together, all of them. She and Ilya. Niko and Alicia.

A lot had happened over the past year. Loss, renewal, beginnings, endings. Most of all, though, love. They'd all found love.

With her fingers linked in Ilya's, she let him lead the way over the small curb of asphalt that ridged the cul-de-sac and to the small patch of scrubby grass beyond. Then into the trees, all of them ducking as they pushed through the line of evergreens to get to the path Ilya had made.

Behind her, Alicia and Niko were also holding hands. Ilya held a golden-leafed limb out of the way so they could all pass. The path beneath their feet was uneven and curving, but none of them stumbled or fell.

Alicia paused at the spot where the old equipment shed had once stood. Only for a moment. The bad memories that lingered there were never going to disappear entirely, but without the shed to hold on to them, maybe at least they could fade.

The sun was beginning to drop on the horizon by the time they got to the clearing, where there had once been an old rope swing, and the rock ledge, where they'd spent so many hours sunning themselves and jumping off into the quarry's water. The day had been warm, but the coming night breeze was chilly. It blew the hair back from Theresa's face as she zipped her jacket up to her throat.

"Look at that." Ilya pointed across the water to the construction. The hotel, higher on the ridge, was nearly finished. The time-share condos had been open for about a month. "I heard the hotel opens next month. Too late for swimming."

"There's always next summer." Theresa looped her arm through his as they stood at the edge of the overhang. "We'll pack a picnic. Rent a canoe."

He laughed, looking at her. "Sure we will."

"It might be fun," Niko said as he and Alicia took their places beside Theresa and Ilya. "You never know."

Ilya pulled a bottle from his pocket and unscrewed the cap. He lifted it in the direction of the condos and hotel. *"Vashee zda-ró-vye."*

"To closing doors and opening windows," Theresa said, and took a small sip from the bottle before passing it to Niko.

"Vashee zda-ró-vye," he repeated. "To health and wealth and happiness."

"To the memory of those no longer with us," Alicia said quietly and took her own sip. "The ones we loved and those we struggle to love."

Jenni. Babulya. Galina, who had not died but who certainly was no longer with them and wasn't likely to be for a long time. Theresa's father, whom she had struggled to love.

"To B's Diner," Ilya said when the bottle came back to him. "And to bees, in general. May the keeping of them never sting any of us!"

Niko took the bottle his brother offered and swigged before putting the cap back on. "Dare you to jump in."

"No way. I like my nuts unfrozen, thanks."

Niko guffawed and clapped his brother on the back. "Like you *have* nuts."

They both fake-tussled for a moment, pushing Theresa's heart into her throat for a few moments when they got too close to the edge. The brothers stopped at the clatter and splash of pebbles being kicked off the ledge and into the water. All of them turned, the four of them in a line, with the sun's final light pushing their shadows out behind them.

In the water, something splashed. Too far away to be the rocks they'd kicked. Something else that rose and gleamed and sent a spray of water into the sky.

"Chester," Ilya said solemnly.

Niko shook his head. "No way."

Alicia stepped forward, shading her eyes to look out across the water. She turned to face them, her eyes bright with tears, but a broad smile on her face. "It's Jenni, I think."

If Alicia wanted to think that, it was all right with Theresa. It surprised her, though, when Alicia took Theresa's hand. Still looking out over the water, the other woman squeezed Theresa's fingers.

"I lost my sister so many years ago." Alicia's quiet voice carried out over the water, lifted on the breeze. "We all lost her, and we will always miss her. But she's never going to be completely gone. Not while we all still have each other . . . however messed up it might be."

Theresa laughed around the lump in her throat. She and Alicia bumped shoulders. "It's a mess, all right."

"A good mess," Ilya said from her other side.

His arm snaked around Alicia's back to pull her closer, as he handed off the bottle to his brother and then hugged her hard with both arms. When the kiss broke, Ilya was smiling.

"Love you," he mouthed.

"Love you, too," she whispered back.

She caught Alicia glancing at them, and for a moment Theresa hesitated. She might always hesitate, just a little, the way she supposed Ilya was always going to have a millisecond's hesitation at the sight of his brother together with his ex-wife. It was complicated and messy, but it was also going to be okay. Everything was going to be more than okay. They were all starting something brand-new.

And it was going to be amazing.